Murder at Maltby le Marsh

A Harlowe & Fitch Historical Mystery
ELIZABETH ROSE

OLIVERHEBERBOOKS

Cover art by Dar Albert at Wicked Smart Designs

Published by Oliver-Heber Books

0 9 8 7 6 5 4 3 2 1

A Note to My Readers

Dear Readers,

The **Harlowe & Fitch Historical Mystery Series** is ongoing with a main thread that continues to develop throughout the entire series. Mixed in with each story is a new murder mystery that is solved before the book is finished. While every installment can be read as a stand-alone, it is advised, and also ideal, to start from the beginning with **Murder at Mablethorpe Castle**, Book 1, and to read them in order. If not, there could be surprises ruined along the way.

There might be cliffhangers, but never for the current murder. And while these are murder mysteries and not romances, there is still a romantic thread woven in as well.

See more notes at the end of this book, but for now, welcome to the world of Harlowe & Fitch where investigations into murders in Mablethorpe and the surrounding areas are underway. A headstrong noblewoman searching for justice, and a stealthy sheriff trying to secure the safety of his town, team up to uncover that which is hidden but needs to be brought to the surface.

Elizabeth Rose

Prologue

Maltby le Marsh Abbey, Late 1300s, England

Hildegard struggled to stay conscious, even with the pain wracking her bruised and beaten body. So tired. So defeated. She knew she was dying after the loss of so much blood. Her abdomen convulsed and blood flowed from between her legs. All she wanted was to be free ... and for justice to be served. The sound of the ringing church bells in the distance echoed in her head as the bricks being set in place started to quickly block out all light. All life. No one would ever hear her or find her inside the abbey's wall.

With her hands and legs bound with rope and a cloth gagging her mouth, she could barely breathe for the lack of air in the small, confined space. Darkness had always frightened her, and she loathed being alone. Now, she prayed for the darkness to consume her and to bring her solace from this world. From her fear and pain. The part that angered her the most was that the truth would never be told. No one would ever know what she'd accidentally discovered and why her life was snuffed out faster than the flame of a candle. The truth would die with her now. Her life was sadly over.

Reaching down with her bound hands, she rested them on

her belly. What would her life have been like if she had made different choices? If she had never come to the abbey in the first place. Or, at least, if she hadn't been in the wrong place at the wrong time.

Swipe, clink, scrape. Swipe, clink, scrape. Each moment of her life counted down as another brick was quickly set into place, the mortar holding the bricks tightly together, creating her tomb. Every second of her life grew shorter as each brick was placed in the wall, and she was left to die.

Nay, she cried out in her mind. With the last of her strength, she used her bound hands, trying to push at the bricks, but only managing to scrape her fingers raw. The pain in her body was unbearable, and she could no longer struggle to stay conscious. Her insides contorted. Sadly, her death would bring about the end of another as well.

"No one can save you now." She heard the muffled words as her murderer whispered through the last hole in the wall before putting the final brick in place.

With the light gone, the darkness claimed her. Hildegard had been sealed alive in her tomb. This would be her final resting place. Yes, it was here and now that she would die.

Chapter One

Murders in Mablethorpe were starting to add up quickly. Sheriff Zachariah Fitch had just solved a case in town, being assisted by his good friend since childhood, Lady Vivienne Harlowe. However, before they could even find a moment to relax or possibly take a deep breath of relief, another murder came calling for their attention. It had only been a day since all the trouble on Rotten Row ended. Or was over for the time being, since there would always be trouble in this bad part of town. Zachariah worked day and night to make the town as safe as it could possibly be. However, that would all have to be pushed aside for now, since he was about to start out on a journey to the neighboring village. Maltby le Marsh Abbey was where another murder had supposedly taken place, according to the town's constable as well as Zachariah's sibling, Sister Magdalena. Already, this trip was not at all what he wanted or expected in the least, even though he'd yet to leave.

"Lady Vivienne, may I have a word with you privately, please?" Zachariah stood in the courtyard of Mablethorpe Castle with his arms crossed over his chest. He eyed the wagon preparing to leave for Maltby le Marsh, not liking what he saw.

3

"Of course, Sheriff Fitch. What is it?" Vivienne sounded chipper and happy today. He wished he could say he felt the same way, but it was far from the truth. When his estranged sister arrived in Mablethorpe, begging for his help, just her presence brought old grievances to the surface.

He took Vivienne by the elbow and pulled her off to the side. Turning his back on the others, he spoke softly so as not to be overheard.

"First of all, I never wanted to take this case in Maltby le Marsh and you know it," he told her. "Why on earth would you agree to it for the both of us without speaking to me first?"

A look of surprise washed over her face. It was quickly replaced with that of insult mixed with determination. "Sheriff Fitch, you surprise me sometimes. Especially since your job as town sheriff gives you jurisdiction over the neighboring village of Maltby le Marsh as well. The abbey needs your help. Your sister needs you! Magdalena is a nun, and you can't turn away a woman devoted to God. It's just not right."

"Magdalena and I are not on the best of terms. And please don't use the excuse of her being a nun to try to get me to do anything."

"Not on the best of terms?" she asked, looking at him from the corner of her eye. "This has something to do with the fact you two haven't even spoken since the death of your wife, doesn't it?"

"What difference does it make? It's in the past and we need to stay away from things that will only stir up more trouble."

"The matter is obviously in the present, as well, since you seem to want nothing to do with her. What happened between you two that made you so stubborn and grumpy? Why won't you come to her aid?"

Zachariah hesitated, not wanting to tell her all about his private life and certainly not his troubles. He'd had nothing but disappointment for years now and he'd rather not dig up old disputes. Mayhap if he gave Vivienne what she wanted, she'd stop asking him about his past.

"Never mind. I'll go to Maltby le Marsh. I'll investigate. I don't care." He waved his hands wildly in the air as he found it hard to tamp down his aggravation.

"You will?" she asked, looking as if she didn't believe him.

"Yes. I said I'd do it. But tell me, why in God's name are we taking all of them with us?" He motioned with an outstretched arm to the wagon filled with people.

Their journey should have included the two of them, as well as Sister Magdalena and Constable Erikson from Maltby le Marsh. No one else. Instead, his daughter's nursemaid, Nairnie, sat on the bench seat of the wagon chattering away and acting like a good friend to his sister, when she'd only just met her. In the back of the wagon was his seven-year-old daughter, Starah, who was singing. Next to her was Lady Vivienne's page boy, Martin. The children were both seven years of age. It had just been discovered that Martin was Lady Vivienne's long lost son, stolen from her during a nightmare that took away her family just after the boy's birth. And to add to this cacophony of chattering, singing, and giggling, came the constant barking of Lady Vivienne's big bloodhound named Grunt, who sat nuzzled in between the children.

"Sheriff, you need to involve your daughter in more aspects of your life. This is a perfect opportunity to do so," explained Vivienne. "And as for Martin, I just found him again after so long and I am not going anywhere without him."

"Well, what about the dog?" He raised a brow. "Surely a hound has no place in an abbey."

"The children love Grunt! You know that. Besides, Grunt has a good nose for sniffing out trouble."

"Or causing it," mumbled Zachariah under his breath. True,

the dog often created problems, but on the other hand, Vivienne was right about him being helpful too. After all, Grunt had been the one to find the last two murder victims. Still, having the children along was only going to be more than distracting, and he wouldn't be able to focus on the case. Not to mention, Nairnie was boisterous and spoke much too loud and freely about whatever happened to be on her mind. Her stories alone of having grandsons and a husband that were all once pirates was not going to go over well amongst monks and nuns. He wasn't looking forward to this trip at all. "Thank goodness, at least that cat isn't in the wagon too."

"Oh nay," said Vivienne. "Starah's cat, Midnight, would only make Grunt go crazy. Wymond is watching Midnight until we return." Vivienne spoke of the young lad who was once the rat-catcher's assistant. The cat knew Wymond well since Midnight used to hunt for rats with him, as well as the man referred to as the Pied Piper.

"Sheriff, will we be leaving soon?" asked Constable Erikson from his position in the wagon. He looked back over his shoulder, the reins gripped tightly in his hand. There was no mistaking the look of distress on his face. Nairnie was laughing raucously, slapping her hand against her knee like an old, crusty sailor as she conversed with Magdalena. Zachariah was sure the poor constable was already at his wit's end and probably getting a headache from all the noise.

"Yes. Let's go," said Zachariah, starting in the direction of the traveling party.

"I agree. We need to get started," Vivienne said, but didn't move at all. Instead, she looked around as if she were searching for someone.

"Now what?" he asked, stopping and turning back toward her. He was not really sure he wanted to hear her answer. "Lord and Lady Mablethorpe are by the wagon if you are looking for them to say farewell." If only it were that easy, but he knew it wouldn't be so.

"Nay. I already said my goodbyes to my aunt and uncle," she told him, tucking a strand of her long blonde hair back into her braid that rested over one shoulder. Vivienne usually kept her head uncovered, or at times even wore her hair long. She didn't abide by the rules of nobles pertaining to how she should look or dress. "However, there is someone else I am waiting on." She continued to stretch her neck, searching the crowded courtyard.

Mablethorpe Castle was her uncle's holding. It was a large stone fortress with thick walls, corner towers, battlements, a drawbridge, and a moat. It was highly fortified against potential attackers. Outbuildings such as a smithy, the mews, and the kennels dotted the inner ward, as well as a pond and small orchard. Positioned close by, but outside the gates, was the village where the mill and the alehouse could be found. Villagers lived in small huts made from wattle and daub. Here is where peasants farmed the land, and all the castle's vast kitchen and pantry needs were met. Meat, fish, grain, and more, along with necessary animal fodder such as hay and oats.

"Lady Vivienne, I would have thought you'd made all the preparations for this trip earlier, while you were waiting for me to arrive from town," Zachariah told her. Vivienne was usually very precise and impeccable with her plans. "By the way, I don't appreciate you putting the idea in Nairnie's head about taking her and Starah with us."

"I didn't. Not really," she told him, still scanning the court-yard for someone. "I just told them last night that Martin and Grunt were coming along, and that I thought it would be nice if Starah could join us too."

"If that isn't putting an idea in someone's head, I don't know what is."

"Well?" Her bright blue eyes sought out his now. "It would be nice. For the children. Don't you agree?"

"This is a possible murder case, not a trip to the fair," he told her. "Give that some thought."

She stared at him, blinking several times in succession before she spoke. "So what are you saying, Sheriff? That you want me to tell the children and Nairnie that they can't come along with us after all?"

Vivienne wouldn't back down and would never change her mind. He knew that about her by now. There was no use in stirring up a heated argument between them. All he wanted was some peace and quiet.

"Nay, of course not," he answered. "Starah is so excited about the trip that I couldn't possibly send her back home now without breaking her heart." He blew a puff of air from his mouth. "Let's be on our way, shall we?"

"Oh, there she is." Vivienne's chin raised as she looked over the heads of the crowd. "Maleine, we're over here. You'd better hurry!" she shouted, causing Zachariah to cringe with her unladylike actions. "We are leaving now and you don't want to be left behind. Maleine, over here." She waved her hand wildly over her head, trying to get the young woman's attention.

"Maleine?" he asked, thinking this was going from bad to worse. "The mayor's daughter? Please don't tell me that you've invited her to go on the trip with us too."

"I did, but this is different." Vivienne smiled and swatted at the air as if that were going to make him stop asking questions.

"How so?" he wanted to know.

"Maleine is going to be joining the order now, since her family is all gone and she's alone."

True, Zachariah had heard the girl say she wanted to join the abbey, but he didn't realize she'd be doing it now! Especially since they were embarking on a murder investigation. This wasn't the time or place for this.

"Vivienne, why is Maleine going all the way to Maltby le Marsh when Mablethorpe Abbey is right here?" He nodded to the large double monastery in the distance, overlooking the town. Mablethorpe Abbey housed both monks and nuns. It was constructed of red brick and sprawled across rolling hills. Surrounding it were flocks of long-haired sheep that were raised by the church for wool trade, as well as for milk and making cheese and butter.

"It's *Lady* Vivienne," she reminded him, since they'd agreed to use their titles and keep their relationship professional. She always seemed to remind him of this when they disagreed on something. "And Maleine has already spoken to Sister Magdalena about joining the order. Your sister is the one who suggested Maleine go to Maltby le Marsh Abbey to train with her as a postulant. Magdalena is so nice. I don't understand why you two don't get along. You used to be even closer with her than you were with your other siblings. Something happened between you and I really wish you'd tell me what it was."

"Enough talking. We have an investigation to start, although I have no idea how that is going to happen with all these people underfoot."

"We'll make it work," she told him, as if it were nothing to get upset about.

"The abbey at Maltby le Marsh isn't nearly as large as Mablethorpe Abbey," Zachariah pointed out. "That might create a little problem with us bringing in so many people."

"Nonsense. Your sister said they take in all travelers, and that there is more than enough room to house us all as guests during our stay."

"There's nothing I can do to change your mind, is there?" Zachariah narrowed his eyes, looking across the courtyard at the little entourage that would be accompanying them. Maleine tossed her bag into the back of the wagon, hoisting herself up to join Martin, Starah, and the dog.

"Maleine, wait!" called out Wymond, the lad who used to be the rat-catcher's assistant. With a crutch under one arm so he wouldn't have to put much weight on his broken leg, he hobbled across the courtyard toward the wagon. His two ferrets followed him, slinking over the cobblestones. Grunt spied them and started barking, and was about to jump down and chase them when Martin grabbed hold of the dog and held him back with Maleine's help. "I'm going to miss you. I'll be waiting for you," Wymond told Maleine. Both he and Maleine were sixteen years of age. Wymond was tall and lanky and had long, scraggly brown hair. Maleine was tall for a girl, and had long, dark hair, almost black and very curly. The boy had eyes for Maleine ever since he'd met her. He'd even offered to marry her after the death of her father, but she'd turned him down.

"Please do not tell me Wymond and his vermin are joining us too, because I draw the line there," Zachariah ground out.

"Calm down, Sheriff." Vivienne gently rested her hand on his arm. "Wymond is staying here at the castle. After all, he'd only be too much of a distraction for Maleine during her training. Not to mention, Grunt would constantly be chasing Chomp and Snuff," she said, referring to the two ferrets.

"And you still believe the others won't be a distraction at all?" He watched as Martin stood up in the wagon, waving his wooden sword through the air while Starah watched him with stars in her eyes, giggling like crazy. Maleine struggled to hold back the barking dog that was still trying to get to the ferrets. Nairnie leaned back over the bench seat, waving a piece of dried beef in the air, trying to attract the hound's attention. When that didn't work, she put two fingers in her mouth and whistled shrilly. Finally, the noise ceased and everyone calmed down.

"You'll thank me in the end," said Vivienne, picking up her skirts and heading quickly toward the wagon. Everyone in the courtyard, from the servants to the nobles, looked on, laughing at the entertainment.

"The last thing I'll be doing is thanking anyone," Zachariah grumbled, throwing his hands in the air once more and heading for his horse. The only thing he could wish for right now was that he'd solve this case as quickly as possible, not having to stay in Maltby le Marsh with these people any longer than needed.

Chapter Two

Vivienne chose to ride in the back of the wagon with the children and Grunt instead of taking her own horse on the trip. This way she could be closer to, and spend more time with, her newfound son, Martin. She honestly could not stop smiling every time she looked at the boy. This was her baby! She was his mother. It would take a while to get used to that.

Martin was her missing baby that she'd only had the opportunity to hold for a few short hours after his birth. Because of thieves on the road, she'd lost her entire family so quickly one night. She'd never even had the chance to name her newborn baby boy. Since it had been seven long years since that happened, Vivienne never dreamed she'd ever see her child again. But life was good now. Fate had brought her baby back to her and given her the chance to be a mother once again. Now, if only she could find her brother Adrian, who went missing that same horrible night. If so, things would be even better. But Adrian had not tried to contact her since he'd disappeared. Her brother knew their aunt and uncle lived at Mablethorpe Castle, yet he'd never shown up there. Sadly, Vivienne realized that meant that Adrian was most likely dead.

They were almost to Maltby le Marsh when Grunt started pouncing on something under the hay in the back of the wagon. It was most likely a mouse that had hidden away on the cart back at the castle.

"Grunt, nay," she scolded her dog, but he didn't stop. And then she saw why. It wasn't a mouse he was after at all. Out from the hay came a quivering little pink nose and long whiskers.

"It's Chomp!" cried Martin, getting to his knees, crawling over and reaching down into the hay, picking up the white ferret to show the others.

"That's one of Wymond's ferrets," said Maleine, holding on to Grunt who looked like he wanted to eat the weasel-like animal.

"Bloody hell," Vivienne heard Zachariah say from atop his horse as he rode right next to the wagon. "What is that thing doing here?"

"Oh, no," said Vivienne, realizing she had promised the sheriff that the ferrets would stay behind. "I suppose it crawled up into the wagon when no one was looking. Sorry about that, Sheriff." She took the ferret from Martin, holding it securely in two hands.

"If Chomp can be here than so should Midnight. Father, we need to go back and get my cat," whined Starah.

"That is never going to happen," he responded.

"I suppose we'd better bring Chomp back to Wymond or he will worry about her," Vivienne mentioned.

"Nay. We are not going back," Zachariah told her. "But I swear to God that if we do, you are all staying behind and I will conduct this investigation with just the constable."

"Zachariah!" gasped Magdalena, blessing herself from the front of the wagon. "Do not use the Lord's name in vain."

"That's for damned sure," said Nairnie. "Especially not around the children."

"Nairnie, please don't curse." Magdalena blessed herself again.

"Ooops," said the old woman, holding her hand up to her mouth. "I guess I am too used to hearin' the pirates cursin' from mornin' til night. It's hard to break a bad habit."

"Pirates?" asked Magdalena, getting another groan from Zachariah.

"We're here," he called out, as they rode up to the gates of Maltby le Marsh Abbey. "Now I want silence from everyone. And hold tightly to those pests or I will personally chain them up."

"Zachariah, I hope you are talking about the animals and not the children." Vivienne scowled at him.

"I was, but now that you mention it ... oh, never mind." They entered the courtyard and he dismounted, coming to the back of the wagon and holding out his hand to assist Vivienne.

"Thank you," said Vivienne, pushing the ferret into his hands and getting out of the wagon by herself. She then helped Starah while Maleine and Martin and the dog hopped out on their own. Constable Erikson aided Sister Magdalena and Nairnie.

"My, this is quite different from Mablethorpe Abbey," commented Vivienne, brushing the hay off her gown as she looked at the small, timeworn building made of red brick. The walls seemed to be crumbling right around them and the whole place lacked life. The few potted plants she saw were dead, and there were puddles of water sitting in the courtyard. Cloistered, or covered walkways, led from a long building on one side of the abbey, connecting to another long building across from it. She figured those were the separate dwelling quarters. One side for the monks and the other for the nuns, since this was considered a double monastery. An old, dingy church with ivy crawling up the walls was at the far side of the abbey. Outside the church was a small graveyard, positioned right next to it.

"Sister Magdalena, you've returned!" Two nuns hurried toward them with a monk following right behind.

"You've brought help. Thank goodness," said the monk.

"Yes, this is Sheriff Zachariah Fitch from Mablethorpe," Constable Erikson spoke up. "He'll be working with me to solve this mystery."

"And me, too. Good day, I'm Lady Vivienne Harlowe from Mablethorpe Castle," she introduced herself.

"Lady Vivienne, this is the Reverend Mother, our abbess," said Magdalena, nodding toward the oldest of the three. "I'd also like you to meet Sister Roberta who is second to the abbess, and is our prioress. Brother Harold is our abbot," she finished.

"Sister Roberta?" asked Vivienne, recognizing that name. "Is your mother by any chance, Wulfhilda, the woman who sells wine and mead at the market square in the town of Mablethorpe?"

"Why, yes. That's my mother. Do you know her?" Sister Roberta was a mature woman who wore the black habit of a Benedictine nun. Over her long tunic was a scapular, like an apron hanging from both the back and front. A simple leather cincture, or belt, was around her waist. Her white coif, a head-piece, consisted of a wimple that covered her neck and cheeks. A long black veil was over the top of her head. She wore a large wooden cross necklace and had her rosary secured to her side. No hair was showing and very little skin—just from her hands and her face.

"Yes, I've met your mother recently," Vivienne told her. "However, she neglected to mention to me that you were a prioress here at the abbey."

"We live humbly and with humility," said Sister Roberta dropping her gaze and blessing herself as she spoke.

"It's an honor to meet you, Reverend Mother." Vivienne paid attention to the abbess next, since she was in charge. She was clothed in the same manner, but her cross necklace was bigger and looked to be made of silver instead of wood. "Is that what you'd like us to call you?"

"Yes. Or you can call me Abbess or Mother Superior if you'd prefer," said the woman, with her nose in the air as studied her guests as if judging them silently. She didn't seem to know how to smile. Vivienne reached down and petted Grunt on the head as he sat patiently at her feet.

"Welcome," said Brother Harold. The monk wore an ankle-length black robe with a scapular over his shoulders as well. A hood covered his head, and he had a rope belt around his waist. A large wooden cross necklace hung from a chain around his neck. A rosary dangled from his side.

"Thank you," answered Vivienne, with a nod of her head.

The Mother Superior looked over at the sheriff's sister. "Who else have you brought back to the abbey with you, Sister Magdalena? There seems to be quite an unexpected crowd."

"We do have a few guests," Sister Magdalena affirmed. "I hope you don't mind, but Lady Vivienne wanted to bring along her son, Martin, as well as the sheriff's daughter, Starah, and her nursemaid, Nairnie. You'll be happy to know that I've also recruited a young woman for the abbey. Her name is Maleine." She put her hand on Maleine's shoulder. Maleine seemed nervous, and looked at the ground rather than at any of the nuns.

"Hello," said the girl softly, cradling the ferret in her arms.

"What is that evil-looking thing?" snapped Sister Roberta, first noticing the ferret.

"That's Chomp. She's not evil. She's a ferret who hunts for

rats," Martin spoke up, stepping forward with his wooden sword in his hand. "And this is Grunt. He uses his nose to sniff out murderers." Martin got down on his knees and hugged the dog around his neck.

"Abbess, I'm not sure all these people should be here. I mean ... considering the circumstances and all," said Brother Harold in deep concern. A crease deepened between his craggy brows. He kept his hands inside his robe, and his hood up, covering the tonsure of hair circling his head. He was an older man, mayhap the age of Vivienne's uncle. He was clean-shaven as all monks were, and soft-spoken. A gentle man indeed.

"Neither should the animals be here," added Sister Roberta. "After all, this is a place of worship, meditation, and prayer. It will be very disruptive to the order."

"I assure you all, none of them will get in the way of the murder investigation," spoke up Zachariah. He threw Vivienne a look of blame, silently relaying to her that he agreed with the others. She didn't care. She'd made a decision to bring them with her and no one was going to send any of them away.

"Weapons are frowned upon in a holy place and not allowed inside the church at all," pointed out the Mother Superior. Her eyes fastened on the wooden sword in Martin's hand.

"Martin's sword is made of wood and can't really be referred to as a weapon," Vivienne explained. "It won't harm anyone. It is more of a toy, really."

"My sword is only a toy?" asked Martin, with a disappointed frown. "But I thought you told me to respect it since it's a weapon, much like the knights use."

"Just don't be using it at the abbey," said Vivienne softly, giving Martin's shoulder a quick squeeze.

"Will you please show us where the body was found?" asked Zachariah, getting right to the point.

"Nay. It isn't a place for children," said the Mother Superior with a sniff. "It would be better for them to wait for you in their quarters."

"I'll stay back with the children," offered Nairnie, pulling Starah to her. Martin was still on the ground with the dog.

"Our rooms at the abbey are small and simple," explained the abbess, with no expression at all on her face. "This is a double monastery, which means the monks and any men who are residing here or staying with us while on their travels will lodge on one side. The females will remain on the other."

"Of course," agreed Vivienne. "We'd have it no other way."

"Constable, will you be staying here as well?" asked Brother Harold.

"Nay," answered Constable Erikson. "My home and family are here in Maltby le Marsh. I'll just be traveling here each day to help Sheriff Fitch with the investigation."

"Sister Magdalena, you'll be in charge of the postulant," instructed the abbess, speaking of Maleine. A postulant was one who was asking to be accepted into the order. There was a period of up to a year where the postulant would be trained and judged in order to be accepted as a novitiate to take her final vows. In the meantime, she would participate in a lot of praying as well as manual labor.

"Yes, Mother Superior, I would be honored to be in charge of the postulant's training. Thank you so much," Magdalena answered with a nod.

"Get the girl a habit to wear. My dear, you'll need to give that weasel to someone else," said the abbess. "As of right now, you are to give up all your worldly possessions to the church. You'll be sharing the dormitory with some of the other sisters."

"Yes, Abbess," said Maleine, handing the ferret to Starah.

"You will live by the rules of poverty, chastity, and obedience from now on," continued the abbess. "Prayer sessions in the church with the rest of the order happen eight times a day. Attending Mass is also a requirement."

"I'm expected to go to church eight times a day?" Maleine's head snapped up and her eyes opened wide. "You must be jesting."

"I assure you, I am quite serious, young lady. I never jest," the Reverend Mother answered, her pinched face showing her distaste for Maleine's free choice of words.

"It is our way of life and expected of you as part of your training now too, my dear," Magdalena told her, smiling kindly.

"That's right," agreed the prioress. "You will also be required to spend quiet time alone reading the Bible, and in private prayer and meditation throughout the day."

"But I don't even know how to read! And more prayers? By myself? Really?" Maleine's frantic gaze flashed over to Vivienne in what seemed like a cry for help.

"Don't worry. I'm sure they will teach you to read, Maleine," Vivienne assured her.

"That all depends. Are you of a high status?" asked the abbess.

"What do you mean?" Maleine looked confused by the question.

"She's not a noble," Vivienne spoke up for the girl. "Although her father was the mayor of Mablethorpe."

"I see. Then your father will be donating a good dowry for you to be here, I'm sure," said the abbess.

Maleine's scared look turned to one of sadness now. "Nay, Mother Reverend. My father will not be sending a dowry."

"Why not?" she demanded to know.

"He is dead." Maleine's voice was so soft it was almost hard to hear her. It seemed as if she had a difficult time talking about this aloud.

"He's dead? Well, then, I'm sure whatever you inherited will be given to the abbey."

"What?" Maleine's big eyes looked up in disbelief. Her father, while being mayor, had too many unpaid debts at the time of his death. Maleine even lost their house in the end. There was nothing at all that she'd inherited.

"I'll make sure that the town council sends a small donation on Maleine's late father's behalf, for her entrance into the abbey," spoke up Zachariah. Vivienne was thankful he'd interceded, since she didn't want the nuns to find out what kind of man the mayor had truly been.

"Since the girl is of a lower status, it is uncommon for us to teach her to read and write," explained Sister Roberta.

"That's right," agreed the abbot. "Perhaps Maleine would be better suited as a lay sister," was his suggestion.

"Lay sister?" Vivienne realized that lay sisters did all chores and physical work and were never truly considered a full-fledged nun, no matter if they'd spent their entire lives at the abbey. She wanted something better than that for Maleine. The girl deserved that much. "I'm sure Maleine will prove to be a good candidate for a choir nun if only given the chance."

"Oh, yes. I do love to sing," said Maleine, finally showing some interest. "I want to be a choir nun, please."

"Nay!" snapped the abbess. "Choir nuns are nobles only. Besides, you would have to know how to read and write which you've already said you can't do. It is out of the question."

"But I want to know those skills," cried Maleine. "I'm a fast learner, really I am."

"Can you cook, Maleine?" asked Brother Harold.

"Well, yes, a little. I often cooked at home."

"Reverend Mother, I suggest she work in the kitchen then," said the abbot in a soft voice.

"Yes, I agree," the nun answered.

"If I work in the kitchen, do I still have to pray so much?" Maleine still seemed worried about all the praying that would be required. As far as Vivienne knew, the girl had probably never even gone to church when she lived back in Mablethorpe.

"Yes, my dear, you'll still have to pray," said Magdalena. "Going to church for the prayer sessions is required of our lay people as well, unless you are preparing a meal for directly afterward. But don't fret. After a while you will look forward to the prayer sessions, I promise. I know I do."

Vivienne heard a little snort from Zachariah when his sister said this, and it made her wonder why he'd reacted in such a manner.

"I'm hungry," Martin whined, standing up and taking Vivienne's hand. "Can we eat now?"

"Yes. When are the meals?" asked Maleine, with longing in her eyes to hear something, anything, she might enjoy more than working and praying all day long.

"Usually, guests eat in a separate hall away from the others," explained the abbess. "But since you are our only guests at this time, you will be allowed to eat with the monks and nuns in the refectory during your stay here."

"When's the meal?" asked Martin licking his lips. Grunt looked up at the boy and whimpered. The dog's long tongue shot out and licked his lips too.

"We will all eat together after Sext," Mother Superior informed them.

"After sex? I thought nuns were supposed to be chaste!" Maleine's eyes opened even wider, almost causing Vivienne to laugh aloud. Vivienne looked over at Zachariah, who muffled his guffaws with a hand to his mouth followed by a fake cough.

"She's speaking of the prayer sessions. Such as Sext ... None ..." Magdalena started to tell her, as if that should mean something to Maleine.

"None? So then, after no sex? Or does that mean no food if you have sex?" Maleine's brow furrowed. "I'm confused."

"Sext is the name of one of their prayer sessions," Vivienne explained before this conversation got any further out of hand.

"That's right," said Magdalena. "Sext is what we call the midday prayers. You'll learn all about it. It's part of your training."

"I'm hungry too," Starah spoke up. "Will we be having haggis like Nairnie makes? Did you know haggis is the innards of a sheep cooked with other stuff, wrapped up in the sheep's stomach? It sounds awful but it's really good." The little girl petted the ferret as she relayed this information.

"We will certainly not be having that!" snapped Mother Superior, looking as if she were about to swoon at the thought of eating animal organs. "We very seldom eat meat here at the abbey, and it is usually only on special occasions."

Vivienne heard Zachariah groan again at this announcement.

"And on Fridays we fast," she continued. "That means, no food at all."

Grunt let out a big sigh just then, and dropped down and put his nose between his paws, almost as if he understood what she'd said.

"But it's not even Lent," said Maleine.

"Och, this is nonsense!" Nairnie threw her hands up in the air in disgust. The Scottish woman was always more than happy to give her honest opinion, even at the most inappropriate times. "The wee ones need food to maintain their strength and to grow. They are no' trainin' to be a blasted monk or nun and shouldna have to fast! God's eyes, let them eat!"

The nuns gasped at her cursing.

Zachariah cleared his throat. "Nairnie, remember where you are now, please. And I'm sure they don't really expect their guests to follow the same rules as those enrolled in the order. Do you?" He looked over at his sister when he said it.

"Of course, not," said Magdalena. "I'm sure we could find food for all of you on a Friday, although there will be no one to cook it."

Before anyone could respond to that, Mother Superior spoke up again. "Erlene, you will be required to work in the fields for the rest of the day after the meal."

Everyone looked around, wondering whom she was talking to.

"I think you mean, Maleine," Vivienne corrected her, seeing that the girl was about ready to cry. She couldn't blame her. When Maleine made the decision to become a nun, Vivienne was sure she had no idea what all was expected in the way they lived and the promises they made.

The bells in the steeple rang out loudly, echoing across the courtyard. Mother Superior's head snapped around to look up at the church. "Sext is starting. I am sure you will all be joining us?"

"I have some things to discuss with Constable Erikson about the case, so that's a nay for me." Zachariah so gracefully removed himself from going to the church with the others.

Vivienne didn't want to attend either. And she knew the children would never sit still that long. She also didn't want to leave the animals unattended. If they did go, Nairnie would most likely stop the prayers to tell the monks and nuns her opinion, and that was not going to be a good thing at all.

"I'm sure Nairnie would like to get the children settled." Vivienne spoke up for them before any of them could say another word.

"I will show our guests to their quarters," offered Magdalena. "Maleine, after the prayer session we'll get you your new clothes."

Vivienne was about to make up an excuse for herself as well, but when Maleine's scared eyes sought her out, she decided she couldn't abandon her. Not now. Not after everything she'd been through lately. Maleine needed a friend and Vivienne decided she would be there for her in her time of great need.

"I'll go with the rest of you to the church," Vivienne offered.

"You will?" Zachariah looked up in surprise, seeming very confused as to why she'd said this.

"Yes, Sheriff Fitch," she told him. "I will rejoin you and Constable Erikson at the meal. For now, I would like to be there to support Maleine."

Maleine let out a deep breath of relief. "Thank you so much, Lady Vivienne." Finally, Vivienne was able to get the smile to return to Maleine's face, even if it didn't quite reach the girl's eyes.

"This way, please," Magdalena told Nairnie, who followed her with the children and animals in tow.

"Constable Erikson?" Zachariah hurried over and the two men walked in the opposite direction, discussing things about the case.

Vivienne joined Maleine, and together they followed the nuns to the church.

"Lady Vivienne, I'm scared," Maleine whispered.

"Yes, the abbess is quite frightening, I agree," she whispered back.

"Not just that," said the girl, looking off into the distance and pointing at the graveyard. Her face paled and a shudder ran through her body. "Please don't think I am addled, but I swear I just saw a ghost!"

Chapter Three

"Aghost?" asked Vivienne, her attention flitting over to the graveyard where Maleine pointed. She saw nothing. "What did it look like? I mean, I saw a ghost back at the graveyard at Mablethorpe, too."

"I'm not sure. It was only for a second or two. He was … white and see-through, I think. And floating. He looked to be wearing a cloak and hood. It happened so fast and then he just disappeared."

"That sounds like the same monk ghost that I saw in the graveyard back home. I wonder if he is the one luring us here."

"Lady Vivienne, please hurry and bring the postulant with you," called out the Mother Superior. "Being late for prayers is not tolerated."

"Maleine, I'm sorry but I am afraid Mother Superior is going to be a lot scarier than any ghost," Vivienne whispered to girl, making them both chuckle.

27

"So where exactly was the body found?" Sheriff Fitch headed into the refectory with the constable.

"Actually, it was discovered in one of the walls of a small room just off the kitchen," responded Constable Erikson. "Or should I say it is still there."

"Show me."

"I think we should wait for Mother Superior and the others. She won't like us disobeying orders."

"You let me worry about Mother Superior." Zachariah didn't care for the nun or anything she had to say. "And what do you mean the body is still there? You didn't move it? It will be starting to decompose and I am sure creating a foul stench by now."

"Nay. It's not what you think. You'll see," said the constable as they walked into the kitchen. The lay brothers and sisters who were preparing the meal for directly after the prayer session nodded at them as they passed by. Still, they didn't say a word. Idle chatter or even meaningful conversations were not allowed unless started by the Mother Superior or someone she'd granted permission to speak.

At the far end of the kitchen, were three small rooms.

"What are those?" Zachariah nodded.

The constable answered. "One is the pantry where bread is kept. The second is a buttery for the wine and ale. And the third is the scullery where the dishes are washed and cleaned and the kitchen utensils and pots are stored."

"Which room is the one with the body?" asked Zachariah.

"The scullery. That one," said the constable, pointing to the correct room. His eyes darted around. He looked quite concerned that the abbess would find them there and they'd be reprimanded.

Zachariah was here to do a job and would wait for no one's permission. He walked into the scullery and immediately noticed the bricks missing in the back wall. The entire kitchen area was constructed of either stone or bricks, hence making it harder for a fire to spread throughout the abbey should an accident happen.

"In there?" he asked, already knowing the answer but somehow wanting the constable to confirm it.

"Yes. I was told by Brother Harold that the wall needed repairing. When the lay monks started removing bricks to put in more mortar, that is when they found her."

"Her? The corpse is a woman, then?" Zachariah walked over to the far side of the room and stopped in front of the open hole in the wall.

"We think so, by the remains of the clothes. They seem to be those of a nun."

"Hand me a candle," instructed Zachariah. The constable lit a candle from a side table and gave it to him. Zachariah stuck his head in the hole of the brick wall, using the candle in order to see into the dark space.

Sure enough, someone was inside. But this someone wasn't a decomposing body as he'd expected. This corpse was mainly a skeleton, wearing what looked like a long black gown that was mostly tattered and torn. The skeleton's hair was cut short and of a deep red color. A short veil crowned her head.

"Do you see her?" asked the constable.

"I do. It seems to be a nun, just like you said. However, her clothes are so chewed up by rats, that it is hard to tell anything for sure."

"Rats?" asked the constable. "Are you sure of that?"

"Oh, trust me, I'm sure. I am quite familiar with rats from my last investigation. I'd say the rodents probably ate her flesh right off her body. It's going to be hard telling how long this corpse has been here. If we knew who she was, it would certainly help answer some questions."

"How long do you guess she's been in there?" asked the constable. "I mean, is there any way you can actually tell?"

"I can't say for sure but can probably estimate. Mayhap a year, I'm thinking. I can't see normal signs of decay because of the rat activity, so it could be several years or possibly even longer."

"Let me take a look," came a voice from behind them.

Zachariah jumped in surprise, not realizing anyone was in the room with them. He turned so fast that wax from the candle splashed onto his hand, causing him to cringe in pain. "Nairnie," he ground out. "Aren't you supposed to be watching over the children?"

"I am," she told him, hurrying to his side. "They're here too. "Starah! Martin! I'm in here," she shouted.

"Please don't yell, Nairnie. Remember you are in an abbey," Zachariah reminded her. "Nobody even talks aloud around here unless asked to do so. You'll have to keep your voice down."

"Sorry," she said in a crackly, hoarse whisper. "Give me the candle, Sheriff." She reached out and took it from him before he had a chance to object. Sticking the lit beeswax candle into the opening, followed by her face, she took a long, good look around. "Och, there's a dead person in here," came her muffled voice, since her head was buried in the opening of the wall.

"Nairnie, we know that. Now back out and give me the flame. I am trying to investigate."

"Hold on. I see something reflecting in the firelight but I can't tell exactly what it is. It is near the head of the corpse. It looks like jewelry to me." She shoved her arm into the hole next. "Blethers, it's too far away. I canna reach it."

"Nairnie, stop it and get out!" snapped the sheriff. "This is a crime scene and you shouldn't be touching anything. You don't belong here, so leave."

"Sorry," she said, backing out and handing him the candle.

"Ye might want to take the skeleton out of there so we can have a better look at it."

"You think so?" he asked sarcastically.

"There's a skeleton? Excellent! I want to see it too." Martin ran into the scullery, followed by Grunt. Starah was right behind them still holding on to the ferret which was squirming around in her arms, wanting to be set free.

"Children, you shouldn't be in here," warned the sheriff.

Martin ran up, pushing his way to the wall but he was too short to look into the hole where the bricks had fallen out to expose the hidden area between the walls. He jumped up and down, trying to see inside.

"Chomp, nay," yelled Starah. The ferret slithered out of her arms, hitting the floor with a thud. The animal immediately ran around the scullery. Grunt barked and chased after it, knocking into everything, sending pots and pans clattering to the floor.

"God's eyes, please tell me this isn't happening," mumbled Zachariah, already regretting allowing Nairnie and the children to come along on this investigation.

"Zachariah! Stop using the Lord's name in vain," scolded his sister Magdalena, hurrying into the room after the others.

"Magdalena, why are they all in here?" asked Zachariah. "I thought you were taking them to their sleeping quarters."

"The children wanted to see the rest of the abbey, especially where they will be eating," explained Magdalena. "I wanted to show them the refectory and kitchen on the way to their quarters."

"The constable and I are trying to conduct a murder investigation here. I cannot do so with all this commotion."

"Yes, it is a little noisy. Mother Superior won't like it at all," agreed Magdalena. "Come, children. It is best if we leave now."

"I have them," said Nairnie, taking hold of Starah's hand. Grunt continued to bark.

"Martin, quiet down the dog," ordered Zachariah.

"I'm trying," said Martin, pulling at the dog's collar as Grunt stood on his back legs, attempting to get into the hole in the wall.

"What is that blasted dog doing now?" Zachariah didn't think things could get any worse.

"He's trying to get Chomp because she just disappeared into the wall," explained Martin.

"Oh, no. That's not good." Zachariah pulled the dog down, sticking his head into the hole again, using the candle for light. "I see Chomp. She's down a little ways and seems to be playing with something by the head of the corpse."

"Mayhap it's a rat," said Martin. "After all, she was a rat-catching ferret."

"Nay. It's not a rat." Zachariah could see something in the ferret's mouth that was reflecting light. "Martin, can you call the ferret to you, please? If so, mayhap I can grab her."

"I don't have the Pied Piper's horn to do that," said Martin.

"Try this." Nairnie handed him an empty bottle.

"What should I do with this?" asked Martin.

"Blow over the top of it," explained Nairnie. "It'll make a whistlin' noise."

"All right." The boy did as told.

Starah nodded. "It sounds a lot like the Pied Piper's horn. Well done, Martin."

"Who is this Pied Piper you keep mentioning?" asked Sister Magdalena.

"Never mind," said Zachariah, noticing that the ferret was coming closer, cocking her head as if she heard the whistling noise and was responding to it. "Keep it up, Martin. I think it's working. She's almost near enough for me to get her." When Chomp got closer, Zachariah grabbed her by the scruff of her neck and yanked the animal out of the hole. The ferret's pink nose quivered as she held something clamped tightly in her jaws.

"What does she have?" asked Martin.

"Constable Erikson, please take this candle." Zachariah gave it to the man and used his free hand to remove the item from the ferret's mouth. "It looks like a brooch of some sort. Perhaps one that is used to fasten a cloak."

"Ah ha! I told ye I saw jewelry," said Nairnie, beaming with pride.

"Good girl, Chomp." Starah lifted her hands. "Father, I'll take her now."

"With pleasure." He gently handed the animal over to his daughter.

Holding the brooch on his palm, Zachariah inspected it closer. It was metal, and looked to be made of pure silver. It had a long sharp pin that was attached to a circular hoop open at both ends. The piece was engraved with an ornate design. The ends looked like snakes with small red rubies for eyes.

"What's going on in here?" came the angry voice of Mother Superior. With her hands folded piously, the nun's robes swept across the floor as she entered the small scullery, followed by Maleine and Vivienne.

"We heard Grunt barking and thought there might be trouble, so we left the prayer service early," Maleine informed them.

"Sheriff Fitch found a clue on the dead person," Martin eagerly explained. Grunt barked as if he were agreeing.

"Sheriff, I thought I told you that the children don't belong here," snapped Mother Superior.

"She's right," agreed Vivienne. "I don't want my son lingering around a murder scene. Nairnie, will you please take the children and the animals to our quarters?"

"I'll show them the way," offered Magdalena. "Come, children."

Finally, after they left, along with the animals, things calmed down again.

"Is this where you found the murdered person?" asked Vivienne, wanting to know facts about the case.

"The corpse is still inside the wall," explained the sheriff.

Vivienne curiously walked over to the hole in the wall, trying to see in, but it was too dark to make out anything inside.

"Yes, this is the place," said Brother Harold. He had entered right behind them. "Some of the bricks were loose and I asked the lay brothers to repair them. When they removed them to start working, they noticed something in the wall and came to me right away."

"May I, Constable?" Vivienne held out her hand and he gave her the candle. She peered into the wall, seeing a skeleton with torn-up clothing. The hands of the skeleton were bound by a rope that looked to be the same simple belt worn by the monks and nuns. There was a rag in her jaws that encircled her head and was tied at the back. The veil on her head told Vivienne this was indeed a nun. "Yes, it was obviously murder."

"Did you find anything else in the wall with the body?" asked the monk, looking at the sheriff who was still inspecting the brooch. "I wouldn't let anyone close enough to touch the body until I told the constable what the lay brothers had found."

"We did find something else," answered the constable. "It is a brooch that is used to fasten a cloak."

"And it looks quite ornate," said Zachariah, inspecting the cloak pin in his hand. "I don't believe anyone in the order would even own such a thing. Would they?"

"Most definitely not," sniffed Mother Superior. "We live simply and do not covet material objects."

"She's right," answered the monk, surveying the pin from

his position. "All possessions are required to be given up when one enters into the order. We all take the vow of poverty."

"Then how would that brooch have gotten inside the wall?" asked Vivienne. She blew out the candle and placed it on a nearby table and then proceeded to pick up the pots and pans that her hound had knocked to the floor.

"It is quite a mystery," answered Mother Superior.

"Sheriff, may I see the brooch?" Vivienne stretched her neck, looking over at Zachariah.

"Of course," he answered, handing it to her.

"It almost looks like something a noble would wear," she said, recognizing the ornate quality of the pin. "I have some brooches similar to this myself."

"Mother Superior, you have a lot of nobles who take vows to become nuns and monks, don't you?" asked the sheriff.

"Aye," she answered. "Some of them are either widows or widowers, but most of them are young. Usually fourth- or fifth-born children in a family. They are sent here to be nuns and monks by their families if their parents cannot find suitable marriage alliances for them. It is too expensive to raise so many children, otherwise."

"What happens to their dowries or their personal belongings once they come here?" asked Vivienne, inspecting the pin.

"They are stored at first and then sold, of course," said Mother Superior.

"The money is used to help support the church and the order," added the monk.

"Does this pin look familiar to either of you?" Vivienne held up the brooch.

"Nay. I can't say it does," answered the nun.

"Not to me," said Brother Harold, looking over with squinted eyes. "Of course, you might want to ask Brother Silas about it. He might recognize it."

"Who is Brother Silas?" Vivienne wanted to know.

"He is our sacrist," explained Mother Superior.

"And ... what exactly is a sacrist?" asked Zachariah.

Brother Harold was quick to explain. "The sacrist's duties include everything from ringing the church bells to being responsible for the care of the entire church. He handles the sacred vessels, as well as liturgical items and holy vestments."

"Yes, Brother Silas holds tremendous responsibility," agreed Mother Superior. "We, at the abbey, count on him for many things. The place could not operate properly without him."

"Does he have anything to do with the dowries taken in from the postulants?" asked the sheriff.

"He does," said Mother Superior. "There is a spot in the sacristy where the items are kept until sold."

"Who has access to this room?"

"Only the sacrist, Brother Harold, and myself hold the key."

"Then Brother Silas is whom I want to talk to," said the sheriff. "Where can I find him?"

"Oh, you can't talk with him now," explained Brother Harold. "He will be busy preparing the host and wine for Mass."

"Then when will he be free?" asked Vivienne. "It is important that the sheriff and I have a chance to question him. He might know something about this brooch."

"This is an abbey," Mother Superior reminded them, her voice terse. "We have a strict structure and there are procedures as well as certain schedules that must be followed and maintained at all times."

"This is also now a murder investigation," Zachariah pointed out. "A woman has been killed, and I won't stop until I find out her identity as well as who took her life. I am Sheriff of Mablethorpe and I have a job to do."

"Sheriff, I appreciate your concern and I want to find the

killer as much as you do," said the nun. "However, your procedures are going to have to wait for now. You'll be required to work around the schedule of the abbey while you're here." The bells started ringing from the church and the nun's head snapped up. "It is time to eat. If you'll all join the others in the refectory, we'll get started."

"What about the body?" asked Vivienne. "We'll need to remove it from the wall and inspect it closer for clues. We'll also have to question everyone at the abbey."

"I hardly think a dead body is going anywhere," said Mother Superior. "And there are only certain times of the day when the monks and nuns are allowed to speak. After the meal is finished, I'll make arrangements for you and the sheriff so you'll be able to move forward with your investigation."

"Thank you," said Vivienne, cutting off Zachariah when she was sure he was about to object. He was devoted to his work, and also not used to taking orders from anyone. Especially not a nun!

"Constable, will you be joining us for the meal?" asked Brother Harold.

"I could use a bite to eat." Constable Erikson rubbed his stomach. Vivienne didn't miss his tongue shooting out to lick his lips.

"Follow me then," said the monk. "Mother Superior." Brother Harold bowed his head and held out his arm. The nun swept past him out of the room, followed by the monk and then the constable.

"I really wish you hadn't accepted this job for us," the sheriff told Vivienne under his breath.

"Sheriff, it is your duty to help find killers and bring about justice for those whose lives were taken." Vivienne handed him the brooch. "You'll have to push aside whatever qualms you have with your sister right now. This case must take priority."

"Yes," he said, speaking to her while his focus remained on the brooch in his hand. "However, it's not about qualms with Magdalena, even if you believe that to be so. I'm afraid that with Nairnie, the children, and the pets along, this case is going to drive me mad before I have a chance to find even a single answer."

Vivienne chuckled. "Don't worry about that. I'm here to help smooth things over," she told him, reaching out and giving his forearm a squeeze. "Shall we join the others in the refectory for the meal?"

"Why not?" he asked sarcastically, slipping the brooch into his pouch. "After all, I suppose eating roots and weeds are the least of my problems at the moment."

Chapter Four

Zachariah sat at the table with the others in total silence as the food was served. Magdalena read aloud from the Bible as everyone consumed the almost all-vegetable meal of turnip and bean porridge, as well as a small serving of a dark, coarse bread with no butter. He stirred the hot porridge, not sure he wanted to taste it. What he needed right now was a hunk of meat to fill his aching belly.

A soft whimper came from under the table, followed by hot breath on his leg. He looked down to see Grunt's sad eyes staring up at him.

"Believe me, you won't want this," he whispered to the dog, finally putting a spoonful of bean porridge into his mouth. He almost gagged. It was bland and in desperate need of some meat as well as seasoning.

"Shhhh," whispered Vivienne from next to him, leaning over to speak directly into his ear. "Your sister is reading from the Bible. Pay attention."

"Why?" he mumbled under his breath, picking up the coarse bread. "Will there be a test on it later?"

Mother Superior cleared her throat, giving him the evil eye.

He took a bite of the dry bread and almost spit it out. He probably would have if the nun hadn't been watching him so closely.

Maleine walked up with a pitcher to fill their cups, already being given a chore to do.

"Finally," said the sheriff, holding his cup up high. Maleine put only a splash of wine in it, and proceeded to pour Vivienne some wine next. "Wait. Fill it up," he told her, still holding his cup high. "To the top."

"I can't," she told him in a soft voice. Maleine's eyes flashed over to the Mother Superior and then back to him again. "I was told that the amount of wine is restricted except on hot summer days."

"It is summer. And I promise it is going to be hot today." Zachariah waved his cup in front of her. "I am not a monk, Maleine, so what does it matter?"

"I don't want to get in trouble on my first day here at the abbey." Fear filled the girl's eyes.

"Don't put her in that position," scolded Vivienne. "Continue, Maleine. The sheriff can have my wine." She pushed her cup over to him, making him feel suddenly guilty. Her cup was only half filled as well. She would need something to wash down this awful meal, so he couldn't possibly in good faith drink hers.

"Nay. You take it." Zachariah pushed Vivienne's cup of wine back to her. "And Grunt can have my bread." He slid the bread off the table, dropping it to his lap, hoping Mother Superior hadn't noticed. The dog gobbled up the bread in two bites, licking his lips afterward. "I'm glad to see someone enjoyed it," he commented.

Magdalena finished reading, putting down the Bible and coming to sit next to Zachariah.

"Oh, it looks like you're nearly finished eating," she whispered to him. "And it seems they forgot to give me a bowl of food."

"You can have mine." He slid the bowl of uneaten bean porridge and the spoon to his sister.

"Thank you, brother, but there is no need to fast on my account," she whispered.

"Believe me, I want to. Now, if you'll excuse me, I have work to do." He got up from the table, ignoring Mother Superior's disapproving gaze. Hurrying out of the refectory, he didn't stop until he heard Vivienne's sweet voice from behind him.

"Zachariah, wait for me."

He stopped in his tracks, noticing she used his name in a familiar way. He rather liked that. Turning around, he saw Vivienne holding up her skirts and running to catch up with him. Grunt trotted along at her side.

"Aren't you afraid you'll be reprimanded for leaving the meal early?" he asked. "After all, it seems there are strict rules that need to be followed at every minute of the day and night while here at the abbey."

"I was never any good at following rules, and you know it."

That made him smile. It was something he admired about Vivienne. She had a mind of her own and didn't let anyone tell her what to do.

"Yes, I do know it. Better than anyone."

"Why did you leave the refectory so soon?" she asked.

"I didn't care for the meal."

"Oh. I thought it might have had something to do with Magdalena. After all, you seem to do anything possible to avoid being with or talking to her. Why is that?"

They walked together slowly across the courtyard.

"Why is it that you never give up trying to get information out of me, even though I've told you it is a personal issue?"

"I consider us good friends. Don't you?"

"Yes," he answered. "You know that."

"If you can't confide in a good friend, then who can you talk to about things that are bothering you?"

"Who said anything was bothering me?"

"It is written all over your face, not to mention your actions."

Zachariah let out a deep sigh. "There's not much I can hide from you, is there, Vivienne?"

She flashed him a quick smile. "Why would you even want to hide anything from me? I mean, I've told you all about my life. You know everything there is to know about me."

As SOON AS Vivienne said the words, she realized she was naught more than a big liar. She hadn't told Zachariah everything about her. There was something she'd kept a secret from everyone except for her aunt and uncle. Her hand went to her chest, covering the ring she wore hidden on a chain under her clothing. It had been given to her by her dying mother. She'd been told it was the ring of King Edward, and that she was the bastard child of their sovereign. Since she still wasn't sure what to think about the whole situation, she'd kept it to herself and had never shared the information with the sheriff. Only her aunt and uncle knew about it, but they'd promised to keep her secret. For now. Since her uncle was planning a tournament soon and she was told the king would be attending, she had every intention to meet King Edward at that time. Mayhap she'd even be brave enough to confront him about being his bastard daughter. But for now, her secret would remain hidden, just like the necklace.

"Let's sit down," Zachariah told her, motioning to a wooden bench that was placed at the edge of one of the cloistered walkways that connected several of the buildings.

"All right," she said, taking a seat. He sat down next to

her, leaning forward and putting his face in his hands. "Did you want to tell me now why you seem to push Magdalena away?"

"It's not like that." He removed his hands from his face, staring out in front of him as he spoke. "You don't understand. You moved away and you weren't around for most of what went on in my family."

"I'm sorry about that, but I had no choice. I had to follow my family. But why don't you tell me about it now? I'd like to be here for you, even if I wasn't when you really needed me."

Those words must have broken through his wall that he always had up to protect himself. He slowly turned to face her, his eyes seeming to drink her in. Mayhap he was finally going to open up to her.

"Vivienne ... I ... I ..."

"Go on," she urged him. "You know you can tell me anything."

"I know I can. You've always been such a close and dear friend to me."

She reached out and took his hand in hers, staring deeply into his eyes. "Tell me everything that is troubling you. And be sure to leave nothing out."

He chuckled at that. "It would take way too much time, sweetheart. Besides, you don't want to know what goes on in here." He lifted his free hand, tapping his forefinger against his temple.

She liked the way he'd called her sweetheart. It made her feel ... special. "I'm sure it's not half as scary as what goes on in here." She imitated his action, tapping her finger against her own temple.

They both laughed, breaking the tension between them.

"Magdalena is the eldest sibling, right?" she asked, even though she knew the answer. Growing up, she'd met each of his three siblings. She probably knew them better than Zachariah knew himself.

"Aye," he answered. "She is the eldest, then comes me, followed by Isaac and my other sister."

"Other sister," she repeated. "You mean Cassandra. Why can't you speak her name aloud? You weren't like this years ago."

"This isn't about her." He pulled his hand away from her. When he looked as if he'd go silent again or possibly get up and leave, she quickly directed the conversation back to Magdalena.

"You're right. We are talking about Magdalena and why you hate her so much."

His head jerked upward and he looked down his nose at her. "I don't hate her. It's just that she is responsible for—"

"For what?" Vivienne could see how hard this was for Zachariah. He had some things buried so deeply within him that it was going to take a lot of prying to uncover them. "Does this have anything to do with Margaret?" she asked, speaking of his late wife.

"Yes." He clenched his hands together and looked down to his lap. "Margaret took it upon herself to care for Magdalena when she got the pox," he said, in naught but a whisper.

"Yes, go on." Vivienne was starting to understand things now. "But Magdalena didn't live with you and Margaret and Starah after the death of your parents because she was a nun."

"Yes, that's right, she joined the order. However, she came to visit me sometimes and stayed at our house. When Magdalena took her vows, I felt as if she'd abandoned me. Mother was already dead, and then, so was Father. I felt as if I had to care for my other siblings as well as my wife and newborn baby. Not to mention, I had a new job, taking over as sheriff in my father's place. It was all so overwhelming."

"I understand. But it wasn't long before your other siblings moved away too."

"I still wish they hadn't. I tried to hold the family together but just couldn't. My family fell apart so fast that I wasn't even sure what had happened."

"Tell me about when Margaret died."

He stared off into the distance as he recalled those days. "Magdalena sometimes came to visit us, staying for up to a week at a time."

"I'm surprised the Mother Superior allowed her to leave the abbey."

"Me, too. Anyway, the last time she came to visit us, she became ill with the pox. She was too sick to send back to the abbey, so she stayed with us. My wife tried to heal her."

"I was away visiting friends with my aunt and uncle at the time, and didn't arrive back in Mablethorpe until the day before Margaret died," she remembered.

"Margaret died of the pox. I still can't believe it," he said, wringing his hands together and staring at the ground. "My wife had sent Starah and me away, not wanting us to catch Magdalena's illness. But she stayed right there with my sister the entire time, to take care of her every need."

"Why would she do that?" asked Vivienne. "Didn't she know how contagious the pox was?"

"She knew," he said softly. "But at the time the town's doctor was away. Margaret had a kind heart and didn't want Magdalena to die all alone. You see, my sister was very ill, and most people don't recover from something like that."

"Even so, that wasn't fair to you and Starah. Margaret must have known she'd end up catching the pox and dying. No?"

"Nay, not really. You see, Margaret had the pox when she was a child and she survived it. We've all heard our entire lives that no one can get the pox twice. We thought Margaret would be safe. However, as we now see, that was untrue."

"But Magdalena didn't die from the pox."

"Nay, she didn't. My wife somehow healed her with herbs and potions. I think she might have even used some good luck charms, I don't know."

"I see." Vivienne was now starting to understand the turmoil going on in Zachariah's head. It had to be so hard to lose Margaret after she had risked her life to save his sister. "But there was no one to heal your wife in the end, was there? And when she died, you and Starah were left to carry on without her."

"Magdalena should have stayed at the abbey instead of coming to visit. She knew I was angry with her for leaving the family that way. I think she was trying to make amends, but it only made things worse between us."

"I hear the pox can travel quickly and there is no real cure. Those who survive it are just lucky."

"Margaret didn't even let me know she'd caught the pox. I heard it from Magdalena after she was feeling better and called for the doctor. I wanted to be with Margaret, but the doctor refused to let me or Starah into the house. God's eyes, why did I listen to her when she asked me to take Starah and leave the house in the first place? If I had been there, I would have known she was sick too. I might have been able to help her. She needed me, Vivienne. And I wasn't there for her. Then I was called away on a case that took longer than it should have taken. When I returned, she was dying, taking her last breaths. The doctor made me stand at the doorway to say my goodbye to her. He wouldn't even let Starah in the house at the time. I guess children catch the pox more easily. Dammit, why didn't I put my family before my job? I will never forgive myself for that as long as I live."

"Stop it!" Vivienne commanded. "Margaret didn't want you and Starah to catch the pox too. She knew what she was doing by not telling you she was dying. There was nothing you could have done to save her. If you had gone to her side to help her, then you would have caught the illness too and passed away as well. If so, Starah would have no parents at all right now."

"Dammit, it is all Magdalena's fault that Margaret's gone." Zachariah smashed one angry fist against his open palm. If not for her, my wife would still be alive today."

"You cannot blame this on your sister!" she told him. "Magdalena was there trying to make amends. No one knew she'd become ill. It was naught but an act of God and you need to accept that."

"Oh, really? I suppose, like the way you've accepted the deaths of your parents and brother? Was that an act of God too?" he asked with a hard edge to his voice.

Her body stiffened. She had never forgiven God after losing her entire family in one night. The sheriff made his point clear, but she didn't like it. "I think we should go now," she said, starting to stand, but he reached up and grabbed her arm and pulled her back down to the bench.

"I'm sorry, Vivienne. It was low of me to say that. I know how much you've suffered. You have been through more turmoil and sadness and hardships than anyone I know."

"Everyone's losses and the things that hurt them are very real to them. I understand that, Zachariah. However, I don't need to remind you that my family was taken from me, and my parents were killed by thieves right in front of my very eyes. I was scared for my life! And I felt so helpless, not being able to save them."

"You'd just given birth, Vivienne. No one expected you to fight back. There was nothing you could have done to change the outcome."

She ignored what he said since she didn't believe it completely. Instead, she continued to talk about his life, not wanting to face her own demons right now. "Margaret died of an illness. My parents died at the hands of horrible people. You cannot compare what happened to your wife to what took the lives of my family. It was totally different. Don't you understand? The deaths of my parents were more than just an act of God."

"You're right. And once again, I am sorry, Vivienne."

"*Lady* Vivienne," she so blatantly corrected him. "You are being naught but a selfish cur to think that you are the only one suffering because of Margaret's death. Did you lay the burden of guilt upon your sister's shoulders because she survived but Margaret didn't? Because if so, that is not fair, Sheriff Fitch. You, out of anyone, should know that innocent people should not be judged as guilty for something that was out of their control."

It took him a moment to answer, and just when she thought he'd run from this, he surprised her with his next words.

"You're right. It's not Magdalena's fault. Not really. I was just cross and needed someone besides God or myself to blame, I suppose."

"Then you will make things right with Magdalena? It has been too long."

"I'm working on forgiving her, because I know that what you say makes a lot of sense. But please, be patient with me. This is difficult. However, even though I really want to make amends with Magdalena someday, I'm just not ... quite ... ready yet."

"Good enough. For now," she said, reaching over and patting his hand with hers. "This is the first step you need to take and I am proud of you for doing so. But you are going to have to sit down and tell Magdalena how you feel about all this, and also that you no longer blame her for leaving to join the order. Or for Margaret's death."

"I will," he said, getting to his feet, busying himself with brushing invisible lint off his tunic. "But for now, I need to focus on the matter at hand. A woman has been murdered, and I ... *we*, need to figure out who she was, and who killed her."

"Then what are we waiting for, Sheriff?" Vivienne got to her feet as well, trying to hide the feelings inside her that the sheriff had poked and brought to the surface. He wasn't the only one who needed to reconcile with his past. But her story was so different. She needed to find answers before she could reconcile with God or anyone for what happened to her family. The only saving grace that tended to soften the blow was the miracle that she'd found Martin, the baby she'd lost seven years ago and that she'd thought was dead.

"Let's go back to the refectory and see about removing the corpse from the scullery wall," he suggested.

"We will," she answered. "But first, I'd like to see my son."

"Yes," he said with a quick nod. "Right now, I feel as if I'd like to see my daughter, too."

They walked side by side back to the refectory to spend time with the children they loved.

Chapter Five

Vivienne awoke the next morning to hear birds chirping from the open window. She turned over in the bed she'd shared with her son, seeing Grunt lying there instead, lounged out as if he owned the bed.

"Grunt, where is Martin?" she asked with a yawn.

"My lady, the children went down to the courtyard to join Sheriff Fitch," said Nairnie, looking out the open window. Nairnie had shared a second bed in the room last night with Starah, while Zachariah slept in his own chamber in a building for the monks and men. It was at the opposite side of the abbey.

"The sheriff's up already?" Vivienne heard this news from Nairnie and sprang out of bed.

"Everyone is up but ye, lassie. Ye ken the monks and nuns rise early for prayer and chores. The prayer sessions of Lauds and Prime are already over, and the bells just rang for the mid-mornin' prayers, whatever they're called."

"The midmorning prayers are called Tierce," she told Nairnie, hurrying over to don her gown. "I can't believe I slept so long. Why didn't you wake me?"

"I tried, but ye seemed to need yer rest, so I let ye be. I took the children for the meal, then left them with the sheriff and came back here to get ye. Sheriff Fitch said he canna wait any longer for ye. They are about to remove the corpse from the wall."

"Oh, nay. Nairnie, I wish you would have woken me." She struggled to put on her gown, feeling anxious and not wanting Zachariah to conduct the investigation without her.

"Let me help ye, lass." Nairnie grabbed the gown from her. She was about to put it over Vivienne's head when the old woman's eyes opened wide. "Why are ye wearin' that?"

"Wearing what?" she asked, still half-asleep. "It's my shift."

"Nay. That!" Nairnie reached out and picked up the ring hanging from the chain around Vivienne's neck. "It looks like it belongs to a king."

"Oh!" She quickly turned away and hid the ring back under her shift. "It's a family heirloom."

"Hah!" spat the old woman. "Unless ye are related to the king, I'd say that is far from the truth. Did ye steal it, lassie?"

"Nay. Of course not." Vivienne reached out and grabbed her gown and proceeded to don it herself.

"Then where did it come from?"

"If you must know, it was given to me by my dying mother." She laced up her bodice.

"Mmm hmm." Nairnie looked at her with one squinted eye, making Vivienne feel uncomfortable.

"It's the truth," she said in a fluster, rushing over and sitting down on a chair to put on her shoes.

"So yer mother stole it from the king, then."

"Nay! My mother would never steal anything. And why do you keep saying it is the ring of a king? Nobles are very wealthy, you realize."

"I ken that. But I dinna remember hearin' that yer parents

were that wealthy. I mean, that ring has a ruby in it the size of my eyeball."

"You are exaggerating, Nairnie. Now just forget that you even saw it."

Nairnie walked over with a boar's bristle brush and started brushing out Vivienne's hair. "Does the sheriff realize ye have that ring?"

"It's none of his business. Or yours for that matter." The brush hit a snag and pulled at Vivienne's head, causing her to jerk.

"I can tell when someone is no' tellin' the whole truth, lassie. What is it that ye are keepin' a secret?"

"What makes you think I am keeping anything a secret?"

"Ye hide the ring beneath yer clothin' instead of showin' it off like most nobles would."

"I am humble. I don't like to flaunt my wealth."

"Hah! Do ye really expect me to believe that?" Nairnie continued brushing out Vivienne's hair.

"Well, it's true." She pushed away Nairnie's hand and stood up.

"Ye wear it close to yer heart, so it must mean somethin' to ye. It's very important to ye for some reason."

"It's just a ring, Nairnie. It reminds me of my mother so I wear it close to my heart. But you are mistaken. It is not what you think it is."

"I've been around a long time, my lady. I've seen treasures and things that once belonged to kings."

"Your grandsons stole from the king?"

"My grandsons stole from whoever they could," she told her. "But I was also handmaid to the daughters of the Legendary Bastards of the Crown. Those three brothers constantly stole from the king."

"You've mentioned them before," said Vivienne, her hand

going to the ring under her clothes as she found herself deep in thought. "So, they are bastards of King Edward?"

"Yes. Rowen, Rook, and Reed are their names," she explained. "They are triplets born of the king's mistress. Because of superstition involving twins, let alone triplets, King Edward ordered them killed at birth."

"That's awful!" she exclaimed. "How did they survive?"

"It's a long story, lass. And one that you might want to hear from them someday, personally."

"Why would I want that?" she asked, meekly, thinking that Nairnie was somehow looking into her mind and figuring out what she'd protected and kept anyone from knowing.

"Ye asked about the bastards before and I found that curious." The old woman walked over and put the brush down on a table. Grunt jumped off the bed and shook and then stretched. His mouth opened wide in a yawn.

"That's because I am curious. I like to know things. That is why I help the sheriff investigate murders."

"Ye are the king's bastard, aren't ye? Tell the truth."

Vivienne gasped, unable to lie to Nairnie now that she'd figured out her secret.

"I ... I ..."

"It's nothin' to be ashamed of, my lady. I dinna ken why ye are keepin' it to yerself."

"Nairnie, there is a lot I don't know about my life. And until I find answers, I'd rather not let anyone know. But, yes, you are right. I am King Edward's bastard. I didn't know it until my mother gave me this ring and told me so with her dying breath."

"Ye are close to the sheriff, I can see that. Ye should tell him."

"I ... can't."

"Why no'? Because he was unable to solve the murder of your parents seven years ago?"

Vivienne's brows arched. "You know about that too?"

"I am good at observin' people and listenin' to not only what they say but to what they are tryin' no' to say."

"Yes. I can see that. Nairnie, will you please keep my secret to yourself for now?"

"I will, lass. However, I think if the sheriff had this bit of information, it might have helped him to figure out your parents' murderers, or at least the reason they were killed."

"I suppose you're right," she said softly. "I guess I didn't consider that."

"Ye dinna like when people keep things from ye when ye are tryin' to solve a murder, so I fail to see the reason why ye kept this secret instead of sharin' it with the one man who could help ye. That is, Sheriff Fitch."

"I know you're right, Nairnie. And I will tell him. Eventually. Just not right now."

"My advice to ye is no' to wait much longer, my lady. Seven years makes a cold trail to follow. At this rate, it might already be too late to figure out who killed yer parents or why they were murdered at all."

"Thank you, Nairnie. For keeping my secret," she said, turning and heading for the door with Grunt at her heels. She stopped and turned around. "Do you really think I should have told Zachariah about the ring when I first got it?"

"I wouldna have said so, if I didna believe it. I have the feelin' ye have been so busy blamin' him for not finding your parents' killers that ye kept evidence from him that might have helped greatly if he had been privy to the information."

"Yes. I do see your point," she said, turning back to the door, feeling no better than Zachariah now and how he'd blamed Magdalena for the death of his wife. Perhaps she was no different from him after all.

"Lay the body out here on this table," Zachariah instructed the constable and the monks as they pulled the skeleton out of the wall. They were in the scullery, but one end of the small room had been set up with a hanging curtain for privacy. Behind the curtain is where he would view the murdered body, searching for clues. On the other side, the kitchen helpers washed their dishes and used the utensils and pots and pans needed to make the meals.

"I'm here," came Vivienne's voice from behind the curtain. Then she pulled it aside and stopped, looking down at the skeletal remains that the men were placing on the table. "Sorry I'm late. I overslept."

"Yes, you most certainly did," said Mother Superior, who hovered, getting in the way as she watched Zachariah's every move. She stood with Brother Harold, smashed in the corner since the area was small and the people were many, making the room very crowded.

"Thank you for the assistance. That'll be all for now," the sheriff told the monks. The two monks bowed their tonsured heads and hurried past Vivienne, leaving the scullery. Grunt poked out his nose from behind Vivienne's skirt, and sniffed the air.

"Sheriff, if there is nothing you need from me, I have things to attend," said Mother Superior.

"Please, don't let me stop you," Zachariah told her.

"Brother Harold will stay to watch the investigation," she told them, hands again folded piously as she left the area. Vivienne stepped aside to let her pass.

"I'm glad I didn't miss the viewing of the body." Vivienne walked up to inspect the remains. Grunt sniffed around the floor.

"Where were you?" Zachariah asked softly.

"I told you, I overslept."

"Well, I was up since dawn," he told her. "By the way, I've asked Constable Erickson to send someone back to Mablethorpe tomorrow with the weasel. He's proving to be too much of a distraction."

"Oh, you mean the ferret. Chomp," she corrected him.

"Whatever you want to call him. Mother Superior didn't like the idea of him being in the abbey either, even though I told her he could hunt rats for her."

"Chomp is a female. But, I agree. It's probably better that she is returned. I'm sure Wymond will be worried about her."

"Sheriff, shall we inspect the body?" asked the constable.

"Yes," said Zachariah, leaning over to try and figure it all out. Pieces of dried up flesh still clung to the bones, but most of it was gone. There were no eyes or tongue to be seen, proving his theory of the rats, since that is what the rodents ate first. Short red hair stuck out from the scalp in all directions, covered by the remnants of a short veil on her head. "It is definitely a woman."

"A nun," said the constable.

"Nay, I think mayhap this woman was only a postulant, and hadn't taken her final vows yet," said Vivienne.

"Why would you say that?" asked the constable.

"Look at her veil." Vivienne pointed. "Although it is chewed by rats it seems shorter than normal. Plus, I don't see a coif. If she were a nun, one would cover most of her face. Brother Harold, I noticed that Maleine didn't have a coif either."

"That's right. Postulants don't normally wear one. Also, their veils are shorter, you are correct," agreed Brother Harold.

"Her hands are bond with rope as well as her feet," said the constable.

"I am guessing the rope was her belt," said Zachariah. "Or, at least, one of the ropes."

"Don't nuns wear leather belts?" asked Vivienne.

"Yes, sometimes," answered the monk. "However, rope cinctures are worn as well."

"What about postulants?" she asked.

"Rope belts are always given to those who have not yet taken their final vows," he explained. "It is meant to train them in their vow of poverty."

"Well, this is good information to have, I guess. One of the ropes that the murderer used to bind her was her own belt. We still have no idea of where the other rope came from." Zachariah inspected the body closer, seeing something inside her ribs. He carefully stuck in his fingers and lifted out a green gemstone rosary, holding it up high for the others to see. "This is a nice rosary, don't you all agree?"

"Yes. It seems quite ornate for a postulant to have," said Vivienne. "Or am I wrong, Brother Harold?"

The monk didn't really seem to be looking at it. "The rosary is one thing that can be chosen by the postulants as well as nuns and monks. Some come into the abbey with a family heirloom rosary, and others are given a rosary as a gift by visitors. Some rosaries are more ornate than others."

"What about those cross necklaces I've seen on the nuns?" asked the constable. "She doesn't seem to have one."

"That's odd," said the monk. "Even postulants are given cross necklaces."

"Mayhap she lost it in a struggle," suggested Vivienne. "We will have to ask around if one was found."

"That's going to be hard to answer until we know exactly when this girl was killed," said Zachariah. "Her red hair should be something to go on to identify her. It's rare as far as hair colors go."

"Yes, it is," said the constable.

"Brother Harold, do you remember any postulants who had red hair?" Zachariah asked the monk.

"I wouldn't be able to say. The girls entering the order have their hair cut and covered immediately after arriving here. Mother Superior would be the one to ask about that."

"We'll be sure to do so," answered the sheriff.

"I'll start asking some of the nuns if any of them remember a postulant here in the past who was a redhead," offered Vivienne. "Mayhap someone will know something about the dead woman."

"Look at her shoes," the sheriff pointed out.

"What about them?" asked the constable. "They seem to have holes chewed in them."

"Nay, those are not holes, Constable. She was wearing sandals when she died."

"You're right," said Vivienne, taking a closer look as well. "Then it must have been warm outside, possibly summer when she was killed. She doesn't seem to be wearing a mantle, so that would make sense."

"Curious," said Zachariah, pulling the cloak pin out of his pouch and holding it out in his palm. "Then if it was warm out, and she had no cloak, this brooch might have belonged to the killer."

"Yes. It could be," said Brother Harold. "Although, why would her killer be wearing a cloak?"

"To hide himself," said Vivienne. "He or she didn't want their identity discovered when they were stuffing the poor girl into the wall. I wonder if she was buried alive."

"My guess would be yes," said Zachariah. "If she were dead at the time, there would have been no need to gag or bind her. The killer was trying to muffle her cries for help and to keep her from fighting back."

Grunt put his front feet up on the table, biting at the clothes remnants near the torso of the dead woman.

"Grunt, don't do that," scolded Vivienne, pushing the dog away. The dog barked loudly.

"Lady Vivienne, can you please remove your hound?" asked the sheriff. "He is going to ruin any evidence that we find."

"I think Grunt is trying to tell us something, but I'm not sure what," Vivienne explained.

"Well, take him outside for now. The meal is going to be starting soon and the lay monks and nuns will need to use this scullery. We only have a short time left. Mother Superior wants the body removed from the refectory before everyone gathers here to eat."

"All right. I'll take Grunt outside and also check with Nairnie on the children," she told him.

"Good idea," he told her. "Brother Harold, is there a place to move the body for now until we can inspect it further?"

"It would be proper to bury the corpse right away," suggested the monk. "However, not in the cemetery since that is consecrated ground. If this woman was murdered, she'll have to be buried outside the perimeters of the churchyard. I'm sorry."

"I'm not yet ready to bury the remains." Zachariah looked over the skeleton as he spoke. "There is still an investigation going on, so I'll need access to the bones until I find some answers."

"Sheriff Fitch is right," spoke up Constable Erikson. "There might still be something we're missing so it would be a missed opportunity if we buried the body so soon."

"I also want a covering placed over the hole in the wall for now," instructed Zachariah. "I'm not yet finished investigating the inside of the wall where we found the corpse."

"I'll have the lay monks see to that right away," said the

monk with a nod. "And I suppose the body can be moved to the charnel house until after the investigation."

"Charnel house?" asked Vivienne from the door, holding open the hanging curtain. She had been lingering instead of checking on the children. "I'm not familiar with that term. What is it?"

"It's an ossuary," said Zachariah. When he saw her look of confusion, he explained further. "A room where exhumed bones are kept."

"Exhumed bones?" she gasped. "Whatever for?"

"The church graveyard is small," explained Brother Harold. "Sometimes we need to exhume those who have been dead for a while in order to have room to bury the newly departed."

"And you place these exhumed bodies in a house?" she asked.

"Yes. It's a stone building that is attached to the back of the church and can be entered from inside the church or from outside in the graveyard," explained the monk.

"If the building is small as you say, then how many corpses can actually be laid out in there?" Vivienne needed more of a visual, but Zachariah realized she wasn't going to like the answer. Still, being a curious woman she wouldn't stop with her questions until her curiosity was totally satisfied.

"My lady, it's nothing like you think in there," he told her, still trying to be vague.

"Then what is it like? Perhaps I'll just have to go and see for myself." She turned to leave but Zachariah rushed forward and took her by the arm to stop her.

"Nay. You first need to be prepared for what you'll witness."

"You say that like it's something appalling."

"It is. You see, the exhumed bodies are not intact. They are ... broken up. The skulls are all piled up, and the arm and leg bones are stacked together according to length."

"What?" Her eyes shot open wide and her jaw dropped. "That sounds terrifying! Why would anyone do such a thing?"

"To make room for the newly departed," said the monk with a shrug. "I'm sorry, my lady, but it is the way it's always been done."

"You don't have to go in there, Vivienne," said Zachariah under his breath. "There is no need, and no one is asking you to enter."

"Of course, I have to go in there." She shook off his arm. "Sheriff, I am not as frail as you think. I assure you that I will not swoon from seeing a pile of old bones."

"I hope not," he muttered, letting go of her arm. "Brother Harold, please bring a horse and wagon to the door so we can easily move the body. I have much work to do."

Chapter Six

"My lady, what are they doing?" asked Maleine, standing next to Vivienne as the monks carried the body of the dead woman out of the refectory and placed her on the cart.

"They are taking the murdered woman's remains to the ossuary," Vivienne told her.

"The what?"

"It's a room stacked up with exhumed bones. It allows space for the newly dead to be buried."

"Oh. That sounds like a horrible place." Maleine held her hand to her mouth. "I hope they won't make me work in there too."

Vivienne took a good look at Maleine. She was now wearing the clothes of a postulant which included a long, dark gown and a short veil. It was so odd to see her this dressed this way. Especially since she was only sixteen. The severity made her look so much older.

"I see they gave you your new clothes." Vivienne smiled, trying to act supportive.

"Ugh. I hate this," complained Maleine, holding out the sides of her gown, its hem brushing the floor.

"Did they cut your hair too?"

Maleine pulled off her short veil, almost causing Vivienne to cry out in alarm. Maleine's beautiful, long dark hair that was almost black and full of curls was gone! Now, she had only a short crop of curly hair, all different lengths. It had been hidden under her veil. "Why did they have to cut it so short?" she asked.

"It is part of the training, I guess." Maleine's hand went to her head. "Of course, I think my hair is shorter than they usually cut it because I was careless in the kitchen."

"What do you mean? Did they punish you by chopping off all your hair?"

"Yes, and no. I had an accident or two in the kitchen, and I think the Mother Superior let out her frustration with the shears in her hand."

"Accident? Are you hurt?"

"Nay, my lady, I am not hurt. I'm just clumsy. Or I've inherited bad luck from my father. I'm not sure which."

"Please, explain."

"Well, I fell and broke a jar of honey. I got it all over my hands and then touched my head and it got in my hair. Mother Superior was furious. She cut the sticky parts out of my hair with her red-handled shears."

"I'm so sorry to hear that."

"I also dropped the long-handled wooden paddle while taking loaves of bread from the oven. A small chunk of the handle broke off. It angered Sister Roberta as well as Mother Superior since the bread fell on the dirty floor. My meal was taken away as a punishment because of that."

"That's not right! I will sneak you some food."

"Nay, please don't, my lady. If anyone found out about it, we would both be in trouble. I will be fine. Much worse things have happened to others. I will endure." Maleine looked as if she was trying to keep from crying. Still, the girl remained steady and strong. Vivienne admired her bravery.

Nairnie had taken the children along with Chomp out to the abbey's orchard, and Vivienne was glad that they were not here right now. She had wanted to spend time with Martin, but realized that the investigation needed a lot of her attention. She wouldn't be able to spend time with her son unless he was at her side, and that wasn't what she wanted. Not when she was on her way to an ossuary. Martin and Starah were so young. They shouldn't have to be exposed to murder and exhumed bodies. They should be playing in the sunshine and running and laughing, like she used to do with Zachariah when they were that age.

"I'm sorry you had to see this, Maleine. Especially after everything you've been through lately. I thought you'd find solace at the abbey, but it isn't quite looking that way, is it?"

"I must admit, being a postulant hasn't been very enjoyable so far." Strain showed on Maleine's face.

"You mean because of your hair and the punishment? Besides that, are they treating you kindly?"

"Oh, yes, my lady. The monks and nuns are very kind, but since we are not allowed to talk except for small portions of the day, it is proving to be quite lonely. I miss talking with you, the children, and even Wymond."

"I can understand that. If I had to remain quiet, I don't think I'd survive five minutes."

They both giggled at that.

"Keeping quiet is hard, but what is even tougher is having to work in the kitchen and in the fields every minute that I am not in church praying. And you know how much praying we are expected to do." Maleine rolled her eyes.

"Yes. It is quite an extreme and overwhelming schedule, I agree. Especially for someone your age." Vivienne noticed more tears in the girl's eyes even though she blinked them away.

"What's the matter, Maleine?" She reached out and placed her hand on Maleine's arm. "You can tell me anything. If it's your hair that is making you so upset, don't let it bother you. Under your veil, no one will even see it."

"I know that, my lady," she answered with a sniffle. "But I used to feel pretty before. Wymond even told me he liked my long hair. And now ... now ..." She started crying this time, not able to hold back the tears.

"Don't worry about Wymond. He's so smitten with you that he would like you even if you didn't have any hair at all."

"I think that's what Mother Superior was trying to do when she snipped my hair so short. I had to beg her not to cut off even more."

"Wear the veil for now," said Vivienne, placing it back over Maleine's head. "Since I don't believe the abbey has any looking glasses, you'll be more apt to forget about your hair if you can't see it."

"Thank you, my lady." Maleine wiped away the rest of her tears. "You are so strong and beautiful. I want to be just like you."

"Like me? Oh, no, I don't think you want to be like me, Maleine. After all, the sheriff calls me nosy and too curious for my own good. He is constantly making me feel as if I'm doing something wrong."

"Are you?"

"Nay. I don't believe so. I vowed to help others find justice for their loved ones who were murdered since I was never able to find my own parents' killers."

"I'm sorry, Lady Vivienne. I didn't know. But you and the sheriff are so good at investigating. I am sure you will find your answers someday by working together."

"I hope you're right," she said, feeling less hopeful with each passing day since it had been seven years now since her family's tragedy. "But right now, I need to concentrate on that poor girl we found buried alive in the wall."

"Buried alive? Really?" Maleine's eyes opened wide. "Why would someone do that to another?"

"Those are the answers we are trying to figure out."

"I want to help, my lady. Please, let me do something toward this investigation that will make a difference." Eagerness showed on her face. She truly meant what she said.

"I don't know about that, Maleine. After all, you have duties to the church now and quite a full schedule. It doesn't seem like you have any extra time to be investigating murders."

"I lost both my parents recently too," she reminded Vivienne. "I want to find justice for others just like you do. Please. Let me be a part of discovering who murdered this poor woman, and help to make them pay for their actions."

Vivienne's heart went out to the girl. She was still so young but had made a decision that would change her life forever. By devoting herself to the church and by being a nun, taking the vows of poverty, chastity, and obedience, she was going to miss out on all the excitement that life had to offer. Vivienne never understood why any woman would ever choose to live this way. Since this had been Maleine's decision, Vivienne had not tried to stop her. But now, Vivienne was starting to wonder if Maleine really wanted this kind of life, after all.

"Maleine, are you having doubts about becoming a nun?"

She hesitated for a moment, sniffled again and then answered. "Nay. Of course not." The girl's gaze dropped to the ground. "I no longer have a family. Besides, my father's bad decisions have made it impossible for me to return home. Everyone will hate me for the things he did. I must stay here and pray. Pray for his forgiveness and for God to lead me down the right path."

"I understand," Vivienne said, not wanting to put any more

pressure on the girl right now. "But just know that if you ever change your mind, my offer of taking you back to live at Mablethorpe Castle with me is still open."

"Thank you, my lady, but this is my cross to bear, not yours."

"I think we all bear each other's crosses in one way or another," Vivienne told her. "By coming together, we only get stronger."

"Yes. And that is why I want to help you with this investigation. So, please tell me what I can do."

"You can keep your ears and eyes open, Maleine. Let me know if you find out anything that might be related to this poor woman's murder. But be careful."

"What do you mean by that?"

"Being an investigator is a dangerous profession," she told her. "I hate to have to say this, but you can't really trust anyone."

"I'm in an abbey now. With holy people. Certainly, they are to be trusted."

"Just because someone takes vows and prays and wears a robe or a habit, it doesn't make them entirely trustworthy," Vivienne tried to explain.

"Are you saying you think that someone inside the abbey killed that poor woman?" Maleine seemed intrigued now. Her sorrow over her hair had suddenly disappeared.

"I'm not saying yes and I am not saying no at this point."

"So, the murderer could still be here?" Maleine's wide eyes looked one way and then the other. "And what about that ghost I saw? Do you think the ghost has anything to do with the murder?"

Vivienne moved closer to the girl and spoke in a soft voice so as not to be heard. "I don't know about the ghost, but all I'm saying is that I find it rather convenient to bury a woman in a wall if the murderer had access to the premises. After all, if the killer was a visitor, I'd think they'd just leave the dead body where it fell and run off. This, to me, seems like a matter bound to the abbey."

The corners of Maleine's mouth slowly curled up into a smile. "I think I am just the person you need. After all, I am living here now. I am sure I can find out information—just give me a chance to try. Tell me I can, and then I will hurry back to my work with a whole new purpose and lots more enthusiasm too."

"You have my blessings, Maleine."

"Thank you, my lady," Maleine answered excitedly and turned to go.

"But mayhap, let's just keep this between us," Vivienne called after her. "After all, Sheriff Fitch already doesn't quite accept me working with him. I don't think he'd be fast to accept having two women helping with the work that he thinks he can do all by himself."

"Lady Vivienne, don't go in there." Zachariah walked out of the charnel house, not wanting her to see all the skulls and bones piled up inside. "It's no place for a lady."

"Sheriff, you know that I will need to go inside and inspect the corpse again with you. We need to conduct a more thorough investigation if we expect to find answers."

He let out a deep breath. "I guess there is no way to stop you, so why bother trying?"

"That's right," she answered with a smug smile, taking a step toward the ossuary.

"Go on in, then. I'll be paying a little visit to the sacrist, since this seems to be one of the only times he is free."

She stopped abruptly and turned back around. "You're going to see the sacrist? Oh, wait for me. I want to question him as well." She hurried to catch up with him as he headed toward the front entrance of the church.

Zachariah smiled inwardly. He knew that Vivienne would want to come along with him if he said that. He also knew it would keep her out of the bone room for now. Her curious nature wouldn't allow him to question the sacrist without her by his side. It worked just as he'd planned. Or at least for now.

"What was the name of the sacrist again? I can't quite remember." She tapped her mouth with the tip of her finger.

"His name is Brother Silas." Zachariah guided her up the front church steps with a hand to the small of her back.

"Brother Silas," she repeated. "That's right. I should have remembered. I'm not sure where my head is lately."

"Mayhap it's on the children who shouldn't be here in the first place?"

"I hate to admit it, but I am starting to think you're right about that."

"Really." He chuckled. It wasn't often that Vivienne admitted she was wrong about anything. "Since we're in agreement, I'll send them back home."

"Nay!" She stopped at the top of the steps and turned to face him. "You can't do that."

"Why not? You just agreed with me that we shouldn't have brought them here."

"They are so excited to be traveling with us. If you send them away now, Starah will be crushed. She'll think you don't want her."

"My daughter knows I need to be gone at times for my job. Besides, she has Nairnie to keep her company. Are you sure it isn't you who is feeling guilt at possibly sending Martin away after you've just found him again?"

"Mayhap you're right," she said softly, turning her face downward rather than looking him in the eye. "I do feel guilty.

And I really want him here with me, but I know now that we shouldn't have brought the children to the site of a murder."

"Then they'll go home."

"Nay. We can't do that."

Frustration filled him. "Lady Vivienne, you need to make up your mind. Do you want them to stay or leave? You can't have it both ways."

"I'd like the children to be able to make the choice if they want to stay here with us or go back to Mablethorpe."

He shook his head, not wanting to let children decide what was best for them. Vivienne was stubborn, but he knew how much this meant to her. She'd lived seven years thinking her baby was dead. He supposed he could see her point for wanting to keep Martin near. "Do whatever you want, I don't really care. Just please make a decision and stick with it. I cannot tolerate you floundering back and forth like a limp fish."

"Limp fish?" she questioned. "That makes no sense at all. And I don't like being referred to in such a manner."

"Then decide." He opened the door to the church and nodded to let her enter first. Once inside, it took a moment for their eyes to get adjusted to the semi-darkness after being outside in the bright sun.

Saint Agnes's was a cruciform church, as was typical for the Catholic religion. A long nave was lined with wooden benches on both sides, leading up to the pulpit in front with the altar. Transepts, making up the arms of a cross, jutted out on both sides, heading to two different directions. The ossuary attached to one, and another room that he suspected was the sacristy was at the end of the other. Directly above the cross section where the passageways met, was a tall turret with a winding staircase leading up to the bell tower, where the bell was rung before each scheduled session of prayers and each Mass.

"Who's there?" A voice from inside the empty church echoed off the walls. Zachariah looked around, trying to determine from where the voice came.

"Greetings, I am Sheriff Fitch and this is Lady Vivienne Harlowe," he called out, making his way down the long aisle with Vivienne at his side. "We are looking for the sacrist, Brother Silas. Do you know where we can find him?"

"I'm Brother Silas," said a man walking out from a shadow and reaching up to light a candle next to the altar. It helped to brighten up the area. He proceeded to come down the three steps to meet them. He turned his back to them, facing a large crucifix mounted on the wall behind the altar. He genuflected and blessed himself and then turned back around. Large arrow-slit styled windows rose up behind the altar, letting in small streams of light every time the sun broke out from behind a cloud. The church itself was made of brick combined with stone, just like the rest of the abbey. It was simple, with open windows, since glass was expensive, and colored glass was usually only donated by the rich or the king. "How may I help you?"

"We would like to ask you some questions, Brother Silas," said Vivienne, causing the man to frown.

"About what?" He raised his brows. "If you two would like to be married, you'll have to speak to Mother Superior and she'll schedule a date."

"Married? No, no," said Zachariah with a nervous chuckle. He couldn't dismiss the thought that when he'd walked down the aisle with Vivienne just now, it did reminded him of his wedding to Margaret. "We are here on a murder investigation, not to be wed."

"Murder?" The monk blessed himself. "Please, this is no place for speaking of the ways of the devil. We can talk outside."

"I'd like to view the sacristy, if you don't mind," blurted out

Vivienne. Zachariah locked eyes with her and she nodded slightly.

"Yes, I would like to see everything as well," he added, thinking mayhap Vivienne was trying to get more information. He supposed any tidbit might help.

"I'm sorry, but I just closed up the sacristy and it won't be open again until tonight before Vespers. Perhaps you could show up early for the prayer service and see it then."

"Nay. We don't have time for prayers." Zachariah felt angry that the monk was denying their request. It almost made it seem like the monk didn't want them in there and that made him wonder why.

"No time for prayers?" asked Brother Silas, dramatically blessing himself again, and closing his eyes to say what was most likely a quick prayer to save their souls.

"I think what the sheriff means is that we are anxious to complete this investigation and return home to Mablethorpe," Vivienne interjected. It was probably a good thing she spoke since Zachariah was about to command the monk to open the room. He didn't like wasting all his time with silly rules.

"Oh, you're here from Mablethorpe?" asked the monk. "I suppose all this has to do with the body that was found in the wall, then."

"Yes, that's right," said Zachariah. "We have a few questions to ask you about the murder."

"Shhhh," said the monk, holding his finger in front of his lips. "Not in here. We'll have to talk outside, instead."

"Fine," grumbled Zachariah, figuring he'd come back later to see the sacristy. Mayhap when this fool monk wasn't even around.

They walked out into the sunshine. Grunt came running up to them, sniffing the bottom of Brother Silas's robe.

"Where did this beast come from?" asked the monk, quickly stepping backward.

"He's not a beast, Brother Silas. He is my bloodhound, Grunt," explained Vivienne.

"He shouldn't be here at the abbey. Animals are not allowed." Brother Silas almost seemed afraid of the dog.

"Mother Superior didn't seem to mind. Much. Besides, Grunt helps us in our investigations," she continued.

"A dog helps you?"

"Yes," said Vivienne proudly. "Grunt has been able to sniff out anything suspicious, and so has even found several dead bodies for us in the past."

"Oh, my," said Brother Silas, eyeing up the dog. "I've never heard of such a thing."

"If you don't mind, we'd like to get to the questions," Zachariah told him impatiently. "We have a lot to do, and are trying our best to keep to the schedule of the abbey."

"Yes, that is good." The monk nodded. "However, I'm afraid I'll be of no help to you at all. I don't know anything about the murder."

"How long have you been sacrist for the abbey?" asked Zachariah.

"I've been the abbey's sacrist for nine ... nay, almost ten years now."

"That long? Then you probably know everyone who comes to or leaves the abbey," said Vivienne.

"Yes. Yes, I suppose I do."

"Do you remember a young female postulant with red hair?" Zachariah waited as the monk put his hand to his chin.

"It's hard to say, since I never see the hair of the women. It is always covered. How long ago do you mean?"

"We're not sure," said Vivienne. "Since the corpse has been

chewed up by rats, we don't have a strong guess on the timeline of when the girl was actually murdered."

"I'm sorry. There have been a lot of postulants here over the years," said the monk. "Some of them stayed and took their vows to become nuns, and others left before that ever happened. You'd have to check with Mother Superior about examining the records."

"Yes, we will, thank you," said Zachariah, seeing that this man was going to be of no help at all. Then he had another thought. "Do you remember when the wall in the scullery was repaired and bricked back up?"

"Well, let me see." The monk looked up in the air, as if in thought. "It was being repaired when I first came here about ten years ago."

"Nay." Vivienne shook her head. "I'm sure the woman's death wasn't that long ago."

"How can you be certain?" asked the monk.

"She can't. She's just guessing. I suppose you can call it ... woman's intuition," said Zachariah. "Was there another time, more recently when the wall had to be bricked up again?"

"The wall in the scullery seems to always be falling down," said Brother Silas. "Yes, I do believe there were several other times when the lay monks had to repair it."

"When was the last time?" asked Zachariah, knowing that was the time they were looking for, since someone would have spotted the body earlier if the woman had been murdered long ago.

"It was just a few days ago when the lay monks went to repair the hole and found the body. I thought you knew that and it is why you are here."

"We do know that, thank you," said Vivienne, blessedly stepping in because Zachariah had no more patience for this man. "We want to know the time before this. When would that have been?"

"I can't give you an actual date."

"Just an approximate one would be fine," said Zachariah through his teeth.

"It was mayhap ... about a year ago, I think. Of course, it might have been two years. I mean, time goes so quickly here at the abbey that it's really hard to say."

"Thank you, that helps," said Zachariah. "So now we know that the postulant was murdered between one and two years ago. Is there anything else you can add?"

"Nay, I don't think so," said the monk. "But tell me, why do you think this girl was murdered?"

Zachariah eyed the monk, wondering if he was truly stupid or just pretending to be. "In case you haven't heard, her legs and arms were bound with rope and she had a gag in her mouth. It is more than evident that she was murdered and didn't accidentally fall into a hole in the wall and just stay there to die."

"Sheriff, please," warned Vivienne with a glare. "There is no need to be crude." She looked back at the monk. "The sheriff didn't mean to offend you, Brother Silas."

"No offense taken," answered the monk. "I only asked such a question because if you knew anything about the church and the order, Sheriff Fitch, you'd realize that sometimes immurement of nuns does happen."

"Immurement?" asked Vivienne. "What is that? I am not familiar with the term."

"I mean that nuns are bricked up into a wall as a form of penance," the monk explained.

"You can't be serious," said Zachariah, finding this hard to believe.

"It's true," Brother Silas continued. "However, it is just temporary, and they are given food and water through a hole in the wall. They are not left there to die. Just to reflect upon their sins."

"Egads, I cannot believe someone who is said to be holy would ever do such a thing to another," spat Zachariah, finding this entire process horrifying.

"I wish I were jesting, but it is true," the monk told them. "If you don't believe me, you can look in some of the books of records and read all about it."

"Where would we find these books with the records?" asked Vivienne.

"They are all kept in the scriptorium. But you will need permission just to enter the room, and then more permission to actually look at the books. And you can't touch them without wearing gloves."

"God's eyes, these rules are silly." Zachariah shook his head, thinking how absurd this all sounded to him.

"Please, refrain from using the Lord's name in vain, Sheriff Fitch." Brother Silas blessed himself again, looking as if he were afraid of being struck down by lightning, the way he directed his gaze to the clouds.

"Whom can we ask for permission to see the books?" Vivienne wondered.

"The armarius, Brother Thaddeus, can help you with that. He is in charge of all the manuscripts and books. Or the abbot, Brother Harold, would be able to help you as well."

"Can't you do it?" asked Zachariah, knowing how much power the sacrist held.

"I suppose I could if the other two are not available to assist you. However, I don't like to overstep my bounds, so you need to speak with them first."

"Thank you, Brother Silas, we'll do that," said Vivienne. "You have been more than helpful."

Hearing her say that almost made Zachariah laugh aloud.

This monk wasn't a help, but seemed to be naught more than a hindrance, slowing down the investigation.

"If that is all, I need to get back to my responsibilities. It is almost time for me to ring the bells for None," said the monk, speaking of the afternoon prayer session that was right before Vespers.

"That'll be all for now. Thank you, Brother Silas." Zachariah turned and walked down the church steps, stopping at the bottom as Brother Silas disappeared back inside the church. Grunt whined and dropped down at Zachariah's feet.

"Well, should we go find either Brother Thaddeus or Brother Harold to let us into the scriptorium?" asked Vivienne, sounding chipper as always, joining him at his side.

Zachariah spotted Nairnie walking through the gates of the abbey with a basket slung over her arm. Martin was next to her, swinging his wooden sword around in the air. Starah was with them, holding that damned weasel clutched in her grip, trying to keep it from running. She seemed to have something in her hand and was feeding the animal.

Zachariah's heart longed to be with his young daughter, Starah. If he wasn't always working, he could be spending time with her instead of pushing her off on Nairnie. Life just wasn't fair sometimes. Why couldn't he have a happy, normal family life? A life more like the way it was before his wife died, and before his parents passed on. Everything seemed to go downhill fast after that. He had no real relationships with his siblings anymore, and it seemed to him as if he had lost his entire family except for Starah. He purposely worked a lot, just to keep himself occupied. But bid the devil, if he didn't start spending more time with Starah, he might lose her too. The last thing he wanted was for his daughter to become a nun and end up in a place like this.

"Sheriff? Did you hear me?" Vivienne leaned forward to

look directly at him. Those bright blue eyes pulled him in, making him feel as if all his problems didn't exist. Vivienne was someone who had always been there for him. Someone he could trust. If only he could have found her parents' murderers, he might feel worthy of her true friendship.

"I'm sorry. What did you say?"

"I said, mayhap our investigation can wait. I think it might do us all good to go for a walk with the children."

"We don't have time for walks. We have work to do."

Her hands went to her hips and she perused him from the side of her eye. "Zachariah Fitch, I know you better than anyone, and I can tell that being here has put you on edge."

"Yes, you're correct. I guess it has."

"Have you spoken with Magdalena yet? To make amends, I mean?"

"I haven't had time. You know that."

"I believe it is important for both of us to actually start making time for the people we love. Now, come with me. I won't take no for an answer." She took his hand and all but dragged him over to the gate where Nairnie and the children stood.

"Father!" Starah ran to him with Chomp clutched close to her chest. "Are you here to spend the day with us?"

"We went to the orchard, but I want to go to the graveyard and look for ghosts so I can slay them with my sword." Martin swiped his wooden sword through the air, almost hitting Nairnie. She jumped back.

"Och, child, be careful with that thing before ye poke out someone's eye," she complained.

"Yes, Martin, please, be careful." Vivienne took the wooden sword away from him. "You'll have to put this away while you're at the abbey. You heard Mother Superior say no weapons are allowed."

"But it's not a weapon according to you, Mother. You said it was just a toy."

Zachariah didn't miss the way Vivienne's face lit up when Martin called her Mother. His heart went out to them both. Then, when Starah leaned up against him, reaching out and taking his hand, he calmed. Yes, Vivienne was right. They all needed to spend time with the ones they loved. Life was too short not to do so.

"How about I borrow a wagon from Brother Harold and all of us go for a ride?" he asked.

"That's a great idea," said Vivienne. "An hour sitting at the creek in the sun would be fun and relaxing."

"I'll go to the kitchen and see if I can rustle up some food to take with us." Nairnie hobbled away with Grunt wagging his tail and following along, as if he knew what she'd said and was looking for something to eat.

"Wait for me," called out Martin, snatching his sword away from Vivienne and running to catch up with them.

"Are we really going to spend some time together, Father?" Starah looked up at him and he saw the doubt in her eyes. It was almost as if she was afraid to be excited about this, thinking it might not really happen.

"I said we're doing it, so we will. Now, why don't you come with me to the stable to get the cart?" He took his daughter's hand and headed away as the little girl chattered about ferrets and dogs and everything that children considered important.

VIVIENNE TOOK a deep breath and released it slowly, thinking that mayhap she was wrong again. Having the children here with them at the abbey could be a good thing indeed. Since it was Zachariah's suggestion to go for a ride in the wagon with the children, there was hope after all, she supposed. She never thought he'd actually push aside his duties to spend time with anyone, but he'd just behaved quite differently. Perhaps he was changing. Mayhap being here with his daughter truly was beneficial for him.

"Lady Vivienne, good day."

She turned around to see Sister Magdalena approaching with Maleine.

"Greetings," she answered with a nod. "I'm so glad to see you both. Where are you going?"

"Sister Magdalena and I spent the morning in the garden, tending to the herbs," Maleine told her. "Now, we are bringing herbs and small loaves of bread to several poor families in the village."

"How nice," said Vivienne. "I am sure they will appreciate the gesture."

"Maleine, we should hurry," instructed Magdalena. "One of the women is about to give birth. We received word of it just this morning."

"Give birth?" asked Maleine, looking terrified. "I don't have to see that, do I?"

"Yes, my dear, of course you do. The abbess thinks you should learn how to deliver a baby, and I am going to show you how it's done."

"Nay!" Maleine made a face. "I don't want to learn that." Her eyes flashed over to Vivienne. "I have no desire to be present at a birth."

"Maleine, I am sure it is all just more of your training," said Vivienne. "Birthing a baby is a part of life and nothing to fear. You are of age now, and need to know about things a woman experiences."

"Nuns don't have babies. I can't even have relations with a man," Maleine retorted. "I don't see a purpose for this kind of training in the least."

"It'll be all right, my dear," said Magdalena in a calm and kind voice. "This might be a difficult birth and I'll need your help."

"Lady Vivienne, do I really have to go?" Maleine almost seemed as if she were about to cry. Or run.

"I have no authority over your training, Maleine," Vivienne explained. "You need to listen to Sister Magdalena since she is your mentor."

"I don't know if I can do this." Maleine wrung her hands, her body stiffening. Fear washed over her face. Vivienne didn't want her to feel this uneasy. Especially when she had no family member to help her through this. Things were happening too fast for the girl.

"I suppose I could join you two in order to assist with the birth if it is needed. I am more experienced than Maleine with something like this."

"Oh, I'd like that, my lady." Maleine let out a deep breath and seemed to relax.

"That might be a good idea," agreed Sister Magdalena. "I would appreciate the help. I've never really been in charge of helping to birth a baby, and have only watched and assisted by handing things over to a midwife or fetching water and other such tasks."

"You haven't aided in more ways than that?" asked Vivienne, thinking this was a lot to expect of anyone. "Why are they sending you then, if you've never been in charge before?"

"Mother Superior thinks I should do it. She says I need to learn to be more of a leader."

Vivienne wondered what kind of a heartless woman Mother Superior really was to send two novices of the act of birthing babies to a woman who sounded as if she were about to have a difficult time giving birth.

"Maleine, are you going to come with us down to the

creek?" Martin ran up to join them with Grunt running alongside. The dog's tongue hung out, since it was already proving to be a hot day.

"Good day, Martin. Nay, I can't come with you, although the creek sounds more inviting than watching the birth of a baby." Maleine frowned again.

Nairnie waddled up with a basket over her arm. Vivienne could see apples and what looked like a round of cheese peeking out from under the towel covering the food. "We're ready to go and I've a few things that might interest ye, lassie." She started pulling the towel away to show her, but stopped as soon as she saw Magdalena. "Och, I didna realize we were no' alone." She quickly covered up the food again.

"It's all right, Nairnie." Magdalena smiled, leaning over to whisper. "I won't tell Mother Superior about what you have in the basket."

"Grunt and I distracted the cooks while Nairnie sneaked the food into the basket," proudly announced Martin, almost making Vivienne laugh aloud. Nothing these two did seemed to surprise her anymore.

The horse and wagon rolled up, with Zachariah driving and Starah sitting on the seat next to him. She held something on her lap.

"Lady Vivienne, it's time to go," the sheriff announced.

"Oh, I'm sorry, but I won't be going with you, after all," said Vivienne, her heart dropping when she saw the disappointed look on Martin's face.

"Why not, Mother?" asked her son. "I thought we were going to spend the day together."

"I want to, Martin, I'm sorry. But I promised Sister Magdalena that I'd go to the village and help her deliver a baby. It is proving to be a difficult birth, and the woman's life could be at risk. They need all the help they can get."

"Oh." Martin's spirits dropped.

"Sweetheart, I promise to spend time with you as soon as I return," said Vivienne, feeling awful about this decision. She wanted to be with her son, but if a woman in labor needed help, she wanted to be there for her as well. Especially since the two women being sent to help her had no real experience in this matter.

"Nonsense," said Nairnie, pushing the basket of food into Vivienne's hands. "I'll go to help with the birth, while ye go with yer son to enjoy the day, as ye should."

"Nairnie, I can't ask you to do that." Vivienne admired the old woman for what she was trying to do.

"Ye didna ask, lass, I just told ye. Besides, I'm sure I've got more experience with birthin' bairns than all of ye put together."

"If you insist," said Vivienne, knowing what Nairnie said was most likely true. She would be a much better choice to be there than any of the rest of them.

"How far is the village from here?" asked Nairnie.

"It'll take a while to walk there," explained Magdalena. "We should get going if we want to be back by dark."

"Nay, we're no' walkin'. Get in the wagon, all of ye. They can drop us off on the way to the creek and pick us up on the way back."

"Nairnie, what a great idea," agreed Vivienne. "Magdalena, you sit in the front with Zachariah and Nairnie. I'll sit in the back with the children and the animals. Starah, do you still have Chomp?"

"Aye, my lady," said Starah, standing up on the bench seat, holding up a small cage with the ferret inside.

"What's that?" asked Martin. "You locked up Chomp? She won't like it."

"My father said if Chomp is coming with us, then she needs to ride in the cage," answered Starah.

"I'm not going to be chasing a weasel around all afternoon," grumbled Zachariah.

"She's a ferret," Vivienne corrected him. "And it's actually a good idea, since Grunt seems to like to chase poor Chomp and scare her to death."

"If everyone isn't inside the wagon in the next minute, I'm calling this whole thing off," Zachariah warned them, his impatience rearing its head once again.

"Come on, Sister, ye can sit next to your brother," said Nairnie as they headed to the front of the wagon. "I'm sure ye two have a lot to talk about."

"I don't agree," said Zachariah under his breath, but Vivienne heard him. As Nairnie and Magdalena walked past her, Nairnie winked.

"Dinna worry about a thing," Nairnie whispered. "Before this is all over, things are goin' to be just the way the good Lord intended."

Chapter Seven

By the time they started back to the abbey, the sun had set and it was already getting dark outside. Vivienne enjoyed her time spent with Martin, Starah, and Zachariah at the creek. It seemed to relax the sheriff when she told him to lie back in the sunshine and close his eyes. He'd actually fallen asleep, and she let him snooze. Everything had been going fine until they returned to town to pick up the women.

"Och, it was a good thing I went with Maleine, since it was a difficult birth," said Nairnie, sitting in the back of the wagon with her legs straight out. She was petting Grunt who had his chin on her lap. "I thought that poor wee laddie would never come out."

"I never want to have children," declared Maleine, sitting between Martin and Starah. "It was bloody awful." She opened up the cage and took Chomp out and held the ferret up and kissed her. "I think I'll just have ferrets instead." Grunt whined. "And dogs," she added quickly, reaching out to scratch the hound's ears.

"Can you have ferrets in the abbey?" asked Starah.

"I thought nuns weren't allowed to have dogs," said Martin.

"Oh, that's right." Maleine put Chomp on her lap, petting her as she spoke. Grunt's head popped up and he watched closely. "Mayhap I should have taken Wymond up on his offer to marry me, after all."

"Maleine, aren't you enjoying being a postulant?" asked Magdalena from the front of the wagon. The nun rode on the bench seat, sitting between Zachariah and Vivienne.

"I'm not sure yet," the girl answered.

"It'll get better, I promise," said Magdalena. "It took me a little while, too, but I feel as if everyone at the abbey is my family now."

Vivienne noticed the quick flash of disappointment coming from Zachariah and figured it was time to intervene.

"Sister Magdalena, your family is Zachariah and Starah," she said. "As well as your brother Isaac, and your sister Cassandra."

"I know that, but none of them seem to want me as their sister."

"That's not true," remarked Vivienne. "Zachariah, tell her she's wrong."

"I thought we agreed not to call each other by our Christian names," he scoffed. "Call me Sheriff, please."

"What? Why?" asked Magdalena. "Zachariah, you and Vivienne have been friends since childhood. I would think by now you'd be close enough to use your Christian names without your titles attached."

"I'd appreciate it if you'd not get involved in my personal business, Magdalena." Zachariah's mood went from happy to stormy all over again.

Vivienne didn't like the way this was looking. It was starting to shape up into a squall. But at least the two of them were talking again, so that was a start. Even if it wasn't on the friendliest terms.

"Everyone in Mablethorpe misses you, Sister Magdalena," said Vivienne.

"Oh, I doubt that." The nun's attention went to her brother. "After all, Zachariah has not even talked to me since Margaret died."

"Don't go there," Zachariah warned her, looking forward as he drove the wagon.

"It was no one's fault. Margaret's death, I mean," said Vivienne. "Isn't that right, Sheriff?" She purposely didn't say his name so he wouldn't have more to complain about.

"Zachariah believes his wife is dead because of me," said Magdalena. "Isn't that right, brother?"

"I said ... don't go there." Zachariah's jaw clenched, and he looked over the side of the wagon now as he directed the horse toward the abbey.

"I suppose I am partially to blame, since Margaret's ministrations caused her to get the pox for a second time," added Magdalena.

Vivienne decided this wasn't the time or place for such a discussion. Everyone was tired and it was late. She needed to change up the conversation before things ended badly.

"We had a nice time at the creek today. I think the children will sleep soundly with all the running around they did with Grunt." She looked over her shoulder and smiled at the children who were petting Chomp now. She didn't like to see the ferret caged, and was glad they'd removed Chomp from her confinement. Not in a hurry to point out this fact to the sheriff, she refrained from telling him. Vivienne was sure he wouldn't agree.

It was quiet in the wagon the rest of the way back to the abbey. When they stopped inside the abbey's courtyard, Mother Superior and Brother Harold were there waiting for them, along with Sister Roberta, the prioress, or second-in-command to the abbess.

"Sister Magdalena, where have you been?" snapped Mother Superior. "It is well past mealtime and you and the postulant should have been back hours ago."

"I'm sorry, Mother Superior." Magdalena spoke as Zachariah helped her get down from the bench seat. "The birth in the village was more complicated than we'd predicted. Thank goodness Nairnie was there to help us."

"Blethers, it was nothin'," said Nairnie with a wave of her hand through the air. Zachariah helped her out of the back of the wagon next. "I was glad to be of service."

"The postulant was supposed to be helping you, Sister Magdalena. Not a visitor," said Sister Roberta.

"The postulant has a name. Her name is Maleine," Vivienne interrupted. "And she was there as well. However, someone with experience was needed. Nairnie was a great help. A true godsend, I hear."

"Well, you are all right on time for Compline," Brother Harold told them. "Brother Silas has just rung the bell."

"Mother, we don't have to go to church, do we?" Martin yawned widely.

"The children are tired and Nairnie will be putting them to bed," announced Vivienne, putting her arms around her son's shoulders and holding him to her.

"That sounds good to me," said Nairnie. "I'm worn out. Come on, wee ones."

"Maleine, we'll have to go to the prayer service," said Magdalena in a soft voice.

"Really?" Maleine's eyes sought out Vivienne and Vivienne nodded slightly.

"It's part of your training, Maleine. Go on."

"Fine," she said with a huff. "But someone will have to take Chomp."

"I'll take her," said Starah, holding out her arms, but the little girl was so tired that when the ferret squirmed, she dropped her.

Grunt barked and gave chase toward the graveyard with the weasel-like animal swerving this way and that, trying to shake the dog off her trail.

"Stop that!" screamed Mother Superior with her hand to her head. "This commotion is not allowed."

"I'll get her," offered Martin, taking off at a run after the animals.

"I'll help." Starah followed.

"Starah! Martin! Get back here," shouted Zachariah. "The graveyard at night is no place for children."

"Shhhh. Please." Sister Roberta held a finger to her lips. "You are being much too loud, Sheriff."

"I'll retrieve them," offered Vivienne. "Sheriff Fitch, mayhap you can take the wagon back to the stable in the meantime."

"Gladly," he said, heading away.

"Maleine, we need to get to church with the others." Sister Magdalena took Maleine's arm and they followed the rest of the clergy to the church where all the other monks and nuns were already gathering in silent groups.

"I'll wait right here since I'm too tired to move," said Nairnie with a yawn.

It was getting even darker now, but Vivienne hurried toward the graveyard after the children. Grunt's loud barking echoed in the air. As she approached the graveyard, the tone of the dog's barks suddenly changed. It was no longer the playful noise of a dog chasing a ferret. This sounded more like ... trouble. Aye, something was definitely wrong.

"Martin! Starah!" Vivienne yelled, running into the graveyard, feeling that twisting in her stomach that was always the harbinger of something bad about to happen.

When she heard the children screaming, wild visions of them being murdered flashed through her head. The knot in her stomach became even worse, making her want to vomit.

"Nay!" she cried, running in the dark, dodging tombstone after tombstone, trying to get to the children to protect them before they were hurt. "Please, protect them," she called out, not sure who she was saying this to, and not sure at this point that it even mattered. All she wanted was for the children to stay safe.

Then, out of the graveyard came Starah at a run, holding on to the ferret tightly. Martin was right behind her, waving his wooden sword wildly in the air. They were both screaming as if someone or something was chasing them.

"Whoa! Stop. I'm here," said Vivienne, grabbing Starah, feeling her little body shaking in fright. "Everything is fine now."

"I'll protect you both," said Martin, his eyes wide as he used two hands to wield his sword over his head.

"Protect us from whom? Tell me what happened. Is someone chasing you? Why are you two so scared?"

Grunt continued to bark from deep inside the church's graveyard.

"It's a ghost!" gasped Starah. "He almost touched us."

"He wanted to hurt us but I scared him away with my sword," blurted out Martin, sounding brave, but at the same time coming close to Vivienne's side for protection. When he leaned against her, she could feel the vibrations of the rapid beating of his heart.

"We need to get Grunt and quiet him down." Vivienne took both of their hands and started to head deeper into the graveyard, but could tell they were hesitant to go.

"I'm scared," said Starah, pulling back. "I want my father."

"Mother, I'll protect Starah, but you need to save Grunt from the ghost." Martin pulled Starah over to him, still holding up his sword. She cradled the ferret against her.

Vivienne didn't want to force the children to go back into the graveyard if they were this scared. "Oh, all right, stay here then. But don't move until I get back. Grunt, come here, boy," she called to the dog. "Grunt, please stop all that barking."

She followed the noise of the dog, stopping dead in her tracks when she saw a ghostly, white transparent figure hovering above one of the gravestones. Grunt was down on his haunches, barking and snapping his jaws at the air.

"Oh ... my ... God," she said, having seen the ghost before in Mablethorpe, but it hadn't been this close up. Now, she could tell that the ghost was a monk for certain, and garbed in a long, hooded robe. She couldn't see the features of his face, but then again, neither did she want to. "Leave my dog alone," she shouted, hurrying over and grabbing Grunt by the collar. She stayed hunkered down on the ground, her eyes fixed on the floating figure just above her. Her heart beat in her throat. Something inside her warned her to run, but another part of her said she had to stay there and figure out who this ghost was and what he was trying to tell her. "Who are you and what do you want?" she asked, feeling foolish talking to a ghost, and not really expecting an answer.

But then the ghost reached out one hand, pointing to one of the gravestones as if he were showing it to her. She was about to ask another question when she heard Zachariah calling for her.

"Vivienne, is everything all right?" came his deep voice from behind her.

She turned her head to answer. "Zachariah, get over here. Now!" When she turned back to the ghost, she realized the spirit had dissipated. Grunt stopped barking and she let go of his collar. The hound hurried over to the gravesite where the ghost had been, and curiously sniffed the ground around it.

"What is it? What happened?" Zachariah ran to her, holding Starah in one arm. The little girl still held tightly to the ferret. Martin was right behind him. "The children are frightened out of their minds."

"Yes, I know," she said, feeling lost for words.

"Well, what scared them?" He looked around the area, but of course saw nothing.

"It was ... a ghost," she said, realizing how silly that sounded. There was no such thing as ghosts. Or was there? Right now, she wasn't sure about anything, other than something had upset the children and the dog. A see-through, floating ... something.

"Father, it was a scary ghost. He tried to eat us," cried Starah.

"I stabbed him with my sword but it went right through him," said Martin, looking at the tip of his sword and touching it gently with his fingers.

"Vivienne, what the hell is going on here?" Zachariah's thick brows dipped together.

"Shhh," she warned him, not wanting him to curse around the children, and not needing the nuns and monks to hear him carelessly rattling off things he should keep to himself. "They are telling the truth. Grunt and I saw it too. It was the ghost of a monk."

When she said that, Starah started crying and hid her face against her father's chest. "I don't want to die," she whimpered.

"Stop this nonsense, all of you," the sheriff commanded. "Vivienne, you are scaring the children. Starah, sweetheart, there is no such thing as ghosts."

"But we saw him," Martin insisted. "He was real and right there by that gravestone." He pointed to where the ghost had hovered before pointing at the grave and then disappearing in a flash.

"You saw something else, perhaps a bird or just the fog, but I assure you it wasn't a ghost." The sheriff's words were strong and would have been convincing if they all hadn't known better.

"I'm not lying," said Martin with a pout.

"They're telling the truth," Vivienne told him. "Like I told you, I saw it too, and not just tonight. It was the same ghost I saw at the graveyard in Mablethorpe. Maleine also saw the ghost right here in the graveyard the day we arrived. Ask her if you don't believe me."

"Why didn't you tell me all this sooner?" Zachariah looked concerned as well as perturbed.

"What's all the commotion about?" Nairnie emerged from the dark, reaching out to hold on to tombstones as she carefully and slowly made her way to them in the dark. "It sounded like someone was bein' murdered out here, with all the yellin'."

Starah screamed at hearing the word murdered, digging her face even deeper into her father's tunic.

"We all saw a ghost, Nairnie," Vivienne explained.

"Not all of us," said Zachariah.

"A ghost?" Nairnie lifted her chin and looked around. "What did it look like?"

"It was a ghost of a monk," Vivienne explained.

"He was right here." Martin bravely ran over and pointed at the standing gravestone.

"Yes," agreed Vivienne. "The ghost pointed at that grave as if he were trying to tell or show me something."

"Well, whose grave is that?" Nairnie walked to the grave and bent over, using her sleeve to brush away the dirt from the engraved name. "It says Brother Theodore. Hmmm. I wonder who he was."

"We need to find out," said Vivienne, anxious to know more.

"Nay. Not tonight," said Zachariah. "Nairnie, I need you to get the children to bed. In the morning, I will have the constable and some of his men escort you and the children and the animals back to Mablethorpe."

"We're goin' home? Already?" asked Nairnie in surprise. "But ye havena found the killer yet, or even discovered who the murdered girl was."

"Lady Vivienne and I will be better able to work if we're not so distracted."

Beside him, Vivienne cleared her throat.

"I mean concerned," he corrected himself. "Concerned for the state and safety of the children."

"Sheriff Fitch, I thought we decided to let the children make that choice if they wanted to stay here or go back home," said Vivienne.

"*You* decided on that, not me. However, I am sheriff and head of this investigation, so I will make the final choice for everyone. I'll do it," he repeated. "No one else."

"Hrmph," mumbled Nairnie.

"I want to go home," said Starah, wiping away a tear with the back of her hand.

"Me too," agreed Martin. "I don't like it here."

"You both want to leave? Really?" asked Vivienne. "Martin, are you sure about this?"

"Yes, I'm sure," the boy answered. "I'd rather be back at Mablethorpe Castle learning how to use a sword properly, so next time I see a ghost I can really kill it."

"Mayhap it's for the best," agreed Nairnie. "Sheriff, I'll have the children and the animals ready to leave in the morning."

"Grunt stays," said Vivienne stubbornly, not happy that the sheriff didn't consult her more about this decision before making it. "And if the children leave here, I want them to stay with Nairnie at the castle until our return."

"Lady Vivienne, I have a house in town," the sheriff reminded her. "Starah is fine there."

"Nay, Father. I want to be with Martin and the knights at the castle until you return to protect me," said his daughter.

"Starah, you can't." Zachariah shook his head. "We are commoners. We don't live at the castle like Martin and Lady Vivienne, and neither do we belong there."

"You can all stay in my chamber," Vivienne told them.

"My lady, I hardly think your uncle will approve of that." Zachariah was not happy with this.

"Then I will write a note and send it with them to be sure there are no problems with the arrangements. I'll direct it to my aunt. She'll see that my wishes are carried out. She loves the children and won't mind having them stay there."

"What about me?" asked Nairnie. "She might no' be so happy to have me there."

"Aunt Ellen likes having other women to talk to," Vivienne assured her. "She'll find your stories of pirates very entertaining, I'm sure."

"No pirate stories around my daughter," instructed Zachariah. "Starah is already frightened enough without having to hear about pirates. Now, everyone get some sleep. Tomorrow morning is going to come quickly."

"Come, Starah. And hold on to the weasel so she doesn't get away again," said Nairnie. "We'll pick up the cage on the way to our quarters."

"Chomp is not a weasel, Nairnie. She's a ferret, and she has feelings." Starah stuck up for the ferret, leading the way out of the graveyard. Nairnie and Martin followed.

"Good night, Martin. I'll be there soon," Vivienne called out, waving her hand above her head.

"Good night, Lady Vivienne," Martin called back. "Come

on, Grunt. You have to go to bed now too, even if you don't like it." The dog looked up at Vivienne with big, sad eyes.

"Go on," she told Grunt, sending the dog running after Martin who had become Grunt's best friend since the boy came to live at Mablethorpe Castle.

Vivienne's smile disappeared and she wrapped her arms around herself in a form of a hug.

"You're upset because Martin didn't call you Mother, aren't you?" Zachariah could sometimes see right through her, she swore.

"Martin's been calling me Mother, and I like it. But he just went back to calling me Lady Vivienne again."

"Give him time. He just found out you're his true mother. He's lived for the last seven years calling another woman his mother. You have to realize that sometimes he'll slip back to his old ways."

"I suppose you're right. Or, at least, when he's not happy with me is when he seems to forget who I really am." She sighed. "I can't help thinking that if I spent more time with him, he'd always call me Mother. I don't want him to ever forget who I am."

"You worry too much, my lady. Now come, I'll walk with you back to your quarters. We could all use a good night's sleep." Zachariah put his hand gently on her arm. His touch was warm and endearing. She felt so tired and wanted to sleep. If for no other reason, to escape her worries and troubles.

"Wait. What about the ghost?" She turned her head to look at the gravestone once more. "We need to find out all we can about Brother Theodore and if he is the ghost."

"Tomorrow is another day, my lady. It can wait."

"But we need to find clues to our investigation."

"If it's truly a ghost, he's most likely been dead for quite a while. I'm sure another few hours isn't going to make a difference." He led her out of the graveyard.

"So, you believe that we saw a ghost then, right?"

The sheriff smiled as they continued to walk. "I believe that you and Maleine and the children and even Grunt believe you saw a spirit, yes. Personally, until I see a ghost for myself, I am not going to believe in them."

"Hrmph," she said with a sniff. "Then I hope the ghost of Brother Theodore haunts you as you sleep. Then you'll believe us."

"Now, now. Is that a nice thing to say?"

"Sheriff, you can sometimes be so rigid in your thinking that you wouldn't believe you were seeing a ghost if one came up to you and bit you on the arse." She smiled as she walked away from him, leaving him standing there with his mouth hanging open, at a loss for words. She swore that she'd have him believing in ghosts before they solved this case, if it was the last thing she ever did.

Chapter Eight

It was sad to have to say goodbye to Nairnie and the children the next morning, but Vivienne realized it was for the best that they left and went back home. After their scare with the ghost in the graveyard last night, Starah and Martin hadn't slept much at all. Every time Grunt made a noise or jumped off the bed, the children cried out, thinking the ghost was there to get them.

"Be good. Both of you. I don't want to hear any bad reports about you when I return." Vivienne hugged Martin, giving him a big kiss on his cheek. The little boy wasn't used to all this mothering and attention. He made a face and wiped off her kiss with the back of his hand. It hurt her in a way, but she realized he was just being a boy.

"I'll be training with Sir Guy if he has returned," said Martin. "I need to hurry up and become a knight."

"Don't rush it. Enjoy being a child while you still can," she told him.

"Father, give me a hug" Starah stood up in the back of the wagon holding out her arms. She had Chomp in her cage at her feet. Zachariah scooped her up, kissing her atop her head and giving her a big hug before putting her back down.

"I'll be home soon," he promised. "Take care of Midnight and don't let her outside at night."

"Wymond is watching her," said Starah. "But I'll trade him Chomp for Midnight," she said, obviously missing her cat.

"You do that, sweetheart."

"Father, I'm afraid the ghost is going to eat you." Starah's bottom lip stuck out in a pout.

"Sweetheart, there is no such thing as a ghost. The sooner you realize that, the better."

"Then what was that we saw in the graveyard?" she asked.

"It was just your imagination. Nothing else." The sheriff put her back in the wagon.

"But Mother saw the ghost too," said Martin. Vivienne smiled at hearing what he called her.

"Is Lady Vivienne just imagining the ghost too?" Starah looked up with big, curious eyes.

"Don't answer that," Vivienne whispered to Zachariah. If he agreed that she'd just imagined the ghost, the children would think she was a liar.

"Grunt also saw him, and dogs don't lie," Martin pointed out in a smug manner.

"All right, then. I think it's time to go," said the sheriff.

"Aye, sit down back there both of ye, before ye fall out on yer heads," warned Nairnie from the bench seat of the wagon. One of the abbey's monks, Brother Cedric, was driving. Constable Erikson was going along to protect them. It wasn't that long of a ride back to Mablethorpe and they shouldn't encounter any trouble, but Vivienne was glad Zachariah insisted that the constable escort them. It was one less worry off her mind about the children's and Nairnie's safety.

The wagon started to move, and Vivienne called out to stop them. "Wait," she cried, running after them. "I almost forgot to give you the missive." She handed the scroll to Nairnie. "Be sure to give this to Lady Mablethorpe, not Lord Mablethorpe. My aunt will make sure there are no problems with all of you staying in my chamber until we return."

"Dinna ye worry, my lady, she'll get it," said Nairnie, sticking the missive down the front of her bodice.

Vivienne chuckled. "Nairnie, what are you doing?"

"I figure, that's the safest place for it. Even if robbers stop us along the way, they'd never look there. And if they did, they'd have broken teeth to show for their tryin'." She smashed one fist into her palm in a punch.

"Have a good trip," Vivienne told them, knowing that with Nairnie along, there was no need for a constable. She was sure even the pirates she used to live with feared her. Nairnie was tough and didn't accept trouble from anyone. Yes, she was a woman whom Vivienne was sure no man would ever want to cross. Or live to tell about it, anyway. Vivienne couldn't wait to one day meet Nairnie's husband. He had to be even bigger and scarier than she was, if they were still together.

Grunt whined, sitting on the ground next to Vivienne. She looked down and petted him on the head. "I know you'll miss them, Grunt, but we have work to do. The faster we solve this case, the sooner you can get back to chasing the ferrets and playing with Martin."

Zachariah came up behind her. "We'll be able to focus more now that they've left."

"I suppose you're right," she said with a sigh, waving her hand over her head as the wagon left through the front gate of the abbey. Martin held up his wooden sword, waving it in the air as he stood up, holding on to the side of the wagon. She could hear Nairnie saying something to him, and reaching over the bench seat to pull the boy back down before he fell out.

"I never thought I'd say this, but I think Nairnie is the perfect nursemaid," Zachariah said with a grin.

"Really?" Vivienne looked at him playfully. "So, are you saying that I was right in hiring her after all?"

His eyes flashed over to hers, interlocking. There was a dangerous look to his handsome face, but his dark eyes seemed playful at the same time. For some reason it caused a flutter in her belly.

"I suppose sometimes you do have your moments."

"As well as you do, too," she said, throwing the rare compliment back to him.

There was a connection between them lately that she hadn't felt before. This didn't seem like just a friendship anymore. It was almost like a flirtatious type of attraction. Before she had a chance to even think about it, they were interrupted by a female's scream.

"What was that?" Vivienne's heart jumped into her throat. "I think someone is in danger."

"It sounded like it came from the refectory. Come on!" Zachariah took off at a run.

Grunt ran with them, leading the way. When they reached the refectory, they burst inside and raced to the kitchen where they found Sister Magdalena sitting on the floor just outside the scullery. Maleine was hunkered down next to her. Several lay monks and lay nuns started to arrive from outside, gathering around curiously.

"Magdalena? What's wrong? Are you hurt?" Zachariah hurried over to help his sister to her feet.

"I'm fine, but it was awful," she said, looking pale and weak. "I wasn't expecting that at all."

"Expecting what?" asked Zachariah. "What happened?"

"Sister Magdalena saw someone in the scullery and it scared her," blurted out Maleine.

"Oh no. Was it the ghost?" asked Vivienne, getting a small groan in return from the sheriff.

"Enough with the ghost stories," he grumbled. "Mayhap he's still in there." Zachariah ran into the scullery and Vivienne followed. Grunt entered the room, sniffing around the floor.

"I'll light a candle," said Vivienne, quickly lighting up the small room only to immediately notice something. "Is that hole in the wall bigger today than it was yesterday?" Even though they'd opened up the wall to get the bones out, it almost seemed as if someone had opened it up even more.

"Aye, you're right. It most certainly is, and the covering is gone too," said the sheriff, walking over to inspect it.

"He was right there." Magdalena joined them. She was being held up by Maleine. The nun pointed to the hole in the wall. "I entered the scullery to get a soup ladle, since it is Maleine's day to help cook in the kitchen. I was instructing her, explaining how to make vegetable pottage. Mother Superior insists we eat that at least once a week, whether it is Lent or not."

"Magdalena, please," said the sheriff. "Just tell us what you saw and relay exactly what happened."

"Well, it was dark in here, so I can't be totally sure."

"Just tell me what you remember. Start from the beginning," he instructed.

"All right, I will. We left Prime before the prayer service ended, but I wanted to get here before the rest of the lay workers in order to have an opportunity to instruct Maleine properly. Talking is not permitted during the preparation of the light breakfast served directly after Prime. The vegetable pottage takes all day to simmer, so that was for later, but I thought it would be good if Maleine and I got an early start."

"You are rambling again," said Zachariah in a gruff voice. "I don't care about the meal. Tell me about the intruder."

"Oh, sorry," said his sister.

"What did the intruder look like?" asked Vivienne, trying to help matters by speaking calmly.

"I'm not sure. He wore a dark cloak and the hood was up over his head. His face was covered."

"He?" asked the sheriff. "So, it was a man then?"

"Well … I can't be certain." Magdalena still seemed very shaken. "I suppose it could have been a woman. Or a man." She looked to the ground and shrugged. "He, or she, knocked me down in their hurry to leave."

"What was the intruder doing in here?" asked Vivienne.

"I don't know, but in the dark it almost looked like he had his arm inside that hole in the wall," the nun answered. "He seemed to be searching for something, unless I'm mistaken. I guess I startled him, causing him to push me down as he ran. After all, like I said, we should have still been in church with the others."

"Yes, we know that. I'm sure the intruder knew that, too." The sheriff took the lit candle and held it up as he peered inside the hole in the wall which had definitely become larger since yesterday. More bricks had been pulled off the wall and scattered onto the floor of the scullery in a haphazardly manner. "I think I see something."

"What is it?" asked Vivienne, coming to the sheriff's side. "Can I help you?"

"Nay. I've got it." He grabbed something and pulled it out, holding it up for them to see.

Maleine gasped. "It's a skull."

"A tiny skull," remarked Magdalena.

Vivienne reached out and gently took the skull from the sheriff, brushing off the dirt and dust. She knew exactly what this was. "It's the skull of an unborn baby," she said aloud.

"It is? What does that mean?" asked Maleine.

"It means that the postulant or nun who was murdered ... was pregnant."

Chapter Nine

Spending most of the day in the scullery, Vivienne assisted the sheriff in removing even more bricks to open up the wall, enabling them to look inside easier. When they had, they'd discovered the rest of the bones of the unborn baby, lying in the same area where they found the adult skeleton. Vivienne had guessed that the fetus was probably about five or six months in the womb when it died.

"This gives the murderer a strong motive," said Zachariah, arranging the tiny bones out on the floor. Grunt came over to sniff them.

The room, by the orders of the sheriff had been closed off while they were investigating. Mother Superior was not happy that she hadn't been allowed inside the scullery, but the sheriff told her this was official business. He also said they'd have a meeting with her and the prioress and the abbot after Constable Erikson returned from Mablethorpe.

"I cannot believe a nun, or should I say nun-to-be was pregnant," commented Vivienne, still feeling around inside the wall for more clues but not finding any.

"It happens," said Zachariah. "In my days of being a sheriff, as well as my father being one before me, I've heard all kinds of stories. Sometimes, the people who you think are perfect and flawless are no less human than the rest of us, having a dark side as well. Even if they are from an order."

"We need to start questioning people," said Vivienne, pulling her hand out of the wall and brushing it off. Grunt sprawled in the corner, sleeping. "After all, a nun or postulant being pregnant would be the talk of the abbey, it would seem. Or, at least, I'd imagine that to be so. I'm sure someone must have known about it. I know if I were the poor woman, I'd want a friend to confide in. She must have told someone."

"Mayhap not," said Zachariah, standing up and stretching. "After all, this is something quite controversial since we are in an abbey. It would be kept secret, I'd think. It would do no one any good, especially not the reputation of the abbey, if word got out about a pregnant nun."

"So, do you think that the murderer killed this poor woman to keep her pregnancy a secret?"

"It looks that way. He might be the one who got the girl pregnant, too."

"Mayhap," said Vivienne, clearly deep in thought. "If it even was a man who killed her."

"I'd bet on it. It had to be someone strong enough to haul her body here and lift her high enough to dump her inside the wall. And fend her off if she was struggling with him."

"I suppose that makes sense," said Vivienne. "But what if the man who was the father of this woman's baby was in love with her? Mayhap she loved him too. The murderer could be someone entirely different. Someone who just found out about her pregnancy, perhaps, and was punishing her for it."

Zachariah stood up, brushing off his clothes. "We'll have to be careful not to point fingers at anyone. But in reality, I think someone in this abbey had to be the father of that child. If the girl was a postulant, or even if she was a nun, she wouldn't have been going anywhere, but rather staying right here in the abbey."

"Not true," said Vivienne.

"What do you mean?"

"I mean, sometimes the nuns and monks do leave the abbey. For example, Brother Cedric is escorting Nairnie and the children to Mablethorpe right now."

"You think Brother Cedric is the father?"

"I'm not saying that. I'm just giving examples. Another is when Sister Magdalena and Maleine went to the village to help birth a baby. Or when the monks and nuns go out to the fields to work, or to the market or the trade fair."

"God's teeth, I hope Magdalena is not involved in all this somehow. Now you've got me worried."

"Don't be. I am sure Magdalena is as faithful and as trustworthy as they come. I just think you need to talk to her."

"I can't talk to her about what happened between us. Not yet." He paced the floor and dragged a hand through his hair. "I wouldn't know what to say. It's been so long."

"That is the exact reason you two need to speak. You need to forgive her. Even though it wasn't her fault that Margaret died."

"How do we keep getting back on the subject of my personal affairs?"

"When I said you need to talk to Magdalena, I didn't mean about personal family things, even if you interpreted my words that way. What I meant was that we need to question Sister Magdalena about the victim. Mayhap she can at least help us discover who the dead woman was."

"You're right. I was too distracted with the children here before. I should have been questioning everyone by now."

"Calm down. We'll get it done. And we also need to figure out how the ghost of Brother Theodore is involved."

That caused Zachariah to stop pacing. He looked over at her, shaking his head. "Lady Vivienne, I think it would be in the best interest of everyone if you'd stop mentioning a ghost."

"Why? I think the ghost lured me here all the way from Mablethorpe. He wanted our help and now he is getting it. I tell you, this monk ghost has something to do with the murder."

"There is no ghost!" he snapped. "And I'll not hear another word about it." The sheriff stormed out of the room, leaving Vivienne feeling frustrated. Why didn't he believe her? They had always trusted each other in the past. Was it really so hard for him to trust her word now? Grunt jumped up and hurried over to lick her hand. She smiled, liking the way animals always trusted and forgave humans so easily.

"You believe me about the ghost, don't you, Grunt? I know you do, because you saw the ghost too. So did Maleine, Sister Magdalena, and the children. Now, we just have to hope that the ghost of Brother Theodore will make his presence known to the sheriff as well."

"Thank goodness you have finally returned. What took so long?" Zachariah and Vivienne met the constable out by the stables later that day when he'd arrived back from Mablethorpe. Brother Cedric was with him, and took the horse and wagon to the stables. The investigation was going slowly. They'd only managed to question a handful of nuns today, since it seemed every few minutes the bells of the church were ringing again and it was time for Mass or another of their many prayer sessions. Even when it was in between prayers, no one would speak with them, since they were devoted to only speaking a few times during the day, when it was allowed. This was really slowing down progress.

"Sheriff?" asked the constable in confusion. "I'm not sure what you mean. We dropped off the old woman and children at Mablethorpe Castle as instructed, and returned immediately. We actually made quite good time."

"How did it go?" Vivienne wanted to know, already missing her son. "Did Nairnie give the missive I wrote to my aunt?"

"Yes, she did. Just as you'd instructed," Constable Erikson assured her. "The children seemed happy to be home, and Lady Mablethorpe welcomed them with open arms."

"Oh, good." That made Vivienne feel better. "I knew she wouldn't turn them away. What about Wymond? Was he there too?"

"Who?" asked the constable, not seeming to know who she meant.

"Wymond," she repeated. "He is the young man who owns the ferrets. I'm sure he was more than worried about poor little Chomp when she went missing."

Zachariah cleared his throat. "Lady Vivienne, we cannot waste precious time with small talk. Remember, we are only allowed to speak to the others for short periods of time each day."

"Of course, I'm sorry." Vivienne wanted to hear more about home, since she missed being at the castle. But she realized that the sheriff was right. Her questions about Mablethorpe would have to wait. Right now there was a lot of work to do regarding the murder investigation.

"There is more questioning to be done and we need to get to it at once," stated the sheriff. "Plus, I am still waiting to see the sacristy as promised."

"Hasn't Brother Silas let you into the sacristy yet?" Brother Harold approached, having overheard the sheriff. The monk pulled a large ring of keys from his belt. "I can open the door to the sacristy for you, if you'd like."

"Finally, we are getting somewhere," said Zachariah, throwing his hands in the air. "We appreciate it, Brother Harold." The small group headed toward the church with Grunt following on their heels.

"Have there been any new findings since I left, regarding the murder?" asked the constable.

"Yes," said Vivienne before Zachariah could answer. "Sister Magdalena saw an intruder in the scullery. He was searching for something in the wall."

"Really?" This seemed to surprise Constable Erikson. "I wonder what the intruder was looking for?"

"We think we know," said Zachariah. "We uncovered the skeleton of an unborn baby from inside the wall. It was right in the same area where we removed the corpse."

"An unborn baby?" A look of confusion spread across the constable's face. "What would that be doing there? And how do you know it was unborn?"

"The skeleton was very small and not completely formed yet," Vivienne told him. "We think it means the murdered woman was about five or mayhap six months pregnant at the time of her death."

"She was pregnant? How awful." The constable shook his head as if he were trying to push away the thought of a pregnant nun.

As they passed by the church's graveyard, Vivienne noticed Sister Magdalena, Maleine, and also Sister Roberta standing by one of the graves. The tombstone seemed to hold their attention.

"Oh, wait. Can we stop here first?" asked Vivienne, her hand on the sheriff's arm as she stopped walking.

"Whatever for?" Zachariah stopped as well, but seemed to be in a big hurry to get a look at the sacristy. He most likely didn't want anything or anyone slowing him down. When he focused on a task, he seemed to think of nothing else.

"I want to show Brother Harold where the children and I saw the ghost. Abbot, can you tell us who Brother Theodore was?" Vivienne asked the monk. "And when did he die?"

"Brother Theodore?" The monk looked over to the grave where the women stood. "He was the eldest monk here, at eighty years old." The group slowly started to head over to his grave. "He died about two years ago, I'd say. From nothing more than old age."

"That is very old," said Constable Erikson. "I don't know anyone who has lived that long."

"This is interesting, but has nothing to do with our investigation so we need to move on," complained Zachariah.

"Wait a minute," Vivienne told him as he tried to walk away. "Perhaps Brother Harold can tell us something that might lead us in the right direction. You never know."

"Did you say you saw a ghost by Brother Theodore's grave?" asked Brother Harold as they continued walking.

"Nay," said Zachariah at the same time Vivienne said, "Aye."

"Well, some of us think we saw it," said Zachariah, following the others to the group of women standing in the graveyard. Vivienne was glad he didn't refuse to join them since Magdalena was there and she was sure he wouldn't want to have to talk to her.

"Oh, Brother Harold, did you hear?" Sister Magdalena waved her arm in the air, beckoning them over. "The graveyard monk ghost was seen again, and not just by us, but by others this time."

"Really?" asked Brother Harold. "Who exactly saw this ghost?"

"Well, of course, I saw the ghost," said Sister Magdalena. "But you already know that."

"And so did I," added Sister Roberta. "It's been happening for a while now, but Mother Superior doesn't want to believe us."

"I can't imagine why," scoffed Zachariah.

"Sheriff, please," mumbled Vivienne under her breath, thinking he was being so difficult since coming here to the abbey. She wasn't sure if it was from the lack of food, too many rules about not talking, or perhaps just seeing his sister, in general. As it was, they were constantly breaking the no-talking rule, so he should be happy for that, at least. "We cannot discredit anything seen or heard by an eyewitness," she continued.

"By all means. Go ahead." The sheriff sarcastically held out his arm.

"I think the monk ghost is Brother Theodore, and that he is trying to tell us something." Vivienne felt excited. This could be a piece of evidence, in a way.

"Brother Theodore is a ghost?" Brother Harold held a hand to his mouth. "What was this ghost doing?"

"Floating around. He even came to me in Mablethorpe, trying to lure me here." Vivienne told him her thoughts. "He's been very lively. The ghost even seemed to bring us right here to his grave. Mayhap he is somehow involved with this murder."

"I find this so hard to believe."

"Why is that?" asked Vivienne. "Don't you believe in ghosts, Brother Harold?"

"Whether I do or not has nothing to do with it," he told her. "It just doesn't sound like Brother Theodore at all."

"Why not?" she asked.

"I highly doubt an eighty-year-old had anything to do with a murder."

"It could be possible, though." Vivienne didn't want to give up on this.

"But Brother Theodore spent the last year of his life in bed, mainly sleeping," continued Brother Harold. "He could no longer walk and was too weak to even speak."

"There you go," said Zachariah. "No eighty-year-old bedridden monk would be floating around. It wasn't him."

"Well, mayhap Brother Theodore's ghost has more energy than he had as a man," said Vivienne with a frown.

"How tall was this ghost?" asked the monk.

"Very tall," said Vivienne.

"Yes, he was," answered both of the nuns, agreeing.

"Well, Brother Theodore was short and very bent over." Brother Harold didn't seem to think the ghost was this old monk who'd died, and Zachariah certainly didn't believe it. Vivienne supposed she could be wrong about this, but why else would the ghost lead them to this monk's grave?

"Mayhap next time, you can ask the ghost his name," said Zachariah with a chuckle.

"I did." Vivienne raised her chin in the air, not amused with his question. "I asked who he was and what he wanted. That is when he pointed at this exact grave."

"Excuse me," said Brother Harold. "But if you'd like to see the sacristy, we need to do it now, before the start of Vespers."

"Let's go." Zachariah held out his arm to escort Vivienne. Vivienne didn't take his arm, but walked in front of him and the constable, next to Brother Harold. Grunt followed silently behind them.

ZACHARIAH COULD TELL Vivienne was upset with him, and he probably couldn't blame her. But he wasn't going to stand there pretending to believe in ghosts when it was all nothing but a figment of the woman's imagination. He was a sheriff, and believed hard facts. Not supernatural entities that weren't really there to begin with.

Constable Erikson spoke quietly to him as they walked to the church. "The women really seem to believe the ghost story, don't they?"

"They've got each other convinced it's true, and now even the children are frightened by the story. I wish they'd stop talking about it, since it is not true," he told him.

"How can you be sure? I mean, they all seemed to have seen this so-called ghost."

"Constable, even if it were true, what difference would it make? We need tangible evidence and hard facts if we are going to make an arrest. I don't think a ghost's word on something is enough to put someone behind bars, do you?"

"Nay, of course not," said the constable, as they climbed the steps of the church. In a few minutes, they were all standing outside the small room of the sacristy.

"Before we enter, I must tell you that everything inside this room is sacred and has its place. Please, nothing is to be touched or disturbed," warned Brother Harold.

"We're just here to look," Zachariah assured him.

"Brother Silas is impeccable about keeping everything clean and orderly. All items in this room are to be respected."

"Of course," said Vivienne. "We'd have it no other way."

The monk put the key into the lock and twisted it, slowly pushing open the door. Zachariah swore he heard a loud, low rumbling noise from inside, but wasn't sure from where it came.

"Oh, I have visitors." Brother Silas stood near a wooden shelving unit on the far wall. He looked startled that they were here. "Brother Harold, you know the rules. You are supposed to make an appointment to be here. Especially with guests present."

"I hope we're not disturbing anything," said Vivienne, ever so politely. "We just wanted to see the sacristy since we heard so much about how impeccable you keep it."

"Yes, well, come in." The monk hurried over to the door to greet them. "But I only have a few minutes. I need to prepare things for Vespers."

"What all is kept in this room?" asked the constable, looking around.

"Everything for the Mass," answered the sacrist. "The holy vestments the priest wears, the sacred vessels used for the communion and the wine, and the holy scriptures as well."

"What about holy relics? Where are they?" asked Zachariah, walking around the room, inspecting everything. Just like Brother Harold said, nothing was out of place. It was clean and orderly. Brother Silas kept things impeccable, seeming to live up to his highly regarded reputation.

"The holy relics are kept in reliquaries, or ornate boxes designed to house them," Brother Silas explained.

"What kind of relics are they?" asked Vivienne.

"Anything from bones and teeth, to the hair of the saints," explained Brother Silas. "Body parts are the most powerful and sought-after relics. Next are items that a saint owned, followed by the least valuable, which are things that the saints have touched."

"Valuable?" asked Zachariah. "Do you mean someone would actually pay to possess a relic?"

"Yes, of course," answered Brother Harold. "Some churches are very competitive about their relic collections. The bigger, wealthier churches buy as many relics as they can get their hands on. The more relics a church has, the higher regard it is given from the bishops and the pope. Not to mention, people travel from far away to go on pilgrimages to venerate the holy relics, hoping to have a chance just to see or touch them."

"You let people touch the relics?" asked Zachariah in surprise, since he didn't think it was allowed.

"On special occasions only. Such as if a bishop or the pope were to visit our church here at the abbey; however that has never happened. Our abbey is small and we don't have a lot of relics yet."

"Can we please see these holy relics?" asked Vivienne. "I would very much like to have the honor of viewing them."

"Who'd want to see body parts of saints?" Constable Erikson made a face.

"They are locked up in that shrine." Brother Silas nodded to an ornate metal cabinet with two doors that sat atop a table.

"Who has the key?" asked Zachariah.

"I do. As well as Mother Superior," answered Brother Silas.

"Let them see the relics," urged Brother Harold, seeming proud that they had them, even if there were just a few.

"It is frowned upon to do so, but I suppose I could make an exception for you, Sheriff Fitch, as well as Lady Vivienne." The sacrist used a small key to open the shrine. He put on gloves before pulling out one of the boxes and slowly opening it to let them view what was inside.

"Hair," said Zachariah, looking into the box. "Red hair."

"Yes. These are some of the rare, vibrant locks of Saint Agnes, whom our church was named after." Brother Silas closed up the box and opened another one.

Vivienne looked inside and shuddered. "Is that a ... toe?"

"Yes, indeed. It's the bone of the big toe of Saint Gerard." Brother Silas put it back and opened yet one more. "Next is one of our most prized possessions. It was the rosary of Sister Genevieve of Paris."

"You have a rosary from a saint from Paris?" asked Vivienne in surprise.

"Oh, yes. The abbey paid a lot of money to get this," Brother Silas told them.

Zachariah didn't think the rosary looked very special at all. It was dingy and almost seemed dirty. It was made of wooden beads and nothing at all of value.

"Show them the piece of wood from the crucifix cross," said Brother Harold excitedly.

"The crucifix cross? You mean the cross that Jesus was nailed to?" asked the constable.

"Yes, that's right." Brother Silas pulled out a small wooden box. "This can only be opened for a second. Air might ruin it, so look fast." He opened the box and before anyone could get a good view of the small piece of wood, he snapped the box shut again. "I'm sorry, but I need to ring the bells for Vespers now, so you'll all have to go. I cannot leave the sacristy unsupervised."

Grunt whined and scratched at the floor over by the long set of shelves that held folded linens and goblets used by the priest for Mass, as well as leather-bound books.

"That dog shouldn't be in here," said Brother Silas angrily, looking over his shoulder as he locked away the relics. "If he disturbs or ruins anything, Mother Superior will have my head."

"I'll fetch him." Vivienne hurried over to the shelves, grabbing Grunt by the collar. "Oh, Grunt, you knocked over a drinking vessel." She picked up the vessel on the shelf and placed it back in the upright position. "Thank you for letting us visit, Brother Silas. We're sorry to have bothered you." Vivienne led the way out of the room, still holding on to Grunt's collar.

"Yes, thank you," said Zachariah, stopping in the doorway. "Brother Silas, when would be a good time for us to question you?"

"Me?" He seemed disturbed by the thought.

"It's just procedure. Everyone here will need to be questioned since we found a corpse in the wall," explained the constable.

"Oh, I see."

"Yes. We need to know if you might have possibly seen or heard anything that might help us to solve this murder," said Zachariah.

"I don't know anything, but if you really need to question me, I suppose tomorrow at this same time would be sufficient."

"Thank you, Brother Silas." Zachariah nodded. "Have a good night."

"Will you be coming to Vespers, Sheriff Fitch?" Brother Silas called out from inside the room.

"Yes. Will you?" asked Vivienne softly, smiling at him. She knew damned well that he didn't like being in a church and would never agree to go.

"As soon as I solve the murder, Brother Silas," he answered, quickly leaving, having no desire to spend more time in a church than he had to. He figured if he said this to the monk, then mayhap all the nuns and monks would be more accommodating to help him, since they were all so eager to get him to church.

Chapter Ten

V ivienne tossed and turned all night, not able to sleep. She kept thinking about the ghost in the graveyard, the poor dead girl in the wall, and now that sweet little baby who never had the chance to be born. How could anyone purposely hurt a young pregnant woman? Why would they even want to? Especially in an abbey.

Not able to rest or drift off, she got up, fumbling in the dark to find her cloak which she put on over her night rail. Grunt was on the bed with her and jumped to the floor, stretching. "Mayhap some fresh air will help me to think," she told the dog. Putting on her shoes, she headed across the room and pulled open the door. And screamed.

"My lady, I'm sorry! I didn't mean to scare you." Maleine stood there, right outside her door. She had her hand raised as if she were about to knock. She wore a long cloak over her bedclothes, as well.

"It's all right, Maleine." Vivienne pulled the girl to her in a hug. That's when she noticed Maleine's body shaking. "What's the matter? Has something frightened you or made you upset?"

"I'm sure I'm just being a simpkin and it's nothing at all." She sniffled and wiped a tear from her cheek.

"Maleine, come in." Vivienne looked up and down the outdoor walkway before she closed the door. It didn't seem as if anyone was watching them, and for that she was glad. "Let me light a candle."

"Nay, Mother Superior requires us to have all lights out at bedtime."

"All right, then we'll talk in the dark. Come and sit on the bed. I'll open the shutters for some moonlight."

After the window was opened and they were both seated, Maleine spoke.

"I was sleeping in the dormitory and kept feeling as if I were being watched."

"Well, there are many nuns in the same room. It could be quite possible that one or even more were watching you," she told her, hoping to help calm her down.

"But my spot is by the door. I could have sworn I heard the door thud closed."

"So, are you saying someone left? Or entered?"

"I don't know. Everyone seemed to be sleeping. I figured I just imagined it at first. Then I needed to use the garderobe, so I donned my shoes and cloak and left. It was spooky. In the garderobe I kept hearing noises."

"Were you the only one in there?"

"Yes. But from the corner of my eye, I thought I saw a hooded figure in the hallway as I opened the door to come back to the room."

"Mayhap it was one of the nuns."

"I don't think so. This figure seemed taller than a woman."

"Are you saying a man was on the woman's side of the abbey? If so, you'd better tell Mother Superior about it right away. That is not allowed."

"Nay. I don't want to say anything. I might get someone in trouble. I mean … I was half asleep, so I probably imagined it."

"Nay, you really saw someone. If not, you wouldn't be so frightened and you wouldn't have shown up at my chamber door in the middle of the night."

"Oh, my lady. I am not sure what to think anymore."

"In the morning, I am going to tell Mother Superior that I want you to sleep here in my chamber with me."

"I can't!" Maleine's eyes opened wide. "I am a postulant now. I have to be with the other nuns at all times. I am in training."

"I don't care about that. If I don't feel you are safe here, then I will take measures to change things."

"I appreciate your kindness as well as your concern, Lady Vivienne. However, I don't want special treatment. It is only going to turn the other nuns against me."

"What do you mean? Is someone giving you a hard time?" Vivienne truly cared about Maleine and felt like her guardian, now that the poor girl had no family. She wanted to get to the bottom of this and help her in any way that she could.

"I think things being difficult is expected when one is a postulant. It seems that nothing is pleasurable or easy."

"Maleine, there is still time to back out of this commitment."

"Nay, my lady. I cannot do that."

"Why not? If you are not happy here, then you shouldn't stay."

"I need to be a nun. To repent for my father's sins, just like I told you."

"Don't think you have to take his mistakes onto your own shoulders. You have enough worries as it is."

"I think I belong here, Lady Vivienne. In time, I am sure I will feel like it is my home, just like Sister Magdalena feels it is hers. The nuns and monks are my new family now."

"I'm sure you're right." Out of habit, Vivienne started to brush back a lock of Maleine's hair, but her hair was very short and didn't need it. Vivienne pushed back the girl's hood and ran her hand over Maleine's head anyway, in a form of comforting her. "I miss your long locks," she said softly.

"Me, too," agreed Maleine. "Mother Superior hacked it up so badly that she might have just had me lay my head on the cutting board while she used the cleaver to chop it off. The hair. Not my head."

Vivienne giggled. "I think mayhap she already did." Using both hands, Vivienne tried to tamp down the curly tufts of dark hair that stuck up in all directions from Maleine's head. They both laughed, breaking the tension plaguing them.

In that moment, the bells of the church started ringing, filling the night air with melodic music.

"Oh, it must be another of those crazy prayer sessions," remarked Vivienne. "I will never get used to this."

"Yes, it is time for Matins," said Maleine with a nod.

"It's the middle of the night, though."

"That doesn't seem to make a difference here at the abbey," Maleine informed her. "I'm sorry, but I must leave now. I am expected to be there. If I'm not, I might be punished."

"I don't want you to be punished. You'd better go, I guess. But do you think it's safe to walk outside by yourself? I mean, when you think someone could be following and watching you, it might not be a smart thing to do."

"I don't have a choice, my lady. All the other nuns will have left together by now."

"I'm not sleepy. I'll join you." Vivienne got up and Grunt followed. "Nay, Grunt. You'd better stay here. Having Mother Superior yelling at you when the sun is not even up yet is not something any of us want to hear."

Grunt seemed to understand. He sighed and jumped back

up on the bed and plopped down, nuzzling his nose between his paws.

"I'll be right back," she told him, opening the door and heading down the cloistered walkway with Maleine. The walkway led past the nun's dormitory and around to the front of the church.

"I don't want to go past the graveyard again." Maleine hesitated, holding tightly to Vivienne's arm. "It scares me."

"Don't let anything frighten you. You need to be strong and brave if you're going to help me with this investigation."

"Me?" Maleine looked up with hope in her eyes. "You want my help? Really?"

"You did express interest in being an investigator like me, did you not?"

"Yes! I would love to be just like you, my lady. Your life is so exciting."

"Well, show me what you can do, then."

"What I can do? I can't do anything." Maleine's brows dipped and she seemed confused. "Can I?"

"You can do anything you believe you can do, my dear."

"No one has ever said that to me before, Lady Vivienne."

"That is because they are not me. I mean, most men don't think a woman should have an opinion or any interests other than waiting on them hand and foot."

Maleine smiled widely. "And you don't believe it should be that way, do you?"

"Of course not! After all, women are the ones with intuition, not men. I believe even as females, we should have minds of our own. No one can tell us what we feel. And we can do so much more than just be at the beck and call of a man."

"My lady! I've never heard you talk this way before."

"Well, I don't say it aloud too much, I suppose. However, I do live by my own standards."

"And so will I from this day on. I truly admire you, Lady Vivienne. I feel strong and confident and capable of doing just about anything when I am with you."

"Good. Now that you have changed your mind about what you can accomplish, you will succeed in helping me with this case," Vivienne told her.

"What can I do?"

"You are with the nuns day and night, Maleine. The sheriff and I can barely get a few minutes a day to talk to any of them, or the monks."

"That's true. I can get closer to them than you can, I suppose."

"I need you to watch everyone closely. And when you can, talk to them and ask lots of questions."

"What kind of questions?"

"Well, let me see." Vivienne gave it some consideration. "I am sure someone remembers a postulant with red hair, just like the hair of the girl we found in the wall."

"Yes, it would seem so. What else did you discover so far? Tell me everything."

"All right, I will. The corpse was also found with an ornate cloak brooch that had snakes with ruby eyes on it. I think it belonged to a noble, since only the rich would be likely to own something of such value."

"Oh, this is good to know."

"She also had a green gemstone rosary on her that seemed much too nice and expensive for a poor postulant or nun to own. And she was most likely about five or six months pregnant."

"Am I supposed to tell the nuns all this information?"

"Only if you think it'll help you gain more. Otherwise, keep the facts to yourself."

They arrived at the church, and Vivienne pulled open the large wooden door. The monks and nuns were inside, singing.

The melodic tones filled the area, seeming so heavenly. There was truly a peaceful feeling inside here.

"Oh, that sounds beautiful," said Maleine. With a smile on her face, she lifted her head and closed her eyes as she listened to the choir nuns sing. Vivienne took Maleine by the arm and together they entered the church. It was lit by dozens of beeswax candles, and the scent of frankincense filled the air. Brother Silas was there, still lighting candles up at the altar. He looked over when they entered, and nodded. Vivienne nodded back in return.

"It seems like everyone is here," whispered Vivienne as they took their seats on the benches at the back of the crowded church. She saw Sisters Magdalena and Roberta as well as Mother Superior, all with their hands folded in prayer. Brother Harold sat with Brother Cedric, the monk who had taken the children back to Mablethorpe. One side of the church was filled with monks, and the other with nuns. For a prayer session in the middle of the night, she was shocked that everyone was present. It truly seemed magical in a way. This made her realize why possibly someone might want to be a monk or a nun, after all.

"Not everyone is here," Maleine whispered back. "Sheriff Fitch is missing."

"The sheriff wouldn't come to church if we tied him up and dragged him here ourselves," she whispered back.

"Why not?" asked Maleine in concern. "Doesn't he believe in God?"

"I'm not sure what he believes anymore. All I know is that he is angry."

"Angry? At you?"

"Nay, not me. Or at least I don't think so. Of course, I do tend to do things that upset him, I have to admit."

"Whom is he so angry with, then?"

Vivienne looked up at the crucifix at the front of the church and nodded. Maleine's gaze followed.

"Oh," she said, understanding now that the sheriff was angry with God. "Shall I pray for him?"

"I think we could all use prayers, Maleine. It couldn't hurt." Vivienne was only here for Maleine's sake. Otherwise, she was just as angry with God as Zachariah was.

The prayer session ended and everyone filed out of the church in silence, heading back to their dorms to sleep until daybreak. When the sun rose, they'd get up and wash and have some bread and ale before heading back to church for Prime at seven o'clock. Prime was the second service of the day.

"Are you sure you don't want to stay in my chamber tonight with me?" Vivienne asked, as they approached the communal dormitory that most of the nuns shared.

"I'd better not. After all, I have very important work to do now," said Maleine with a wink, following the rest of the nuns into their chamber and closing the door behind her.

Vivienne was about to go back to her chamber, when out of the corner of her eye, she swore she saw her hound. "Grunt?" she said in surprise, heading toward the refectory, following after him. "How did he get out?" she spoke to herself, knowing she'd closed him inside her room. Hurrying after him, Vivienne noticed that the door to the refectory was open a little. She looked around, not seeing him, and figured he had gone inside.

Slowly pushing open the door that led through the eating area, she walked silently toward the kitchen. "Grunt?" she whispered in a soft voice, just loud enough for her dog to hear her, but not loud enough to wake the nuns and monks. "Are you in here?"

She was about to turn around and go back to her room when she jumped, hearing the sound of a pot or pan clattering to the floor. Her heart beat furiously. Anxiety coursed through her.

Thoughts of what Maleine had told her about seeing a figure and swearing someone had been watching her, filled her head. Was somebody here now? Were they watching her or luring her here on purpose? Perhaps it was the murderer or mayhap the ghost. Or was she being silly and was it just her hound? When she heard Grunt bark once, she let out a deep sigh of relief.

Vivienne barged into the kitchen, pushing open the door that was ajar. "Grunt, what are you doing in here, you silly dog?"

"He's hungry, just like me," came a deep voice in the dark. Then, with the strike of a flint, the light of a candle lit up the room and she saw Zachariah sitting on a bench at one of the kitchen work tables. In front of him was a knife, a smoked leg of mutton, a round of cheese, and a loaf of bread. Grunt was under the table with his chin on the sheriff's lap.

Vivienne started laughing. "I should have known I wouldn't find you in church but that you'd be here in the kitchen instead."

"Come. Join us," said Zachariah, holding out a chunk of cheese on the tip of the knife. "It's not much, but it'll certainly fill our bellies."

"Should you be in here stealing food from monks and nuns in the middle of the night?" She strolled over and sat on the bench next to him, her gaze dropping to the large leg of mutton in front of him. "And where did you find that?"

"It seems some of the nuns and monks eat better than the rest. I found meat hidden in a small smokehouse off the kitchen. That is, a place that we were not shown. And for the record, I don't consider this stealing." He popped the chunk of cheese into his own mouth since she hadn't taken it. "I think of it as ... pay."

"Pay? Pay for what? We haven't done anything yet."

"Hush up, and eat." Once again he offered her the tip of the knife with a chunk of cheese on the end. "Who knows if we'll even get any food at all today. It might be a fasting day or some other such nonsense."

She giggled, taking the cheese with two fingers. Breaking off a piece, she gave it to Grunt before putting the rest in her mouth. Zachariah picked up the leg of mutton, taking a big bite.

"Mmmmm," he moaned in delight, closing his eyes as he chewed and swallowed. "So good." He looked handsome and dangerous at the same time, the jumping light of the candle casting shadows against his tanned skin.

"Is this the reason you've been so grumpy lately, Sheriff? Because you've been hungry?"

"I think that is a safe assumption, my lady." He held the leg of lamb up to her mouth. She was about to reject it, but the delicious, smoked aroma tempted her and she instantly realized that she was hungry too. She bit down and used her teeth to tear off a hunk, catching a loose piece and laughing as she ate.

"I feel so naughty," she told him, as he quickly ate another bite of the meat.

"You are not naughty. You are only quenching an aching hunger deep within."

Why in the world did he have to say that? It only managed to make her feelings of attraction toward him become even stronger. When he offered her more meat, she shook her head and backed away a little, not wanting to be so close.

Grunt whined and Zachariah gave him the rest of the mutton leg. The dog eagerly pulled it under the table and started to gnaw on it.

Zachariah tore off a hunk of brown bread and handed it to her. Then he ripped off a little for himself.

"Well, it all makes sense now, I guess," she said, and bit into the bread.

"I can't think straight when I'm starving." He slid a wooden goblet over, and then picked up a bottle of wine and poured some for her. "Have a bit of wine."

"Wine?" She took the cup and had a sip, handing it back to him. "Mmmm, that is good. Where did you find it?"

"I can't tell you all my secrets, my lady. You just have to know where to look." His gaze focused on her over the rim as he lifted the cup and drank down the wine. His brown eyes seemed to dance with amusement in the soft light of the fire. She started to have that tingly feeling inside again. It must be attraction. But she couldn't feel this way. Not with Zachariah, her best friend. And certainly not here in such a holy place. She needed to quickly think of something else. Anything other than the sheriff.

"Maleine came to my chamber tonight," she told him, trying to change the subject.

"I know. I came to your room to see if you were as hungry as I was. That's when I saw the two of you heading to the church."

"And you didn't follow?" She teased him, knowing it was the last place he'd want to be.

"I heard Grunt's stomach growling, so I let him out of the room and took him with me to the kitchen."

"Grunt must have come looking for me after the prayer service. I saw him and followed him here."

"Vivienne, I don't feel as if this investigation is going well at all. Do you?"

She heard him call her Vivienne without her title, but didn't correct him. Right now, she rather liked the intimate way it sounded. And felt.

"I'm sure it'll get easier soon."

"Why do you think so? Everything we do here seems to be such a struggle. We're never going to find answers when no one seems very willing to help."

"Things are about to change for the better."

"What makes you say that?"

"Maleine is our inside assistant now," she told him proudly.

"What?" He stopped chewing and looked over at her.

"She is around the nuns and monks all day long. She can speak to them easier than we can. Plus, I told her to keep her eyes and ears open."

"Well, I hope that helps." He offered her more wine, but she refused. He downed the rest of the contents and thunked the empty cup down on the table. "If I don't soon start finding answers or clues regarding this murder, I swear I am going to give up being a sheriff altogether."

"Nay, you won't. Don't say that since you know it's not true. You love your work too much to ever leave it." She reached under the table and took the bone away from Grunt, not wanting him to get splinters in his mouth.

Zachariah looked at her, and this time in the firelight, she saw sadness fill his eyes. Zachariah Fitch had never looked so forlorn. "I'm trying to get used to leaving that which I love. Since it seems to be my destiny, anyway," her told her, then got up from the bench, brushed the crumbs off his clothes, and blew out the candle. "We'd better get some sleep now before the damned bells wake us up again."

Vivienne wasn't sure what he meant by the comment about getting used to leaving that which he loved. Did he mean his wife? His parents? His job? Or was it something even more? Could he somehow possibly be talking about ... her?

Chapter Eleven

Vivienne stepped inside the ossuary the next morning, stopping in her tracks when she saw the horror that awaited her there. Besides seeing the skeleton of the body they'd found in the wall, there was so much more. Sunlight blared in through the open door, lighting up the room covered with bones. Skulls were stacked up like stones against one wall, reaching all the way to the ceiling. The other walls were lined with ribs, legs, and arm bones, all piled atop each other like nothing more than logs for the fire.

"Go on in," said Zachariah from behind her as he held the door open. "Unless you'd rather not. That's all right, too. I can inspect the body again by myself."

With her eyes fastened to the exhumed bones, her heart hurt for these people who had lost their lives and then been dug up and displayed in such an insensitive manner. Not to mention, the exhumed bodies had been torn apart. How could holy people do such an awful thing? Even if there wasn't enough room in the graveyard, there was no possible good reason in her mind for an action like this.

"Vivienne?" came his deep, cool voice from behind her. She

felt the heat of his hand on her shoulder. "You need to decide. And know that I will never think less of you if you turn around and walk out of here right now. If I were you, that is what I would do. This isn't meant for everyone. Certainly not a lady."

"Nay," she said, with a shake of her head. "I will do everything and anything it takes to help find that poor woman's killer." With shaking legs, she slowly took a step into the room. The feeling of dread immediately encompassed her. So much death. Such deep sorrow. It was as if she could feel the pain and anguish from each of the bodies that had been moved there.

"Sheriff, I'm here," called out Constable Erikson, as he walked up the few steps behind them. "Are we going to inspect the corpse again?"

"Aye," said Zachariah, gently moving Vivienne aside so that he and the constable could enter the building.

"I'll close the door for privacy." The constable reached out for the door but Vivienne stopped him.

"Nay!" She held up her hand. "Please ... leave it open. I want the fresh air."

"Is everything all right, my lady?" The constable gave the sheriff an odd look.

"Lady Vivienne is fine," he answered for her. "It's just that this place is not for the faint of heart. It might take her a while to get used to it."

"Yes, I can see why." Constable Erikson walked into the room, reaching up and picking up a leg bone with a foot attached. "It's almost as if these bones are going to get up and walk away by themselves." He chuckled, pretending to make the leg walk on its own.

"Nay, don't say or do that," said Vivienne, trying to catch her breath. This was quite overwhelming. "And please, don't touch the bodies in such a disrespectful way."

"I don't see the problem," said the constable with a shrug. "I mean, they are dead so I don't think they'd object to anything I do or say."

"Constable, please," said Zachariah with a nod.

"Whatever you say." Constable Erikson threw the leg bone back to the pile, causing several of them to tumble to the ground. Vivienne jumped back and held her hand to her heart.

"Shall we take another look at the bones of the strumpet then?" The constable had the nerve to smile when he said it.

"I am sure this woman was not a strumpet," said Vivienne, straightening her shoulders as she spoke.

"She was pregnant, wasn't she?" asked the man, walking over to the table and looking down at the bones. "That means she was a loose nun."

"That means nothing of the sort." Vivienne defended the dead woman even though she knew nothing about her.

"How can you say that?" asked the constable. "She was in an abbey and they all take vows of chastity, don't they?"

"Everyone has moments of temptation, even monks and nuns, I'm sure," said Zachariah.

"It could be more than that," Vivienne told them. "Mayhap this poor girl was raped. Did you ever think of that?"

"That could be the case," agreed the sheriff. "But once again, until we can discover her identity, we won't know anything about her for sure."

"Sheriff, it is stuffy in here and too cramped for the three of us." Vivienne wasn't enjoying this at all.

"I agree," said the constable. "Perhaps you should leave, my lady. After all, this is work for those with experience. Leave this to me and Sheriff Fitch. We'll handle everything."

Vivienne's gaze shot over to Zachariah, begging him silently for help. He looked at her and let out a sigh before answering.

"Constable, Lady Vivienne is experienced in murder investigations and has helped me solve several cases in the past.

Perhaps it would be more beneficial if she stays and if you talk to Mother Superior instead."

"What?" It was obvious by his expression that Constable Erikson couldn't believe what he was hearing.

"Yes, I'd rather stay here with Sheriff Fitch," said Vivienne. "We work well together."

"You can start lining up times for us to question the inhabitants of the abbey," Zachariah told the constable.

"You're choosing her over me? Really?" The constable didn't look at all pleased by the sheriff's decision. However, Vivienne was more than happy that Zachariah was standing up for her and her wishes.

"This has nothing to do with choosing anyone over another," explained the sheriff. "We have limited time and need to move quickly. I feel that the Mother Superior would be more apt to grant your request, since you're a constable and Lady Vivienne has no real authority in this investigation."

Vivienne's smile slowly faded. She wasn't sure if he meant this, or was saying it only to make the constable feel more important and also to get him to leave.

"I'll start work on it right away, Sheriff." The constable brushed past Vivienne and left the ossuary. Vivienne heard the constable greet someone, and looked out the open door to see Maleine, Sister Magdalena, and Sister Roberta approaching. As so often, the nuns had their hands folded in prayer.

"Sisters. Maleine. Good morning," Vivienne called out the door to them, happy they were there.

"What are they doing here?" grumbled Zachariah.

"My lady, we have something to tell you." Maleine walked up the two stones steps leading into the ossuary and was about to enter, but Vivienne stopped her.

"Wait! Don't enter," she said with an outstretched arm. "We'll talk out there instead." Vivienne quickly led Maleine back down the steps. She was sure that seeing all those exhumed bodies would frighten the girl, and she didn't want her scared again the way she'd been last night. "What is it?" she asked, once they'd joined the other women.

"You might want to call my brother to join us," suggested Sister Magdalena. "This is important information."

"Oh, all right." Vivienne turned around to call to him, only to find Zachariah already headed down the steps after them.

"I heard her," he said, stopping in front of the nuns. "We have a lot of work to do and very little time to do it," he announced. "Magdalena, this had better be important."

"Sheriff, please. Be kind," Vivienne urged him under her breath, before turning back to the women. "Go ahead, Maleine."

"I was talking to Sisters Magdalena and Roberta, and it seems they think they know the identity of the dead woman," Maleine told her.

"That's wonderful!" exclaimed Vivienne, feeling proud that Maleine had come up with new information regarding the case so quickly. The girl was already proving to be a valuable asset.

"They know her identity? How? We haven't even been able to figure it out," said Zachariah.

"Is it true that the dead woman had red hair?" asked Sister Roberta.

"Yes, that's right," said Vivienne. "Vibrant, red hair."

"And she was dressed like a postulant instead of a nun?" questioned Sister Magdalena.

"We believe so," answered the sheriff. "Do you think you know who she was?"

Magdalena looked over to Sister Roberta and nodded. "Yes. We both remember a postulant with red hair who used to be here about two years ago."

"That's true," agreed Sister Roberta. "Her name was Sabina.

She was only eighteen years of age, and a very kind girl with a loving heart."

"Really," said the sheriff. "Now we are getting somewhere. Do either of you know anyone who might have wanted her dead?"

"Nay," said Sister Magdalena. "She was a sweet girl, but did seem troubled about something when we saw her last."

"That's right," agreed Sister Roberta. "She was getting close to taking her vows. But a few days before it was to happen, she mysteriously disappeared."

"Was she excited about taking her vows?" asked Maleine.

"I can't say she was," said Sister Roberta. "I mean, yes, at first. But as the time of her training period neared its end, Sabina almost seemed to be changing her mind about staying here at the abbey."

"What do you mean?" asked Vivienne. "Did she say something about it to either of you?"

"I have to admit, she told me she wanted to leave the abbey, but we all have said that once or twice when things got rough," said Sister Roberta. "I didn't really think anything of it."

"Did she have a ... a lover?" asked Vivienne.

"I don't know about a lover," said Magdalena. "But she was good friends with a monk. What was his name?" She looked over at Sister Roberta.

"I think it was Brother Benedict, wasn't it?"

"Yes, Sister Roberta is right," said Magdalena. "Brother Benedict. He disappeared about the same time as Sabina."

"Didn't you ask Mother Superior or anyone where they went?"

"We were told they both left the order to go home to their families." Magdalena looked like she wanted to say something else.

"What is it, Sister Magdalena? Tell us everything," said Vivienne. "Even if it doesn't seem important."

"It's probably nothing."

"Magdalena, Lady Vivienne is right," said the sheriff. "If you know something, tell us. It might be a clue in finding Sabina's killer."

"It's just that I swear Sabina said she didn't have any family. None besides those at the abbey, whom she considered her new family."

"Like me," said Maleine softly.

"Didn't you ask anyone about her background?" was the sheriff's question.

"We are taught not to ask questions, and, as you know, we are not even allowed to speak much." Sister Magdalena looked around. "We'd better get back before someone sees us here. I am supposed to be in the orchard, working with Maleine."

"And I need to be stitching with the other nuns. I'll be noticed if I'm missing." Sister Roberta hurried away and Sister Magdalena followed.

"Maleine," said Vivienne, taking the girl by the arm as she was about to walk away too. "Thank you. You were very helpful."

"You're welcome," said Maleine with a proud smile. "I just wish I was appreciated as much for all the manual labor I've been doing here at the abbey. This isn't quite what I expected at all when I enrolled."

"I'll speak to Mother Superior about you being trained to read and write if you'd like."

"I would like that, my lady. However, mayhap later. Right now we have to find a murderer, if one is still about. Thank you. But I must go now." She gave Vivienne a quick hug and then ran after the two nuns.

"You are quite fond of Maleine aren't you?" asked Zachariah.

"Yes. I do like her," said Vivienne, watching the girl go. "I feel sad for her after all the tragedy she's been through. I just hope she finds solace here at the abbey."

"I'm sure she will. She's been very helpful, and now we have something to go on. After we inspect the corpse again, I think we need to have a little meeting with the Mother Superior."

"Of course. But do you think she will know anything about all this?"

"She was with us in the scullery. She knows about the red hair and the girl being a postulant. If my sister and Sister Roberta remembered Sabina, I'm sure Mother Superior knew her as well."

"That's true," said Vivienne. "I wonder why she didn't tell us about Sabina?"

"Mayhap she has something to hide."

"Mother Superior? I highly doubt it."

"Well, then she'd better have a damned good explanation for keeping this information from us."

"Mother Superior, can you tell us about the postulant named Sabina who used to be here at the abbey?" asked Vivienne later that day. Vivienne, the constable, and the sheriff sat at a table set up outside in the graveyard where the questioning was being held. It was the only place that was supposedly not too sacred for something like this, according to Mother Superior.

"There was a girl here a few years ago by that name," said the nun, sitting in a chair across from them.

"Tell us about her," said the constable.

"She was close to taking her vows, but never did."

"Why not?" asked Zachariah.

"It's personal, Sheriff. Why does any of this matter?"

"Did she have red hair?" asked Vivienne.

"I don't remember. I suppose mayhap she did."

"Mother Superior, you need to tell us everything you know about Sabina," the sheriff explained. "If you hold anything back and we discover it, you could be in a lot of trouble. Your position of being the Mother Superior will not help you."

"What on earth are you talking about?" Mother Superior lifted her chin in the air. "I thought we were going to talk about the murder investigation. What does any of this have to do with the postulant, Sabina?"

"We think it was Sabina who was murdered and bricked up in the wall." Vivienne watched for the nun's expression.

Mother Superior's brows dipped and she shook her head. "Nay. That can't be. Sabina left us to go back to her home in Northumberland."

"Did you get confirmation from her family that she ever got home?" asked the sheriff.

"She didn't have any family. Just a few friends there as far as I knew. Sheriff, I am sure this is not the dead woman from the wall."

"How can you be certain of that?" asked Zachariah.

"Because, the girl left the abbey. I just told you that."

"Did you actually see her leave then?" asked Vivienne.

"Nay, I was busy at the time. Brother Silas handles those kinds of things for me. He is very responsible."

"So you don't think he was lying?" asked Zachariah.

"Never," said the nun. "Sheriff, I don't even like that you would ask such a question about someone from the abbey."

"Was Sabina close with anyone?" asked Vivienne.

"Well, yes. She was very close to Brother Benedict," answered the nun.

"And where is this Brother Benedict now?" asked the constable. "We'd like to question him as well."

"Nay, you can't." The nun looked down. "He's no longer here either."

"Are you saying that he left the order too?" asked Vivienne. "That isn't normal, is it?"

"He did leave. Both of them did." Mother Superior seemed like she knew more, but was holding back.

"You need to tell us everything," Vivienne reminded the nun.

"If not, you could be considered an accomplice to the crime," said Constable Erikson.

Her eyes opened wide. "Nay! I am no accomplice and there was not a crime involving these two, I tell you."

"How can you say that?" asked Vivienne.

"I say it, because I was the one who sent them both away."

"Why?"

"Because Sabina was pregnant, and Brother Benedict was the father. There, I said it. Are you happy now?" Mother Superior sat there, shaking her head with her jaw clenched tightly.

"We'll be happier when we find the girl's killer," answered Zachariah.

"Did Brother Silas see Brother Benedict leave too?" asked the constable.

"Yes," said Mother Superior. "He watched them both ride out the gate together."

"Mother Superior, the bones of the fetus we found with the murdered woman tell us that Sabina was at least five or six months pregnant," said Vivienne. "Didn't you know long before you sent them away that Sabina was in that way?"

"I had my suspicions, but it was hard to tell with Sabina.

She wore a loose gown, of course, and only near the end did I think her thickening middle was more than just her gaining weight."

"You should have told us this before," snapped Zachariah.

"I didn't think it was relevant," the woman answered. "Oh, do you really believe the murdered woman was Sabina? That is awful."

"We do," said Zachariah. "And now, we need to find out what happened to Brother Benedict."

"I don't know," she answered. "Like I told you, I believed they both left the order to live together and raise a family, even though we tried to keep it a secret by telling others they just left the order. It wouldn't do well for the reputation of the abbey if anyone knew the truth about the pregnancy."

"Nay, I suppose not." Vivienne wondered how anyone could worry about the reputation of an abbey at a time like this.

Mother Superior continued, "They were not welcome here anymore, so I didn't think anything of it when they never returned. They weren't supposed to."

"You mean, they weren't allowed to," Vivienne corrected her.

"Who can we talk to that might know more about Brother Benedict and his whereabouts?" asked the constable.

"I suppose the abbot would be the one to contact about that."

"Thank you, Mother Superior, we'll talk to Brother Harold." Zachariah stood up, and so did Mother Superior.

She was about to leave, but turned back. "Sabina seemed to be a good girl, but just lost her way, I suppose. I saw that Brother Benedict was fond of her. Mayhap too much. I should have stopped them from ever being together. I feel like this is my fault."

"No one is blaming you, Mother Superior," said Vivienne,

standing up as well and trying to comfort the woman. "And I assure you that we will find Sabina's killer, and he or she will be put behind bars and made to pay for their heinous crime."

"I don't want word about this getting out," said the nun. "My abbey will be ruined if that happens. I will not have its name and reputation slandered because of the mistakes of those two young people."

"Don't you think it's a little too late for that now?" asked Zachariah. "Word is already out about a dead body found in the wall of the scullery. We will need to file reports, as well as to give everyone an explanation and viable answers as to what happened here."

"We cannot undo such a tragedy, Sheriff," said the nun. "Exposing the truth about the girl is only going to hurt the abbey. I don't see why you can't talk about her murder without saying she was pregnant."

"Because, the two matters might be related," Vivienne explained. "Don't you want justice to prevail? Doesn't Sabina deserve our help in figuring out why someone killed her? Don't let her death have been done in vain."

"I suppose you're right." Mother Superior blessed herself. "God will punish the guilty and reward the innocent."

"Not always so, Reverend Mother," said Zachariah. "After all, it looks so far as if Sabina was innocent, and she was far from rewarded."

"Hrmph," mumbled the nun. "I'd hardly say being six months pregnant while training to be a nun was innocent. I just wish I had realized sooner what was going on right under my nose. How could I have been so blind?"

"How long was Sabina here at the abbey?" asked Vivienne.

"She was here about a year. Why?"

"Then her pregnancy happened here without a doubt."

"I told you, it was Brother Benedict. He was much too

friendly with her. I hope when you find him that he gets what he deserves," she said with a sniff, turning and walking away.

"I think we need to speak with Brother Harold next," suggested the constable. "Shall I go fetch him?"

Just then the bells started to ring and all the monks and nuns emerged from inside the buildings, heading in silence to the church for another prayer session.

"Don't bother," said Vivienne. "It is noon and everyone is consumed with prayers. Dinner will be served immediately afterward in silence, as one of the nuns reads from the scriptures. Then they'll all go directly back to work afterward."

"Arrgh," growled the sheriff. "I feel so confined with all these blasted rules."

"Try to stay calm, Sheriff," she told him. "Hopefully, this will all be over very soon."

Chapter Twelve

The rest of the day had been fruitless for trying to get any new information on the murder case. Like Zachariah said, the rules of the abbey were really slowing them down. It was almost as if someone were purposely trying to prevent them from accomplishing anything. Vivienne felt tired and weary. She was also worried about Martin back home. All she wanted to do was to spend time with her son. Instead, she was here, dealing with uncooperative nuns and monks, and a ghost of the past that was making her seem addlepated to Zachariah. She wished the sheriff could see the ghost too.

"Come on, Grunt. Let's go to bed." She headed down the cloistered walkway to her room.

Compline, the last prayer session of the evening, had just ended. Even though it was only seven o'clock, the monks and nuns went straight to bed afterward. If they couldn't sleep, they were expected to spend time in self-introspection or personal prayer. It wasn't even dark outside yet, and it did seem ridiculous. But since the order had been to rise at two in the morning for more prayers, and then be up for the day a few hours after that, she supposed it all made sense in some odd sort of way.

"Goodnight, Lady Vivienne. And Grunt."

Vivienne turned around to see Maleine's smiling face. She wasn't with Sister Magdalena, but with a young nun whom Vivienne had yet to meet. Grunt went right over to the young woman and sniffed her hand. The nun smiled and petted Grunt on the head.

"Goodnight, Maleine. Who is your friend?" Vivienne walked over to join them.

The nun wouldn't talk, but just shook her head and put a hand over her mouth. She was a young woman who seemed to be about Vivienne's age of twenty-three.

"Oh, that's right. Talking is not allowed. Sorry," apologized Vivienne. "I can't get used to these strange rules of the abbey."

"Nay, that's not it. Not really, even though I shouldn't be talking either," said Maleine in a soft voice. She scanned the area, making sure she hadn't been observed breaking the rules. "You see, Sister Ernestine is mute. She is unable to answer you."

"Oh, I'm sorry. I didn't know," said Vivienne. "It must be so hard for you, Sister Ernestine. Did this happen at birth?"

"The answer is no," Maleine answered for her. "When she was a child, seven years old, she fell and hit her head on a rock. That's when it all happened. She lost her hearing as well as her ability to speak. Her parents then gave her to the nuns to raise as an oblate, never to leave the abbey again. When she became of age, she took her vows."

Sister Ernestine looked over at Maleine and used some hand gestures, opening and closing her fingers, somehow talking to Maleine.

"Sister Ernestine said she likes your dog."

"Maleine, how do you know what Sister Ernestine is saying?" asked Vivienne curiously.

"I've been learning gestural communication using the hands like the monks use during times of strict silence. Like this." Maleine moved her fingers quickly in different positions, sometimes even crossing them, opening and closing her hands and moving them in different positions in front of her and in the air.

"A language without words, just using the hands?" asked Vivienne. "How fascinating. I'd like to learn it someday too."

"It comes quite easy to me for some reason. I am still learning, but I rather enjoy it." Maleine smiled widely, saying something back to her new friend with her hands and arms, causing the girl to laugh. Then Sister Ernestine used her hands to say something back to Maleine.

"Ooops. Ooooh, I see." Maleine laughed as well, and corrected her hand motions.

"What is it?" asked Vivienne.

"I thought I was telling Sister Ernestine that I liked your dog too, but I guess I really said I'd like to get a hog."

Vivienne giggled, noticing they were attracting the attention of some of the nuns. "Mayhap you two should go now," she whispered. "I don't want to get you in trouble."

Once again, Sister Ernestine looked at Maleine, saying something with her hands.

"She wants to know if you found any more clues about who killed Sabina," Maleine relayed her friend's message.

"Nay, not yet," Vivienne answered. "Did she know Sabina?"

"You can speak directly to her, my lady," Maleine told Vivienne. "Even though Sister Ernestine cannot hear, she is able to reads lips."

"Oh. All right. Sister Ernestine, did you know Sister Sabina?" asked Vivienne.

The nun nodded and then conveyed her message to Maleine, using just her hands again.

"Sister Ernestine says to tell you that Sabina was not a Sister, since she hadn't yet taken her vows. She was only a postulant. Like I am. She also said yes, she and Sabina were friends."

"Really." Vivienne liked the sound of this. "I wish to talk to you more about her," she said, eager to get more information on the deceased woman. Sister Roberta and Mother Superior walked up before Vivienne could gain any more answers.

"Sister Ernestine. Maleine. You know the rules. No talking," Mother Superior reminded them in a stern tone. "Now you will both be punished tomorrow, and be expected to clean up the ossuary since the sheriff and his friends messed it up."

"The ossuary?" gasped Vivienne. "Oh, Mother Superior, you cannot ask them to do that. Besides, Sister Ernestine wasn't even talking. She can't talk."

"I am in charge here, Lady Vivienne, and I would appreciate you not telling me how to run my abbey." The Reverend Mother was stern.

"It's my fault they were talking. Blame me, not them." Vivienne tried to help her friends.

"I do blame you, my lady," said Mother Superior. "Since you've arrived at the abbey, too many rules have been broken because of you, the sheriff, and that dog."

Sister Roberta spoke up next. "I'll make certain they go directly to their chamber, Reverend Mother." She collected the girls and swept them away.

"I suggest you get to your room as well, Lady Vivienne. And no more talking." Mother Superior didn't wait for an answer, but hurried away and disappeared into the dark, leaving Vivienne and Grunt standing there alone.

"If she's so angry about a little talking, she'll hate the fact I'm on the female's side of the building right now," came a male voice from the dark.

Vivienne spun on her heel to see Zachariah standing in the dark cloistered area, with his back against a stone column and his arms crossed over his chest. His tunic was unbuttoned a little, and she couldn't help noticing dark chest hairs poking through.

"Zachariah, what are you doing here?" she asked in a hoarse whisper, hurrying over to him, checking her surroundings for hovering nuns trying to catch her breaking the rules. Grunt ran over and jumped up, putting his front paws on the sheriff. Zachariah bent over and petted the dog with both hands.

"I never thought I'd be so happy to see you," he said to the dog. Or at least that's whom she thought he was talking to. "I swear I'm going to go mad before I leave this godforsaken place."

"Shhhh. Don't say that!" Vivienne couldn't believe what she heard coming out of the sheriff's mouth. "Remember, we are in a holy place."

"I wouldn't call it holy." He stood back up. "Not with murder, sex, and lies going on here."

"What do you want?" she asked him, looking around once more. "Don't you realize you are jeopardizing everything by being here? If either one of us gets Mother Superior any angrier, she's going to throw us out on our ears before we close this case."

"We wouldn't want that now, would we?" He yawned, and she could tell this investigation was wearing on him as well. For some reason, even meeting up with the Pied Piper on Rotten Row hadn't been as terrifying as to think what would happen if Mother Superior caught them together ... just talking. "Good night, my lady. Sleep well." Zachariah headed toward his own quarters on the other side of the courtyard.

"Good night, Sheriff Fitch," she said, thinking that being here with him made this all seem just a little better. "Sweet dreams."

Heading to her room with Grunt at her side, she entered in the semi-darkness, not bothering to light a candle. She flopped down on the bed, pulling the blanket over her, so tired that she didn't even reprimand Grunt for sleeping on the bed with her, even though she realized that if Mother Superior found out, there would be hell to pay.

"We'll be home soon," she told her hound, slowly petting him with her eyes already closed. "Tomorrow is another day," she mumbled, already drifting off to a dream world where hopefully things would look better.

Chapter Thirteen

Vivienne was having her recurring nightmare again, and there was nothing she could do to stop it ...

Suddenly, Vivienne felt her stomach twist into a knot. She couldn't help feeling that something was horribly wrong, or perhaps about to happen. The twisting feeling inside her gut felt like the sharp blade of a dagger, such as the one she had strapped to her side. The last time she felt this way was six months ago when she'd lost her husband, George, after he was kicked by a horse and died. She reached down to touch the hilt of her blade, feeling odd. The thought flashed through her mind that she'd need her dagger tonight for protection, although she had no idea where this thought came from. The feel of the cold, sharp metal in her hand was so opposite of the warmth of new life from her baby pressed up against her.

After her mother took the baby from her, Vivienne had finally dozed off, but was abruptly woken after not too long. What roused her was the sound of neighing horses and the jerk of the wagon as it halted, coming to a complete and sudden stop. She heard voices, and they sounded menacing, if she wasn't mistaken.

"Off the wagon," commanded a gruff male voice.

"Nay. Leave us alone. We just want to pass," her father replied, doing all he could to protect his family, she was sure. Vivienne's heart sped up. She realized these roads were filled with bandits, and perhaps they were about to be robbed. Her fingers closed over the hilt of her dagger strapped to her side. She would fight to help protect her family if need be.

The next thing she heard sounded like a sword being drawn from a scabbard, followed by the sounds of a struggle. Slowly, she pulled her blade from its sheath and rolled over in the hay, trying to see what was happening.

"Abiathar!" shouted her mother. "Nay!" she screamed and started crying.

Before Vivienne could get to her knees to look over the back of the bench seat, she heard the sickening sound of a body hitting the ground.

"Kill her, too!" commanded another man.

"Nay," Vivienne mumbled to herself, pushing up to a half-sitting position to see what was happening. She saw her mother struggling with a man as he pulled her off the wagon and to the ground. The basket with Vivienne's baby in it was still on the bench seat. Vivienne started to panic. She needed to get to her baby as well as to help her poor mother. Since her father was so quiet and not protecting them, she was sure he'd been killed.

"Sister, what's happening?" Her brother rubbed a sleepy eye, looking up at her from under the hay.

"Adrian, stay down," she warned her brother in a hushed voice. "We're being attacked by outlaws. Keep quiet, so they don't know you are here."

"Who won't know?" he asked, and she silenced him with her finger to his lips.

"Mother is in trouble. I have to help her as well as protect my baby." Not wanting to be seen, Vivienne quietly flipped over the far side of the wagon, letting her feet silently drop to the ground.

She hoped to be able to sneak up to the front of the wagon and grab the basket with her baby, without the ruffians noticing her. It was night and very dark, so that would give her cover. Only a partial moon lit the sky, but was mainly hidden by clouds.

Gripping her dagger tightly, she crept around to the front of the wagon, scared because she knew she was still weak from giving birth. How would she fight off a full-grown man? Especially in her condition? Her toe hit something on the ground. When she looked down, she saw the bloody, lifeless body of her father lying in a crumpled heap. Biting her tongue so as not to cry out, she quickly hunkered down to check for signs of life. His throat had been slit and there was no hope he could survive such a heinous act. He was no longer moving.

It was too late for her father, but mayhap she could still save her mother and her son. She was their only hope now. Slipping her dagger back into her waistbelt, she reached down and took her father's sword from his hand. Since he was only a foot soldier, he didn't own one of the longer, heavier swords mainly used by knights. His was a shorter, lighter blade, devised for closer, hand-to-hand combat. Therefore, Vivienne was able to lift it, having learned from her father how to use it, at her insistence.

Gripping the hilt of her father's sword in two hands, Vivienne slowly stepped around the front of the wagon, just in time to see a shadowy figure stab her mother with his sword and then throw her body to the ground. Too scared to even speak, she froze. Standing in the dark, fear consumed her, making her feel as if she were in hell.

"Someone's coming. Hurry, let's get out of here," came the voice of another shadowy form atop a horse. The man who stabbed her mother withdrew his sword and headed toward his waiting horse.

"Mother! Nay!" screamed her little brother. Vivienne's head

snapped around to see Adrian standing in the hay in the back of the wagon, looking over the edge, terror on his face.

"Dammit. There's someone else," shouted the first bandit to the second.

"Kill him, too," commanded the ruffian's companion. "Leave no witnesses."

The first man rushed over, but Vivienne wasn't about to let him kill her brother too. Guilt already ate away at her that she wasn't able to save her parents. She stepped out in front of the attacker, wildly swinging her father's sword in the air. Mayhap it was her anger controlling her actions, but somehow she managed to stab the man on his right shoulder with her blade. The tip stuck into his flesh and she was sure she felt the blade meet his bone. Quickly, she pulled the blade back, seeing the blood oozing from the man's wound.

"Aaaaah!" the attacker screamed, one hand gripping at his bleeding shoulder from where Vivienne had struck him.

"Dammit, there's a girl here, too," shouted the other man from his horse.

The fighting frightened the horses, causing them to rear up and paw at the air, whinnying loudly. The wagon jerked and her brother fell back in the hay with his feet in the air. Then the horses took off down the road at a run, pulling the wagon along with them. The sound of Vivienne's crying baby from the bench seat inside the basket caused her to panic and become furious all at the same time. Even in her weakened state from just having given birth, Vivienne's motherly instincts kicked in and she fought like a lion. She started swinging the sword wildly at her attacker as she lunged forward, stabbing at him over and over again. All the while she gritted her teeth. No one was going to kill any of her family and get away with it! She was so angry right now, that she wasn't even scared. She wanted both of these outlaws to die.

"You bastard! I'll kill you for what you've done," she shouted, causing him to actually back away from her now. His sword dangled from his fingers as he gripped his bleeding sword arm which she had injured. God's eyes, she wished she had severed his arm all together.

"Let's go," called out the man's friend from his steed. "Someone's coming."

The man she'd struck mumbled something under his breath that she couldn't decipher, but it sounded as if he said the words, 'too soon'. He then turned and ran, mounting his horse, taking off with his friend, leaving her stranded all alone.

"Vivienne," came her mother's soft cry from the ground. Vivienne spun on her heel and ran to her mother, dropping the sword and falling to her knees at her mother's side.

"Mother!" she cried, cradling the woman's head atop her lap. "They killed Father. And the horses ran off with Adrian and my baby." Tears gushed from her eyes as she looked down at her mother bathed in the scant light of the partial moon that broke through the clouds. "Mother, please don't die too! Do not leave me, I beg you. I need you!" Vivienne said the words, but knew that all the wishing in the world wasn't going to change what happened here tonight. Blood covered her mother who clutched her abdomen and moaned in pain. There was no use denying that the woman was not going to live. Her mother lifted her hand, yanking at a chain around her neck until the chain released. Then she slowly held out her closed fist to Vivienne.

"Take ... this ... Daughter. For you ... and the baby."

"Mother, what are you doing? What do you mean?"

"Listen ... to ... me."

"I need to get you help. I think I hear horses coming down the road. I'll signal to the riders." She started to stand, but her mother's hand on her arm stopped her.

"Too ... late," came her mother's soft reply as her eyes started to close. "Go to ... your father. He ... will protect ... you ... and the ... babe."

"Mother, didn't you hear me? Father is dead!" she screamed. "I can't go to him for help. It's too late! I need to find Adrian and my baby."

"Wait." The woman opened her fist and Vivienne looked down to see a gold ring with a ruby gemstone embedded in it dangling from the chain. It was something her mother had been wearing around her neck, although Vivienne had never known it. "This is ... your father's."

"Mother, what are you saying?" Vivienne cried. "You are delirious from the pain. Father doesn't have a ring like this. He is only a poor foot soldier." She picked it up in two fingers, taking a better look at it in the moonlight. "This is gold. With a ruby! It must belong to a very rich noble, or mayhap even a king."

"Yes. King ... Edward. He's your ... father. Don't ... tell ... a ... soul."

"M-my father?" Vivienne thought for a moment that she had heard wrong. "Mother, what did you say? You are hurt and talking nonsense. Mother, can you hear me?"

Her mother became deathly still. When the light of the moon broke through the clouds once again, spilling over her mother, Vivienne saw that the woman stared up at her with open eyes that held no life at all within them. Just like her father. Now her mother was drained of all life too. There was no doubt in Vivienne's mind that she was dead. She had just lost both her parents in a matter of minutes. This couldn't be happening. She had to find Adrian and the baby. Bid the devil, her stomach ached and her body started shaking. She looked down to see blood on her gown and it wasn't from her parents or the man she'd stabbed. It was a result of giving birth and still not being healed. Her head dizzied. The sound of approaching hoofbeats pounding on the earth echoed in her ears. Then, she *felt as if she couldn't breathe and everything went black around her.*

Vivienne's eyes shot open and she lay frozen atop her bed on her back. There, at the foot of her bed, was a ghostly figure staring at her. At first, she had thought it was her deceased mother or perhaps her father. Part of her wanted it to be them. If so, she'd know they were still with her and watching over her.

Blinking a few times, her vision cleared and she finally got accustomed to the darkened room. That's when she realized it was the ghost of the monk whom she'd seen in the graveyard, and he was now standing in her room at the foot of her bed. He lifted his arm and without turning his head, he pointed out the window. She was too frightened to even scream. His face didn't show, being covered by his hood. Still, this dead monk seemed to be trying to tell her something.

"B-Brother Theodore? Is that you?" she managed to squeak out, her body trembling.

Grunt's head popped up, and when he saw the ghost, he jumped up in the bed and started barking ferociously.

"Hush, Grunt," she commanded, grabbing her hound and pulling him to her to keep him from waking the others in the abbey. Then Grunt quieted down, but when she looked back to the foot of the bed, the ghostly monk was gone.

Zachariah had already questioned a dozen monks and nuns by the time Vivienne showed up the next morning in the graveyard with Grunt at her side.

"Good morning. Or should I say good afternoon?" he teased her. "Sleeping well, were you?"

"Nay. On the contrary, I had my recurring nightmare again." She sat down on the empty chair next to him feeling tired and drained of all her usual spirit. "Where is Constable Erikson?"

"He's in the ossuary watching Maleine and Sister Ernestine clean up. And what do you mean, your nightmare? The one about your family?"

"That's the one. Why is the constable watching them? Does he think they will steal some old bones?"

"Mother Superior trusts no one. It was her idea. So was it the same as always?"

"My nightmare?"

"Yes."

"No. I mean, yes, it was, and I was surprised I still dreamed about losing my baby, even though I've found Martin. I guess I just miss him and can't wait to be with him again."

"I miss Starah too. The sooner we tie ends up here, the faster we'll be home. Let's go talk to Sister Ernestine while they are cleaning. Mayhap she knows something."

"She's a deaf mute, Zachariah. But Maleine can communicate with her using her hands as a language. It seems Sister Ernestine was friends with Sabina."

"Oh. No wonder she was so quiet last night. I just figured she was observing the rules of silence. It's good to find someone who was close to the deceased."

"I thought you already knew all this. Didn't you see and hear me talking to Sister Ernestine and Maleine last night in the cloister?"

"Nay, not really. I walked up just as they left. Now, let's go inside."

"Wait a minute," she told him, looking back over her shoulder at the grave of Brother Theodore. "I saw the ghost again. At the foot of my bed last night. When I asked who he was, he pointed out the window at the graveyard."

"Vivienne, not the ghost again, please. We don't have time for this." He gave her quite a look of frustration.

"I mean it. I'm not making this up. I think he is trying to tell us something."

"Well, I suppose we'll never know what it is then, will we? Unless he spoke to you, of course. Do ghosts do that?"

"Nay, don't be silly. Of course he didn't speak. He's a ghost, Zachariah."

"And he didn't use any hand motions to communicate with you? Like the way Sister Ernestine does, or so you say?"

"That's not funny. Although he did use his arm to point out the window."

"Like I said ... forget about it, sweetheart." He started to walk away but stopped in his tracks when he heard what she next had to say.

"Sheriff, I'd like to exhume the body of Brother Theodore."

Zachariah slowly turned around, realizing that Lady Vivienne never ceased to surprise him.

"You what?"

"You heard me. I think Brother Theodore might be trying to tell us that there is a clue in his grave. We need to dig him up to find out for sure."

"My lady, I am not going to ask permission to do such a thing unless we have some real proof."

"I have proof."

"The ghost doesn't count. We can't just go around exhuming bodies."

"What difference does it make? After all, all those bodies in the ossuary were exhumed just to make room for more. I'll ask Brother Harold about it, if you don't want to do it."

"Nay, I'll talk to him about it, but I still say it is a waste of our time."

"I know you don't believe there is a ghost, but I saw him,

Sisters Roberta and Magdalena saw him, and so did Maleine, Martin, and Starah. And Grunt. That is too much evidence to ignore."

"I said I'd ask Brother Harold. Now come. Let's get inside the ossuary and see if we can talk, or should I say *sign*, to Sister Ernestine before that meddling Mother Superior catches us trying to do our job again and stops us."

Vivienne didn't seem quite as reluctant to enter the bone room this time, but Zachariah was still there for her if she needed his support. She entered without hesitation which surprised him. He supposed it was because Maleine and Sister Ernestine were inside. Knowing her, she wanted to protect the girls from whatever spirits might be rising from the exhumed bodies.

"Constable," said Zachariah with a nod as they entered the small building.

"Sheriff, I've been looking over the body of the deceased girl again, but cannot seem to find anything new."

"Thank you for trying. I think we've gotten all we can from her."

"Sheriff Fitch, we are finished sweeping the floor and stacking up the bones," announced Maleine. "May we go now? Neither of us feels comfortable here." Her big eyes swooped from one side of the room with the stacked skulls, over to the dead body so still on the table.

"Not quite yet," he told them. "Maleine, Lady Vivienne tells me that you can talk to Sister Ernestine using just your hands."

"Yes, that's right," said Maleine. "Was there something you wanted me to ask her?"

"I hear she was friends with the dead woman."

"Yes, she was."

"I'd like to know if she knew that Sabina was pregnant, and if so, who impregnated the girl?"

"I'll ask her." Maleine turned to her friend, already moving her hands with grace and speed, but before she could relay the answer, Vivienne spoke up.

"She didn't know about the pregnancy. And she has no idea who the father might have been."

"My lady, that was very good," stated Maleine. "You are truly a fast learner."

"Thank you." Grunt sauntered inside and Vivienne reached down to pet him. "I spent the morning learning that language of signs from Sister Magdalena."

"So that's where you were," said Zachariah, wondering why she'd bother with learning this way to talk with her hands. After all, there was so much to do regarding the murder case. Vivienne sometimes didn't make the wisest choices.

"My lady, may we go now?" asked Maleine. "We still have to help in the orchard before the next prayer session."

"Yes, thank you," said Vivienne, using her hands to sign the words to Sister Ernestine.

Sister Ernestine smiled and used her hands to answer Vivienne before she and Maleine left the ossuary.

"That was very impressive," said Zachariah, as he followed Vivienne out of the building and down the steps. "You are a very talented woman, Lady Vivienne."

"Thank you, Sheriff. But if I had more talent, I'd have this murder case solved by now."

"We'll do it together. I see Brother Harold heading this way with Brother Silas and Brother Cedric. This might be a good time to ask them some questions, as well as to find out if we can exhume Brother Theodore's body."

"Did I hear we're going to dig up a body?" asked the constable, coming down the steps of the ossuary to join them.

"Yes," Vivienne answered.

"If we're allowed to do so," added Zachariah.

"They can't say no to us," the constable assured them. "After all, we are investigating a murder."

"Then let us begin," said Zachariah, waving the monks down. They silently walked over to join them.

"Are we needed for questioning?" asked Brother Harold.

"Yes." Zachariah cleared his throat. "And Abbott, we'd like to ask your permission to exhume a body from the graveyard."

"Exhume a body?" gasped Brother Cedric. "Whatever for?"

"Lady Vivienne has reason to believe that there might be some evidence concerning the case in one of the graves."

"Which one?" Brother Silas wanted to know.

"In the grave of Brother Theodore who died two years ago," Vivienne answered.

"Does this have something to do with those rumors of seeing a ghost in the graveyard?" scoffed Brother Silas.

"It's not a rumor. It is true," Vivienne assured him.

"Brother Harold, we cannot allow the bodies of our Brothers to be dug up for no reason," protested Brother Silas.

"I agree," chimed in Brother Cedric. "Brother Theodore was our oldest and wisest monk. Let him continue to rest in peace."

"That's just it," said Vivienne. "He's not resting in peace. He has been coming to me trying to give me a message."

"What message?" asked Brother Harold.

"I ... I'm not sure." She looked over at Zachariah for help.

As much as Zachariah wanted to side with the monks on this, he realized he had to support Vivienne. She would do the same for him. "It is crucial to the investigation. We are trying to move things along so the abbey can get back to normal."

"Mother Superior won't like this," said Brother Silas.

"She has nothing to say about exhuming a monk," Brother

Harold told them. "Sheriff, I give you my permission to exhume the body of Brother Theodore. However, I will have the monks do it for you. Certain ones are skilled in digging graves and handling the bodies."

"All right, then," he answered with a nod. "When can they start?"

"I would rather proceed with this plan after the sun sets," said the abbot. "It would be best if we did this when most of the nuns and monks are already in their rooms asleep for the night. That way, we will avoid any unwanted questions or possible confrontations."

Confrontations? From monks? This sounded like an odd thing for Brother Harold to say, but Zachariah didn't want to question it. It was a good thing that the monk had agreed to the crazy plan. As far as Zachariah was concerned, he wanted to get this over with as soon as possible and without anyone watching.

Vivienne held a lantern, watching the monks exhume the body of Brother Theodore that night. The sheriff and constable stood by as Brothers Cedric and Silas as a lay monk called Brother Grayson dug up the grave.

"Did any of you know a monk called Brother Benedict?" Vivienne asked, not wanting to waste time. They'd wanted to question the monks earlier, but of course the bells rang and they all ran off to pray again.

"Of course," said the abbot. "We all did."

"What happened to him?" asked Zachariah.

"He just disappeared one night." Brother Grayson spoke as he shoveled dirt to the side. He was a big man who looked twice as strong as the rest. He was said to be the head gravedigger.

"Disappeared?" asked Constable Erikson. "How so?"

"He didn't disappear," said Brother Cedric. "He left with a postulant girl, didn't he?"

"Was her name Sabina?" asked Vivienne, knowing full well it was, but wanting to hear if any of the monks changed the story. Grunt sniffed around in the dirt that was piling up fast.

"Yes, I think so," answered Brother Cedric.

"She and Brother Benedict were intimately involved," Brother Silas blurted out.

"Brother Silas, it is not proper to speak of one of your Brothers in that manner," warned the abbot.

"Nay, we want to hear the truth, so please do," the sheriff told them. "The dead woman was Sabina, and we are looking for this monk we hear was her lover."

"Are you saying Brother Benedict killed Sabina and bricked her up in the wall?" asked Silas.

"We don't know." Vivienne reached out and pulled Grunt back, not wanting her hound to fall in the hole or get hit by flying dirt or possibly the hard end of a shovel.

"I heard them arguing, just before they left," Silas told them.

"What was the argument about?" asked the constable.

"I'm not sure," said Silas. "I was up in the bell tower, getting ready to ring the bells for Compline, and I saw them in the cloister down below. It seems Brother Benedict was very upset about something."

"Mayhap it was because he found out he'd impregnated the girl," said the constable.

"That makes sense. Benedict would do anything to protect his reputation. He was next in line for being abbot," Brother Silas told them.

"Is that right?" asked Zachariah.

"He was," admitted Brother Harold. "Of course, I already

held the position and he wouldn't have had a chance to be abbot unless I was dead."

"Could it be that Brother Benedict and Sabina were supposed to leave here together?" asked Vivienne, trying to check Mother Superior's story.

"Yes, they were," said Brother Silas.

"You must tell us what you know," the sheriff warned him.

"All right. I didn't want to say anything since Mother Superior asked me to keep it a secret, but we both knew Sabina was pregnant."

"How did you know?" asked Zachariah.

"Brother Benedict confided in me," said Brother Silas. "He told me it was his baby and that they wanted to leave and raise a family together."

"Did they leave?" asked Vivienne, knowing full well that Mother Superior told them Brother Silas watched them go.

"After I heard them arguing, I came down from the bell tower," said Brother Silas. "I gave them the message that Mother Superior wanted them to leave the abbey."

"What did they say?" asked the constable.

"They almost seemed relieved to be going," said the monk. "Although they both still seemed angry with each other."

"So they left then?" asked Vivienne.

"I watched them ride out the gate together," said Brother Silas.

"Yet, we found Sabina's bones in the bricked-up wall," commented the sheriff.

"Yes. I don't understand," said Brother Silas with a shrug. "Unless they just wanted us to think they left, and Brother Benedict came back with her and killed her and put her in the wall."

"Something sounds off about all this," said the constable.

"All I can tell you is what I know and what I saw, I'm sorry," said Brother Silas. "I don't understand it at all either. This whole thing is very odd indeed."

One of the shovels clanked against something in the ground. "I think I hit the body," announced the gravedigger, Brother Grayson.

"Everyone stop!" shouted Brother Harold with a hand in the air. "We don't want Brother Theodore's bones damaged."

"He's dead, so what does it matter?" mumbled the sheriff. Vivienne shot him a look and held her finger to her lips, silently warning him to be respectful and not to say things like that.

"We'll have to lift him out carefully," instructed the abbot.

"I'll help," offered the constable, stepping into the hole to help lift the bones of the oldest monk at the abbey. With the two of them and Brother Cedric, they managed to bring the wooden box with the body out of the ground and laid it down next to the grave. The coffin was already rotting and pieces were missing.

Vivienne let go of her dog and rushed forward, holding up her lantern, eager to find answers.

"Lift the lid," instructed the sheriff.

"Wait!" Brother Harold stopped them. "First, we need to say a prayer."

"Is this really necessary?" The look of aggravation on the sheriff's face couldn't be missed.

"Go ahead, Brother Harold. I think it would be a nice gesture," Vivienne spoke up.

After they'd prayed, Zachariah was the one to open the lid of the coffin. "Bring the lanterns closer," he instructed. Vivienne and Brother Harold brought their lanterns over and held them up to light up the man's remains inside the coffin.

Squeamishly, Vivienne peeked into the coffin, curious enough to want to see. "He's already decomposed and only his bones remain," she said in surprise. This wasn't at all what she'd expected.

"The coffin is damaged so the body decomposed fast," Brother Grayson pointed out.

"We need to check inside for anything that might connect him to the postulant who was murdered," said the sheriff.

"Be careful not to disturb anything," the abbot warned them.

After Zachariah and Constable Erikson examined the inside of the coffin, Zachariah made his announcement. "The only thing we can find is his rosary and the cross he is wearing around his neck. Brother Harold, does this all look correct?"

Brother Harold peered into the dark coffin, trying to see. "Aye. It was all he owned."

"I don't see anything that would connect him to the dead girl, do you, Sheriff?" asked the constable.

"Nay. I'm afraid not." Zachariah looked over at Vivienne and slowly closed the coffin's lid.

"It is starting to rain," said Silas. "We need to bury the body again quickly and get back inside."

Grunt looked down into the hole and started barking.

"What is it, Grunt?" asked Vivienne, walking over and holding her lantern over the empty hole. "I don't see anything."

"Mayhap he sees that ghost you were talking about," said Brother Silas with a chuckle.

"I did see a ghost, and I'll ask you to please refrain from judging me with your laughter."

"Get the coffin back inside the hole and cover it up quickly," instructed Brother Harold, as the rain started coming down faster.

"Lady Vivienne, go inside and keep dry," said Zachariah. "There is no need for you to stay here."

"My monks will finish up as well as close up the ossuary,"

said Brother Harold. "There is no need for any of the rest of you to get drenched."

"Thank you, Brother Harold," said Zachariah. "And I'm sorry about the inconvenience we've caused you."

"Yes, thank you," said Vivienne, feeling very disheartened. "Grunt, come on," she called. Her hound still sat there staring into the empty hole. "It's time for bed."

"I'll return in the morning, Sheriff. Good night." Constable Erikson waved his hand in the air and headed toward the gates of the abbey, on his way to his home in the village.

"Are you happy now?" asked Zachariah, as he escorted Vivienne back to the dormitories. Grunt followed along with them.

"I don't understand why we didn't find anything. I was so sure we would find something in the grave to help us with the murder case. The ghost is the one who told me to look there."

"It's just your imagination carrying you away, my lady."

Vivienne didn't like hearing the sheriff talk this way. "Good night, Sheriff Fitch. I hope you sleep soundly." She hurried toward the side of the abbey that housed the females. Grunt led the way.

"Lady Vivienne, wait. Please."

"I have nothing else to say. Good night." She hurried into her room, the door being unlocked since none of the doors except the sacristy had locks. Disappointed that this was another dead end, she quickly changed into her bedclothes and jumped under the covers. Grunt got up on the bed with her. She reached out and petted him behind the ears. "I just don't understand it, Grunt. I was so sure that the ghost of Brother Theodore was trying to tell us something. This just doesn't make sense. I am sure there is something that we're missing."

It wasn't long before she fell asleep. She kept dreaming about graveyards and ghosts, and when she heard Grunt barking, she shot up in bed with her eyes wide open, sure she was going to see the ghost in her room again. Sadly, there was no one there.

"Having bad dreams too, Grunt?" She rubbed behind his ears and he settled back down. "Well, mayhap tomorrow will be a better day." Grunt whined and stared at the door. She wasn't sure if he saw someone, but she didn't see anything. "Go to sleep, Grunt. We have a lot of work to do on the morrow."

Chapter Fourteen

Zachariah was already in the refectory eating his lumpy porridge when Vivienne arrived the next morning with Grunt at her side.

"You look lively today," he told her, lifting a spoonful of the awful gruel, closing his eyes as he slipped it into his mouth. Damn, he couldn't wait to get back home to some of Nairnie's wonderful cooking. At the rate things were going, he'd be so skinny by the time he left here that he'd look no different than the skeletons in the ossuary.

"Zachariah, I discovered something." Vivienne slid onto the bench next to him. The refectory was filled with monks and nuns all having their morning meal.

It surprised him that she hadn't called him sheriff. Well, at least that meant she was no longer angry with him. He hoped.

"What is it?" he asked, about to eat another bite of porridge, but deciding to put it down. His stomach couldn't handle any more.

"Last night, Grunt barked, and I think he saw someone or something in my room."

"Please don't tell me it was that ghost again." He grabbed for his cup, downing some warm ale.

"I don't know. I didn't see anyone, ghost or human. However, this morning I found something written in the dust atop the table in my room. I copied it down on this paper to show you." She held up a piece of paper and handed it to him.

"Let me see that." He took the paper and opened it, reading aloud the words that were scribbled on the paper. "It says, *Dig Deeper*. What the hell does that mean?"

"Zachariah, stop the bad language!" His sister walked up with Maleine. Magdalena held a tray of small loaves of bread, while Maleine had a pitcher and was refilling everyone's drinks.

"Oh, good. Bread," he said, grabbing a loaf off her tray and holding it up to his mouth. "I never thought I'd be so happy to be eating coarse, brown bread."

Grunt whined, resting his chin on Zachariah's lap.

"You can get your own. This one is mine," he told the dog, taking a big bite of bread and chewing. It was dry as usual and very hard to eat. Still, he had no choice unless he wanted to starve, so he swallowed it.

"More ale, Sheriff?" Maleine held up the pitcher.

"Yes. Please. Lots of it." He held up his cup and Maleine filled it while Sister Magdalena headed down the table handing out the small loaves of bread.

"What is that?" asked Maleine, noticing the note in his hand.

"Nothing," he said, placing it on the table.

"What does it say?" the girl asked, not yet able to read.

"I found a message scribbled in the dust on a table in my room this morning, Maleine," Vivienne told her. "I copied down the message on this piece of paper. It says to dig deeper."

"Dig deeper? What does that mean?" Maleine filled a cup of ale for Vivienne.

"We're not sure yet." Since Vivienne missed out on the bread, Zachariah slid the rest of his toward her to share it. He wouldn't have done so if he had known she was going to give half of it to her hound.

"I heard you dug up the body of a monk in the graveyard last night," said Maleine, her eyes dancing with excitement.

"Who told you that?" asked Zachariah. "I thought everyone was asleep."

"I heard it from Sister Ernestine. She read the lips of the monks just minutes ago when they first sat down. They were softly discussing it." She looked around and then leaned over and whispered, "It's quiet time now."

"Of course, it is," complained Zachariah.

To their surprise, Mother Superior stood up to make an announcement.

"Excuse me, but I'd like to tell everyone that today we are having an unplanned visit from the Bishop of Lincolnshire. He'll be joining us at Tierce, so we don't have much time to prepare for his arrival."

"Tierce? When is that again?" Zachariah whispered to Vivienne.

"It's at nine o'clock. Two hours from now," she whispered back.

"Brother Silas will be displaying all the relics during the prayer session which will actually be a Mass today," the nun told them. "This is a very important day. You will all have the opportunity for veneration of the relics." That seemed to bring about a lot of happy whispers from the monks and nuns.

"Veneration of the relics?" asked Zachariah.

"She's talking about praying over the relics, or even touching or kissing them," explained Vivienne.

"Oh, wonderful." The sheriff downed some more ale.

"This might be a good opportunity to get a better look at them," she told him.

"I don't see what it matters," he whispered back. "We need to focus on our investigation."

"I agree. And that is why I think we need to dig up Brother Theodore's body again."

"What?" said Zachariah, louder than he should have.

"Please, refrain from talking," scolded Mother Superior, looking in his direction. "Now, everyone finish up eating and start preparing for the bishop's arrival."

"This is going to set us way back," complained Zachariah.

"Not necessarily," Vivienne leaned over and whispered again. "Actually, this might be exactly what we need."

"I don't know what you mean, but I have a feeling I am not going to like whatever you are planning in that complicated little mind of yours."

She actually giggled. "I think you are going to absolutely hate it."

"Great," he said, pushing his empty cup away. "Then what are we waiting for? Let's get to my daily dose of aggravation."

"IF ANYONE WOULD HAVE TOLD me I'd be agreeing to dig up a body in a graveyard rather than to have to sit through a Mass with the bishop, I never would have believed it until today." Zachariah shoveled dirt off the grave of Brother Theodore while everyone else was inside paying attention to the bishop and venerating the holy relics. "Never mind. Actually, yes, I would believe it."

"I always knew you'd do anything to get out of going to church," Vivienne told him with a smile. Grunt rested on the ground watching him dig. "You'd better dig faster if we're going to finish this before the Mass ends."

"If you want to pick up a shovel and help, it will go a lot faster."

"Oh, there you are, Sheriff. I wondered why I didn't see you in the church." Constable Erikson walked over from the church to join them. "What on earth are you doing?"

"I'm digging up a grave, Constable. What does it look like I'm doing?" muttered Zachariah.

"Didn't we already do this yesterday?" The constable seemed confused.

"I found a message in my chamber this morning that said *Dig Deeper*," explained Vivienne. "I think someone is trying to tell us that we need to look in the ground under Brother Theodore's coffin."

"Really? Who left the note?" asked the constable.

"It wasn't a note actually. It was scribbled in the dust atop a table," she told him.

"Someone came into your room at night to scribble a message in the dust?" asked the constable.

"Possibly," she said, playing with the scrap of paper. "Or ... it might have been a ghost that did it, since mayhap it takes too much strength for a ghost to actually talk."

"Well, next time ask the ghost if he has enough strength to dig up his own body," said Zachariah, wiping the back of his hand across his forehead.

"How would a ghost leave a dust message?" asked Constable Erikson. "Do ghosts have fingers?"

"I don't know." Vivienne shrugged.

"What does it matter?" snapped the sheriff. "Constable, pick up a shovel and help me before I break my damned back."

"Yes, Sheriff Fitch. I'd be happy to, although I have no idea why we're doing this now." Constable Erikson picked up a shovel and started to help uncover the grave.

"We need to hurry before Mass is over. If not, Mother Superior is going to see us and stop us," said Vivienne, trying to urge them to work faster.

"What is it exactly that we're looking for?" Constable Erikson shoveled dirt away as he spoke.

"We're not sure yet." Vivienne peered into the hole. "But I'm certain it has something to do with the murder."

"Is someone really trying to tell you something in secret?" asked the constable.

"That's what I think. Oh, look. I see the coffin," said Vivienne excitedly, pointing at it.

"We'll have it out in a few minutes." Zachariah started shoveling faster.

Before long, the coffin was removed and placed beside the grave, just like the monks had done yesterday.

"Shall I open it?" asked Constable Erikson.

"Nay. Keep digging." Vivienne got down on her knees and peered into the hole. It was a lot easier in the sunlight to actually see anything. Before long, Grunt started barking again, pawing at the dirt around the hole.

"Quiet that hound down," commanded Zachariah. "All we need is for everyone inside the church to hear him."

"He's trying to tell us something. Look!" Vivienne pointed at what seemed to be an edge of a blanket. "I think there is something or someone buried down there. That is, below Brother Theodore's coffin."

"Bid the devil, I think you're right," said Zachariah, dabbing the sleeve of his tunic against the perspiration beading his brow. "Constable, help me pull it out of here."

"Aye, Sheriff."

Sure enough, when they lifted what they'd found, it looked

to be a body wrapped up in a blanket. They placed it on the ground and Grunt sniffed it curiously.

"Are we going to unwrap it, or wait for the monks and Mother Superior to arrive?" asked Constable Erikson.

"Nay! Unwrap it now," said Vivienne. "Hurry! We don't need anyone or anything slowing down this investigation any further."

"I agree," said the sheriff, reaching out and removing the blanket from the corpse. While the body was already decomposed and nothing but bones, it was clear that the deceased man had been a monk. He wore the robe of a monk, and a large ornate cross around his neck that had a small green stone embedded in the center of it. The corpse's wrists and feet were bound with rope, just like Sabina's had been. However, the dead monk did not have a gag in his mouth.

"I told you someone else was buried here," said Vivienne excitedly. "The mysterious message in the dust was right. And I think now I know exactly who the ghost was, and it wasn't Brother Theodore, after all."

"Who do you think this is?" The constable shrugged.

"I'll bet anything that this is the body of the missing Brother Benedict," she told the men.

"I think she might be right," came a man's voice from behind them.

They all turned around to see Brother Harold standing there with his hands folded.

"Brother Harold. I thought you were at Mass in the church," said Vivienne, looking shy about being caught.

"I was. But when I looked out the window, I saw you three here digging up Brother Theodore's body again. I came to stop you."

"I found a message written in the dust in my room this morning." Vivienne handed the piece of paper to Brother

Harold. "I wrote down the words." She continued to talk as the man squinted and pushed his face closer to the paper to read it. "I thought someone was trying to tell me to dig deeper in this grave, and so we did, and we found something too."

"Brother Harold, you said you think this is Brother Benedict's body. How do you know that?" asked the sheriff.

"I don't know for sure, but I have a feeling Lady Vivienne is right," answered the monk.

"Come take a look." Zachariah waved him over. "Does the monk's cross necklace look familiar? Mayhap you can identify him by that. He also has his wrists and feet bound, so it definitely looks like another murder."

"Yes," said Brother Harold, taking a few steps toward the body that everyone was crowded around. He cocked his head, viewing the man they'd just dug up. "I was the one to give Brother Benedict that cross necklace. It was part of the promise that he'd succeed me as abbot if anything happened to me. But then he disappeared along with the postulant, and that was the last I saw or heard of either of them."

"Why would Brother Benedict leave the abbey if he was promised the position of abbot someday?" asked Zachariah. "It doesn't make any sense."

"It does if he was the father of Sabina's baby," said Vivienne. "Mayhap he was willing to give up the position of possibly being abbot in order to marry Sabina and start a family with her. They might have wanted a new life. Together."

"Brother Benedict did fancy the girl," said the monk. "Although I hardly think he would have killed her."

"He wasn't the murderer," said Zachariah. "This proves it. The same person who murdered Brother Benedict is most likely the one who bricked Sabina up in the wall of the scullery."

"Brother Harold, was immurement really something that happened at an abbey?" asked Vivienne, thinking about what

Brother Silas had told them days ago. He had said that sometimes nuns were punished and bricked up into walls until they prayed for forgiveness.

"It is true. Sometimes, immurement does happen. However, I've been here at Maltby le Marsh Abbey for a long time now, and I can honestly say that I have no knowledge of it ever happening here. Until now, mayhap."

The bells rang, signaling that Mass had concluded.

Brother Harold looked over at the church and then back to them. "You'd better take Brother Benedict's body into the ossuary for now. And hurry and place Brother Theodore back into the ground and cover him up quickly. I don't want to have to explain to Mother Superior why I allowed this to happen during Mass with the bishop."

"Yes, we'll do that," said Vivienne. "Thank you."

"I'd like to keep this to ourselves for now," said the sheriff. "Until we know more."

"Yes, that's a good idea," agreed Constable Erikson. "The least number of people who know, the better. That way if the murderer is still here, he won't be alerted that we are getting closer to identifying him or her."

"Thank you, Sheriff, for believing in me," said Vivienne.

Zachariah wiped his brow once more and picked up the shovel. "Nay. Thank *you*, Lady Vivienne, for not only providing me morning exercise, but also for giving me a damned good excuse for not going to Mass."

Chapter Fifteen

Vivienne stood at the back of the church with Zachariah, as the Mass given by the bishop had ended. The procession of nuns and monks had now reached the back of the church, and were preparing to go outside so everyone could talk freely and meet with the bishop personally. There was a lot of commotion. Vivienne felt they could easily use this to their advantage.

"I think we should go up to the altar and venerate the relics," she whispered to the sheriff.

"Nay. I don't want to. Besides, the Mass is over. They'll be putting the relics away quickly. It's too late."

"Then I'll be waiting in the sacristy to see them there instead."

"What for?" he asked.

"I don't know, but I feel like mayhap the relics might have something to do with the murders." Instinct made Vivienne want to go there.

"You might be correct. I didn't think of that. All right, let's go."

"Wait." She took him by his arm. Grunt had followed them

into the church and was standing quietly behind them. "It might be better if you distract the sacrist while I sneak into the sacristy and have a quick look around first, before he puts the relics back. In case we've missed anything else."

"And how do you propose I do that?"

"Well, here comes your sister and Maleine now. Mayhap they can help you."

"How?" He looked at her oddly.

"Figure it out." She pushed him forward, nudging him toward Sister Magdalena and Maleine before Zachariah could object.

"Lady Vivienne, I was searching for you," said Maleine.

"Hello, Zachariah," said his sister. The sheriff just grunted.

"Maleine, walk with me," said Vivienne, wanting Zachariah to be alone with his sister so he would actually talk to her and confide in her again. Vivienne's hopes were that somehow they would make amends before this case was closed and they left the abbey.

"Grunt, what are you doing here?" Maleine smiled and reached down to pet him.

"Maleine," Vivienne whispered. "I want to sneak into the sacristy, but I don't know how to get in if it's locked."

"Oh, that's easy," Maleine told her. "It's not locked right now. I saw Brother Silas open the door just moments ago, preparing to return the relics to their secure location."

"Good. Then come with me," she said, pulling the girl along with her as she made her way through the crowded church, heading to the sacristy. Grunt trotted along behind them, his nose sniffing the air. "I'll need a lookout."

"Oh, all right. I can do that, my lady. I like helping you with your investigations."

Vivienne waited in the shadows until she saw Brother Silas

replace some relics and then walk out of the sacristy, heading over to the altar to collect the rest of them.

"I'm going in," she told Maleine, seeing Sister Magdalena and Zachariah walking up to speak with Brother Silas. "I told the sheriff to distract the sacrist."

"Good idea. Plus, I'll stop Brother Silas if he returns before you exit the room."

"Thank you, Maleine. You are a true friend, not to mention a wonderful asset to have around."

"Don't get too used to it," she told Vivienne. "After all, once you leave and I take my vows, we might never see each other again."

Vivienne's heart almost broke hearing the girl's words. "Nay, don't say that." She reached out to give Maleine a quick squeeze on her shoulder. "We will always be in contact and remain friends forever."

"Do you promise?" There was no doubt Maleine was trying to be strong, holding back her tears.

"I promise," said Vivienne with a smile, turning and entering the sacristy before Brother Silas returned. Grunt entered the room as well, sniffing around the floor.

The first thing she did was to walk over to the open reliquary, to inspect the boxes that had already been replaced. Carefully opening the first box, she remembered this was the one that held the piece of the cross that Jesus Christ died on.

"That doesn't look like much at all," she said aloud, inspecting the sharp shard of rotting wood. If it truly was from the crucifixion cross, she had expected it to be vibrant, filled with holy powers, or at least in good shape. This piece of wood smelled moldy, looked rotten, and didn't seem any different than the coffin they'd dug up in the graveyard. "Oh well." She closed the lid and opened the next box. It was the toe of Saint Gerard. "Ugh," she grunted, slamming down the lid and pulling over the last of the three relic boxes. She opened the lid to find the hair of St. Agnes.

"My, that hair is very red," came a voice from behind her.

Startled, Vivienne spun around with the box still in her hand. "Maleine, you scared me." Vivienne's hand went to her heart. "I thought you were acting as my lookout."

"I was, but I wanted to be more involved in this investigation. What did you find?"

"Nothing much," she told her. "Just some rotting wood, a toe bone, and some hair."

"That hair makes me think of the poor girl who was murdered."

"You mean Sabina?"

"Yes. Sister Magdalena told me that Sabina had such vibrant red hair that Mother Superior thought she was spawned by the devil. She instructed Sabina to never remove her veil in the presence of anyone."

"That could be why not many knew her hair color," commented Vivienne. "We'd better get going. I don't want to be caught." Vivienne put the box back and turned to leave.

Grunt was over by the bookcase, sniffing and pawing at the floor.

"Come on, Grunt," said Maleine. "We have to leave now."

"Wait a minute." Vivienne walked over to her hound, looking down at the floor. "Grunt is the best investigator I know," she told Maleine.

"Why? Did he find something?"

"I believe so. Look at those scratch marks on the floor. They are in the shape of an arch. It almost seems as if something was slid, or moved, doesn't it?"

"I guess so. What does it mean?"

"I'm not sure, but I think this entire bookcase might move." Vivienne put her hand on it, trying to see if she could budge it.

However, that was when they heard Brother Silas's voice outside the partially open door.

"He's coming!" gasped Maleine.

"Quick! Get behind the door," said Vivienne, pulling the girl along with her to hide.

"What is this door doing open?" They heard Brother Silas say, "I am sure I closed it."

"Mayhap it blew open," said Zachariah.

"Yes, the church gets quite windy when the front doors are open like they are now," added Sister Magdalena.

"I'm scared," whispered Maleine. "I don't want to be punished."

"Shhh," said Vivienne, holding on to Maleine's arm.

The door to the room opened, and Vivienne made sure they stayed hidden behind it.

Grunt was over by the reliquary and started barking.

"Oh, nay," whispered Maleine, clamping her hand over her own mouth.

"What is that dog doing in here?" spat Brother Silas. He hurried across the room with another box or two of relics in his hands. Grunt jumped up on him and one of the boxes fell to the floor. "Nay! That is the rosary of Saint Genevieve," shouted Brother Silas. The rosary hit the floor, beads breaking off and rolling everywhere.

"Let us help you pick it up," said Sister Magdalena, bending down to do so.

"Now is our chance to sneak out," whispered Vivienne, taking Maleine by the arm and sneaking out of the room. The sheriff looked up and saw them but said nothing.

"Yes, let me help too," he told Brother Silas.

"Nay! Just leave," the monk ground out. "And take that bloody hound with you."

Vivienne and Maleine didn't say a word until they were

outside the church. The large crowd of nuns and monks were waving goodbye as the Bishop of Lincolnshire sat atop his horse with his guards surrounding him as they exited the abbey.

"That was a close one," said Vivienne, letting out a deep breath.

"I'm sorry I let you down, my lady. I should have stayed at the door as instructed." Maleine looked so defeated.

"Don't worry about it, Maleine. You did nothing wrong. I see you have a strong curiosity, just like me and I respect you for it."

"Thank you for being my friend, Lady Vivienne. I have no one else."

"Don't say that. I am sure you'll have many friends in time, living here at the abbey."

"I hope so." Maleine looked down at Grunt. "Thanks for helping us, Grunt." She got to her knees, hugging the dog around his neck. Grunt licked her face, making Maleine giggle.

"Good boy, Grunt," said Vivienne. "You knew just what to do, as always."

"I wish we had the time to investigate that bookcase closer," Maleine told her, standing again. "Do you think something is hidden behind it?"

"I'm not sure, but I intend to find out."

"Are you going to break into the sacristy when everyone is asleep?" Maleine's eyes opened wide in excitement.

"It is a thought," said Vivienne with a shrug. She saw Sister Magdalena and Zachariah walking out of the church. It was odd to see both of them smiling for a change.

"Over here, Sheriff," she called out, waving her hand in the air. The two walked over to join them and stopped.

"That was a little bit perilous wouldn't you say?" asked Zachariah in his deep, sexy voice.

"Did you find anything?" whispered Sister Magdalena, her eyes scanning the area as she spoke.

"The sheriff told you?" asked Vivienne, not sure they could trust anyone at this point.

"My brother told me nothing," said the nun. "However, it wasn't hard to figure out something was going on when he came up to me and said he wanted us both to go look at the relics together on the altar before the sacrist put them away. Then, when I saw your hound in the sacristy, I knew you were doing some investigating."

Mother Superior and Sister Roberta were close by, and Vivienne saw the abbess look directly at them and then start walking toward them.

"I think we should talk about all this later," said Vivienne. "We are about to have visitors."

"Oh, nay. Here comes Mother Superior." Maleine's body stiffened.

"Don't worry, my dear. I'll handle the abbess," said Sister Magdalena in a soft voice. Vivienne was starting to like Sister Magdalena even more. Before she was a nun and when they were children, she and Vivienne used to get into trouble together at times. Magdalena had always admired Zachariah and followed him around wherever he went. She would always do anything for him. Anything that would gain her the approval of her brother.

"It's time to get back to work in the kitchen," said Mother Superior, walking up with the prioress. "What are you two doing out here? There are a lot of people to feed."

"It's my fault, Reverend Mother." Sister Magdalena folded her hands and bowed her head. "I wanted Maleine to see the bishop since this is such an important day. We'll get back to the kitchens immediately. Come along, Maleine."

"Yes, Sister Magdalena," answered Maleine, hurrying away with the sheriff's sister.

"Were you two at Mass today as well?" asked Sister Roberta. "It was crowded in there but I don't remember seeing you."

Vivienne and Zachariah exchanged glances. Vivienne was sure it would be a sin to lie to nuns. Still, they were going to have to say something. "We feel lucky to have just caught a glimpse of the bishop on this special day," she answered.

"Oh, yes, you are so lucky to have seen him." Sister Roberta's face lit up. "Our abbey was blessed to have the bishop choose to visit us the way he did. And he was very impressed by the relics we have gained through the years. The more relics, the more attention the bishop gives. We don't have many so I was surprised he even came here. However, I think we look important in his eyes now."

Mother Reverend didn't seem to want to talk about the bishop anymore. "That's enough, Sister Roberta. We must refrain from talking more than is necessary. You know the rules."

"Forgive me, Mother Reverend." Sister Roberta bowed her head.

"Did you two get a chance to venerate the relics?" Mother Superior was giving them the evil eye with one eyebrow raised. Or at least it looked evil to Vivienne. She wasn't sure if nuns were just strict or supposed to act mean at times. And why didn't they stop asking so many questions?

"I don't consider myself worthy enough to venerate relics," Zachariah answered, making Vivienne feel a sense of relief. That is, until she heard the rest of what he had to say. "However, Lady Vivienne was lucky enough to get a closer look at the holy items. Weren't you, my lady?"

Right now, she really wanted to strangle him. Why couldn't he have just stopped after proclaiming himself unworthy?

"Yes, I can honestly say that I never thought for the life of me that I'd ever get that close to holy relics," answered Vivienne, side-stepping the truth once again, glancing at the sheriff from the corner of her eye. It wasn't a lie. Then again, she knew it wasn't truly the answer to Mother Superior's question either. Vivienne had been very close to the relics today and actually held the boxes in her hands. Even so, she wasn't about to tell Mother Superior she'd sneaked into the sacristy and helped herself to relics, just to add to her curiosity, hoping to find answers in their murder investigation.

"Actually, Sisters, we're glad the two of you are here," said the sheriff, making Vivienne wonder what he was up to now. "We wanted to ask you both some more questions involving the murders."

Mother Superior's brow raised once again. "Did you just say murders? As in more than one?"

Vivienne's heart dropped. How were they going to explain this without actually lying?

"Sheriff Fitch, was someone else besides the postulant killed?" asked Sister Roberta.

Vivienne was sure they weren't going to get out of this one so easily, since Zachariah accidentally slipped up and said something that they weren't yet ready to announce. She figured secrecy now was pointless. After all, the nuns were going to hear about their findings sooner or later, so she decided to just tell the truth.

"Yes, we discovered there were actually two murders," she told the women.

"Two?" asked Sister Roberta, looking confused.

"We found the body of Brother Benedict buried in the same grave as Brother Theodore," she blurted, immediately receiving an angry glance from Zachariah.

"You what? When did this happen? Why wasn't I told?"

Mother Superior fired questions faster than Vivienne could possibly answer them.

"Brother Benedict is dead?" gasped Sister Roberta. "How sad and awful. I didn't know that."

Vivienne realized they were now in big trouble. Telling them about the dead body was one thing. But admitting that they'd dug it up during the bishop's Mass was probably going to get them thrown out of the abbey before they had a chance to investigate anything further. Either that, or they were going straight to hell when they died. Mayhap she should have chosen her words more carefully. Too late now.

"Mother Superior, we didn't want you distracted, with the bishop's visit and all," said Zachariah. "We planned on telling you right afterward. Whenever you'd like to see the corpse of Brother Benedict, you are welcome to come view it in the ossuary."

"The prioress and I will be there soon. Right now, we have things to attend to. Come, Sister Roberta."

"Yes, Mother Superior." Sister Roberta followed the other nun as they both hurried away in silence.

Grunt barked at them as if telling them off, and then he settled down quietly at Vivienne's feet.

"I knew that would get them to leave," said Zachariah, brushing his hands together to remove the dirt from the gravedigging. "Did you find any clues in the sacristy, my lady?"

"I did. I think the bookshelf moves and there might be something hidden behind it," she relayed her findings. "However, I didn't have time to try it before we were interrupted."

"Yes," said Zachariah, clearing his throat. "Sorry about that. I did my best to distract Brother Silas, but he was focused on the relics and I couldn't slow him down."

"We'll have to go back to the sacristy later and break in to do it, I guess."

"Nay. I am a sheriff and respected, and I won't risk my reputation by sneaking into places we don't belong. Especially not locked rooms. Mayhap if we just ask Brother Silas about it, he'll invite us in. Mayhap the moving bookcase isn't even a secret," suggested the sheriff.

"Do you really believe that?" Vivienne's hands went to her waist. "Everything around here seems to be a secret. I am willing to bet it has something to do with these murders."

"You're right. We'll need to get in there. I'll try to see if mayhap Brother Harold can let us in again."

"Don't say anything about this to anyone," Vivienne warned him. "We have no idea at this point if we can even trust the abbot or Brother Silas or any of them."

"True. But right now, I'd like to have a closer look at Brother Benedict's body."

"Me too," she said, leading the way. Grunt kept pace at her side. "Thank goodness for Grunt, or Maleine and I would have been discovered in the sacristy. Grunt proved to be better at distracting than either you or Maleine."

"Speaking of Maleine, why was the girl even in the sacristy?" asked the sheriff. "She should have been guarding the door for you."

"She was, but then she decided she wanted to help me."

"My lady, you need to be careful. Like you said, we don't know whom we can trust."

She stopped in her tracks, not liking what she just heard. "So now you are telling me not to trust Maleine?"

"I know you are fond of her, but think of her background and what happened with her father."

"Sheriff Fitch, I trust Maleine completely. And I think you need to lower your guard just a little. At least when it comes to people who are close to us."

"I don't know what you mean."

"How did things go with your sister?"

"Oh, that. All right, I guess I understand. However, to be honest, I am not sure I can trust Magdalena either."

"Zachariah, she is your sibling! How can you even say that?"

"I can't help it. Right now, you're lucky I don't suspect you, too."

"We have to trust some of them. Besides, Maleine and Magdalena are helping us. You are wrong about them. I trust both of them with my life."

"Mayhap you're right. It doesn't matter." He shrugged. "Sometimes there is no telling what someone is really thinking, I suppose."

"Like you? After all, I am having a hard time telling exactly what's in your head lately."

"I am just thinking about solving this murder."

"You need to make amends with your sister. Margaret's death was not Magdalena's fault and you know it. I can see that she feels bad about what happened. You need to tell her that she doesn't have to feel guilty and neither does she need to hide away from you in an abbey any longer."

The sheriff's mood became instantly sullen. "I don't want to talk about my personal life. Let's focus on the task at hand, shall we?"

"Of course. As always." She decided it would be fruitless to try to discuss this now. Zachariah was stubborn and didn't like to admit he was ever wrong. He also seemed to put his work before his family more than he should. Mayhap later, when the case was solved, she'd be able to bring him to his senses and show him what was truly important in life. Before it was too late and it was gone.

They entered the ossuary, the feeling of death surrounding her immediately, and making her terribly uncomfortable. This was not an inviting place to visit and she could not wait to leave.

Just being in here with all the skulls and body bones was going to give her more nightmares than she was already having.

"Let's take a look," said Zachariah, uncovering the skeleton of Brother Benedict. His gaze went immediately to the big, ornate cross he was wearing that held an interesting green stone in the center.

"I can't help feeling as if I've seen that stone before," she commented.

"Like in a rosary, perhaps?" Zachariah opened his pouch and pulled out the rosary they'd found on the body of Sabina. It dangled from his fingers, the green gemstones glittering in the sun streaming in from the open door.

"Yes! You're right. It looks exactly like the same kind of gemstone, doesn't it?" She plucked the rosary from his fingers and held it up against the stone on the Brother Benedict's necklace.

"It certainly seems so. But what does that mean?" He leaned over to study the pieces.

"I'm not sure," she told him. "And I also don't know why the murderer wouldn't have stolen this rosary or Brother Benedict's necklace after he slayed them. That must mean the killer wasn't after wealth or riches. He or she must have had some kind of personal grievance with the murdered couple instead."

"My guess is that Sabina struggled with the killer and was put into the wall while she was still alive. That is probably why her wrists and feet were bound and there was a gag in her mouth. Also, the murderer might not have known she had that valuable rosary on her."

"That makes sense," she answered with a nod, still inspecting the monk's skeleton. "And I think that cloak pin belonged to the killer. Mayhap Sabina pulled it off of him in the fight and he didn't know she even had it."

"Possibly," said Zachariah. "If the murderer had to hide

Brother Benedict's body quickly, perhaps he didn't have time to steal the monk's cross."

"Do you think Brother Benedict was also alive when he was buried?" asked Vivienne.

"Nay. He wasn't gagged." The sheriff looked over the body.

"But his wrists and feet are bound by rope." Vivienne didn't like looking at dead bodies, but this one was naught but a skeleton, and so it wasn't as gruesome as some of the murder victims she'd seen in the past, like the ones on Rotten Row.

"The killer could have stabbed him. Look, he has a crack in his rib."

She looked closer to see that the he was right. "I see some blood stains on the blanket, too."

"He must have bound him to make it easier to move the body by himself."

"Don't you find it odd that when the gravediggers put Brother Theodore's body into the ground two years ago, they didn't notice that Brother Benedict was already in there?"

"Perhaps it happened at night and it was dark. Mayhap it was even raining at the time. It could be that they were in a hurry and never even saw Brother Benedict already down there in the hole."

"Or, what if someone who dug the grave, mayhap even all of them, were involved in the murders," she suggested, hoping it wasn't true.

"There are too many questions as well as other factors in play here," he told her. "We'll need to find out more about when Brother Theodore was buried and who all the people were who put him in the ground to begin with."

"I agree."

Grunt put his front paws on the table and started sniffing Brother Benedict's foot. His tongue shot out to lick the bone.

"Nay, don't do that! Get down, Grunt," she scolded her

hound. "You shouldn't put your nose on a dead man's body, let alone lick his foot." She pulled her dog away, and that is when she noticed something. "Sheriff, this monk seems to be missing a toe."

"Dammit, did Grunt pull it off?"

"Nay," she told him. "He was just trying to show me."

"Mayhap it fell off in the grave. After all, the monk wasn't even buried in a coffin."

"I don't think so."

"Why would you say that?"

"Because, the toe that he is missing is his big toe."

"So?"

"Mayhap it means nothing, but I can't help thinking of a relic I saw today in the sacristy. It was the big toe bone of Saint Gerard. Or at least, that is what someone wants us to believe. However, I am wondering if it is possibly the toe of Brother Benedict instead."

Chapter Sixteen

"Thank you for inviting me to join all of you to help with stitching the altar cloths and the priest's vestments," said Vivienne the next day, sitting with several other nuns. Sister Roberta was in charge.

Vivienne looked from one nun to the next. They all kept a straight face and didn't say a word to her. She and Zachariah had already questioned these nuns, but learned nothing new about the murders. She really needed to speak with Sister Roberta, but wasn't sure she'd have a chance at this rate.

"Sister Roberta, will you join me for a moment out in the cloister?" she asked in a soft voice.

The prioress nodded, put down her stitching, and got up and walked out the door with Vivienne. Once outside, the nun seemed to relax.

"I know talking is frowned upon, but you need to understand that the sheriff and I are trying to find a murderer," Vivienne explained. "We need all the help we can get."

Sister Roberta looked both ways before answering. "What can I help you with, my lady?"

Finally she was getting somewhere.

"I was wondering if you could tell me anything about the items we found with the body of Sabina."

"Items?"

"Her green gem stone rosary, for instance?"

"I don't know what you are talking about. No one in the abbey has a rosary made from gem stones. We took the vow of poverty and wouldn't have anything so luxurious as that."

"Really. Well, where do you think she got it? I mean, it was found on her body so I am guessing it was hers. She must have brought it here with her when she came to the abbey."

"Sabina came from a simple home. She didn't have a lot of money and gave very little in the way of a dowry. I didn't want to accept her here at the abbey, but Mother Superior, for some reason, said she saw potential in Sabina. She felt the girl would make a good nun."

"You didn't want to accept her because she didn't have enough money to give to the abbey?" Vivienne thought this a very shallow form of judgment.

"You don't understand, my lady. The abbey has been broke for many years now, and is at risk of being closed down," the nun told her. "The reason for the bishop's visit here today was because he needed to see things for himself."

"What do you mean?" asked Vivienne.

"We don't have the means to fund the order. He has been trying to close us down and after today, I am sure he will succeed."

"What? I don't understand." This came as a surprise to Vivienne. "Certainly, he must have been impressed with the valuable relics that your church has."

Sister Roberta slowly shook her head. "We have too few relics at the abbey for us to be considered important. Some churches, the ones that are successful, have dozens more."

"Well, can't the relics that you do have, be sold? You can use the funds for the upkeep of the abbey, no?"

"Yes, that is what will happen now. Thanks to Brother Silas having attained those relics for us in the first place, our abbey might be safe. For a little longer, at least. He will sell them to whichever church pays us the most."

"So Brother Silas is going to save the abbey? Where did he purchase the relics from in the first place?" asked Vivienne.

"Brother Silas is our sacrist, and has many connections," explained Sister Roberta. "With his help, he has secured us more relics just in the past few years alone than this abbey has ever had. Every so often, he sells them, but he always manages to get more money than he paid in the first place. I am not sure where he buys them. It could be from other churches, a fair or town market, mayhap even from an impoverished noble. He is quite skilled at tracking them down."

"But how does he do that? I don't understand."

"He's been given access to the abbey's coffers. When he hears of a relic that goes up for sale, he buys it at a low price. Then when pilgrims arrive to pay homage, he sends back word of the miracles that have taken place because of the relics. He then sells those same relics as needed for much more than he's paid. He is very smart."

"What miracles?" asked Vivienne. "You can't really tell me that old body parts of saints or just something they owned or touched is bringing about miraculous healings."

"It's true," said the sister. "We've all seen it happen. It is so sad when the holy relics that have brought about miracles must be sold. However, the abbey must be able to sustain itself with very little help from the church in order for the bishop to think it is worth keeping open."

Seeing Mother Superior heading their way, Vivienne

thought it best to stop talking. "Thank you, Sister Roberta. You have been much help."

The nun bowed her head and folded her hands and slowly walked back to continue her stitching.

"Lady Vivienne? Are you distracting the sisters again?" asked the Mother Superior.

"Not at all," she answered. "I was actually looking for you. I thought you might like to join me in the ossuary. After all, you did want to see the body of Brother Benedict, didn't you?"

"Mayhap at a later date. I have an appointment to keep."

"Of course."

Vivienne watched Mother Superior head over to the church. Brother Silas opened the door and let her in. Interesting. This must be who her appointment was with. Vivienne started to suspect everyone, and was wondering if Mother Superior and Brother Silas had something to do with the murders.

"Lady Vivienne?"

"Yes?" She turned around to see the sheriff standing there with Brother Harold.

"The abbot will escort us to the scriptorium now so we can view the abbey's past records. Will you join me?" asked Zachariah.

"Of course," she said, being in deep thought. She wanted to take this time to question Brother Harold while no one else was around. "Excuse me, Brother Harold, but do you remember the day when Brother Theodore was buried?"

"Yes, of course I do. Why do you ask?"

"Who buried his body?"

"Our gravedigger, Brother Grayson, was in charge of digging the hole. Brothers Silas and Cedric always attend each funeral as well."

"Were you there too?" asked the sheriff, obviously seeing where she was going with this.

"I was there for a short while, yes. But it began to rain, so I headed back to the creek to help the lay monks collect the drying laundry before it was dampened by the approaching storm."

"What time of the day was this?" asked Vivienne.

"It was late in the day. I remember it was already getting dark since it was so dreary. Like I said, we had bad weather that day."

"So Brother Theodore's body had to be buried quickly?" she asked.

"Yes. Sometimes Brother Grayson waits until the rain lets up, which he did that day, now that I think about it."

They stopped at the door to the scriptorium, where monks copied manuscripts and illuminators painted the drawings on the pages with bright colors.

"I will let you enter, but only for one hour. And you cannot speak to any of the monks who are working," Brother Harold instructed. "Do you understand?"

Vivienne wondered how anyone survived not being able to communicate with each other. In her opinion, without talking, there wasn't much else to do.

"We understand," said Zachariah. "We'd like to see the books that contain the records from two years ago first."

"Then any records talking about past immurements," added Vivienne.

"Oh, I'm sorry, but I wouldn't know which records contained information about immurements," said the monk. "However, I can provide you with the books from the past two years."

"That would be fine. Thank you," said Zachariah.

"I will show them to you, but you must use gloves to touch them," the monk explained. "Only one candle is allowed, so you'll have to share it between you. I will leave to go to the prayer session, and then return for you in an hour."

"Thank you," said Vivienne. "You have been very accommodating."

Once inside the scriptorium, Brother Harold donned his gloves before bringing the books they wished to view to a long wooden table. He put them down reverently and proceeded to slowly open them up. Next, he placed the lit candle in between them. Then he handed them each a pair of gloves. "Be sure to wear these gloves at all times. Leave the books here on the table and I will return them to the proper shelves when I come back to get you," he said in a whisper before leaving.

There were only two other monks in the scriptorium at this time. She recognized one of them as Brother Cedric, the monk who had taken the children back to Mablethorpe. She nodded at him and smiled. Even though he made eye contact with her, he didn't acknowledge her presence in any way.

"Let's start looking," whispered Zachariah, putting on the gloves. They were thin white gloves made of linen that the scribes used when handling the books.

Together, they started flipping slowly through the pages, reading what they could.

After a while, she ventured to speak to the sheriff again. "What exactly are we looking for?"

"I have no idea. Anything that might help us with the case. Anything involving the dead monk and nun, I guess."

Even though they read quite a few things in the records, they found nothing about Sabina or Brother Benedict leaving the abbey, her being pregnant, or the two of them being in love. Matter of fact, they found very little about them at all.

It was nearing the time for them to leave, and still they'd found nothing that might help them solve the case. One of the monks got up and left, and Brother Cedric proceeded to put some books back on the shelf as he prepared to go as well.

Vivienne was about to close the book when the painting of a woman holding a rosary took her interest. She stopped, scrolling down the page, reading about Saint Agnes, the patron saint of the church. She reached out and tapped Zachariah on the arm. When he looked over at her, she pointed to the book.

"Look," she whispered. "Saint Agnes has been painted by the illuminator as having dark hair."

"Yes. So?"

"It doesn't look red in any way, does it?" she asked him.

"I guess not."

"And look at this painting of Saint Genevieve. She is holding a rosary," Vivienne continued.

"It's green," he said, snapping closed the book he was viewing, taking interest in what she was saying and showing him.

"The rosary relic I saw in the sacristy was definitely not green," said Vivienne. "It was brown. And the hair from Saint Agnes that we were shown was red, not black."

"Something doesn't add up here," said Zachariah.

"We don't always have the proper colors to illuminate a drawing." Brother Cedric walked out from the darkness, having overheard them talking. Or perhaps he'd been spying on them, Vivienne wasn't sure. "However, we do the best we can."

"Did you illuminate this drawing of Saint Agnes?" asked the sheriff.

"Nay," said Brother Cedric in a soft, half-whispered voice. "I am a scribe, Sheriff. I copy script. That book was illuminated by our most talented monk, but he is no longer here."

"Who was he? And where did he go?" asked Vivienne.

"His name was Brother Benedict. He illuminated that book," said the monk with a nod. "And as you know ... he is dead."

Vivienne jerked when she heard the monk say this. They'd been careful not to tell too many people about finding Brother Benedict's body. Still, Brother Cedric seemed to know all about it.

"What makes you think Brother Benedict died?" asked the sheriff. "I thought word was that he and Sabina left the abbey together."

"Sheriff, do not take me for a fool," said Brother Cedric, seeming very insulted. "You have found Brother Benedict's body buried in the grave with Brother Theodore and you are storing his bones in the ossuary."

"That's right," said Zachariah. "But who told you?"

"Even though not much talking goes on at the abbey, I assure you that the walls have ears."

"What does that mean?" asked Vivienne.

Before Brother Cedric could answer, the door opened and Brother Harold, Brother Silas, and Mother Superior all walked into the scriptorium. Vivienne quickly blocked the book, not wanting them to see what they'd found.

"It's time to go," said Brother Harold softly.

"Did you find what you were looking for?" asked Brother Silas, trying to see around her.

"Sheriff Fitch and Lady Vivienne were questioning why the painting of Saint Agnes has different colored hair than the relic we hold," Brother Cedric explained. "And why Saint Genevieve is holding a green rosary in the book, but the rosary we have in the reliquary is brown."

Vivienne wanted to die. Why did Brother Cedric have to tell them that? Nothing in this place was a secret, unless it was something being kept from her and the sheriff.

"What do you mean? Let me see," said Brother Silas, gently pushing his way in between Vivienne and the sheriff to look at the book. He took the lit candle and held it closer to the page.

"Ah, yes. You are quite right in questioning this. You both are very clever, indeed. However, being the sacrist, I must tell you that the real relics are not always put on display, for fear of them being stolen."

"So, you're saying that the red hair in the box and the brown rosary are not the real hair and rosary of Saints Agnes and Genevieve?" asked Vivienne.

"No, they are not," admitted the monk. "We keep those in a special hiding place that is known only to me and Mother Superior."

"Where is this hiding place?" asked Zachariah directly.

Brother Silas and Mother Superior exchanged worried glances.

"We are trying to conduct a double murder investigation," Vivienne explained. "We are not going to steal the relics. We just need to know where they are."

"And we'll need to see them," added the sheriff quickly.

"Go ahead and tell them, Brother Silas," Mother Superior gave the monk permission. "After all, we want to do anything we can to help the sheriff and Lady Vivienne find the killer."

"Of course," said the monk with a bow of his head. "But mayhap it would be better if we just showed them instead."

Finally, Vivienne felt as if they were going to get answers. If they showed them the secret room that was hidden behind the bookcase, then mayhap they were more trustworthy than she'd thought.

They followed the monk and abbess to the church, and entered the sacristy right behind them. Vivienne almost wished Grunt was with her now, since he had a keen nose for sniffing out trouble. But she couldn't bring the dog into the scriptorium and had instead left Grunt with Maleine and Sister Ernestine as they washed clothes down by the river.

"So, where is this secret room?" asked Zachariah.

"How did you know it was a room?" asked Brother Silas.

"I just guessed." Zachariah flashed a quick smile.

"It's behind the bookcase," Mother Superior told them.

Sure enough, Brother Silas went over and pulled on the end of the bookcase. It swung out in an arched motion and opened to reveal a small room right where Vivienne had thought one would be.

"Light a candle, Brother Silas," instructed Mother Superior.

"Aye, Abbess." The monk lit a beeswax candle, and the small enclosure lit up in dim light. It was a much smaller area than Vivienne imagined it would be. It was just a tiny enclosure with three shelves. On those shelves were boxes that matched identically to the ones that were in the sacristy holding the relics she'd witnessed earlier.

"These are the real relics." Brother Silas opened a box, showing them locks of much darker hair that almost looked black. He closed it, and opened another box, showing them a piece of wood that looked much newer than the piece of the supposed crucifixion relic she saw earlier.

"Why didn't you bring out the real relics when the bishop was here?" asked Vivienne suspiciously. "After all, you made everyone think those were true relics and they were all venerating them. That disgusts me."

"Lady Vivienne, it was I who told him not to bring out the true relics," said Mother Superior. "I explained to the bishop your suspicions that the murderer might still be here at the abbey. He agreed that it was in everyone's best interest if the true, valuable relics stayed locked up until you caught the killer. We couldn't take a chance of having them stolen. The state of the abbey depends on them."

"Didn't the bishop want to see the real relics?" asked Zachariah.

"Of course," said the nun. "That is why Brother Silas brought the bishop up here before the Mass to show them to him."

"I see. Thank you for explaining," said Zachariah, sounding satisfied by the explanation.

"What about those other boxes?" asked Vivienne, eager to see if the green rosary was in there. "We'd like to see those as well."

"Mother Superior, it is time for me to ring the bells for Compline," said Brother Silas.

"Yes, we must not be late. Please close up the wall and the sacristy immediately," said Mother Superior. "I'm sorry, Sheriff, but you and Lady Vivienne will have to leave the room at once. We cannot let you stay here without one of us in attendance."

"Take this wine," said Brother Silas, handing the bottle to Zachariah. "It is a fine wine given to us by King Edward himself many years ago. It is stronger than most. We were saving it for a special occasion. But since you two are working so hard to solve this murder case, you deserve it."

"Nay, we couldn't," said Vivienne, not wanting anything from the king. Her hand went to the hidden necklace she wore beneath her clothes.

"Yes, I insist," said Mother Superior. "Enjoy the night off and just relax. Being here at the abbey must be taking quite a toll on both of you. I know how hard it is to adapt to our life and rules. Being away from your children and the town of Mablethorpe, and especially the castle for you, Lady Vivienne, must make it very hard to adjust."

"I will not deny that," mumbled Vivienne.

"We're sorry to have to make you leave, but the abbey runs on a tight schedule, you realize," said Brother Silas.

"We understand," said Zachariah, holding on to the bottle of wine as they were escorted out of the room and the door locked up tightly behind them.

"Just one more question before you go," said Vivienne.

"Please, but quickly," said Brother Silas. "My duties call."

"Where did you get the fake relics?"

"Shhhh," said Brother Silas, looking around.

"You must keep this a secret," said the abbess. "It would not bode well for any of us if everyone knew."

"I'm sorry. I will keep it quiet," Vivienne promised. "I am just curious as to where the items were attained."

"I got them from the gravedigger, Brother Grayson," the monk told her. "I don't know where he got them, but I am guessing they were from some of the bodies he's buried."

"Thank you," said Vivienne, watching the nun and the monk walk away. "Do you believe them?" she asked Zachariah.

"I'm not sure. But if they had something to hide it doesn't seem likely they'd show us the real relics in the secret room."

"Nay, it doesn't," she agreed. "Plus, they gave us a bottle of expensive wine. Could it be a bribe, trying to keep us quiet about what we just learned?"

"Most likely," he said. "They seem really worried about having their relics possibly stolen."

"I hear it happens all the time," she answered. "Relics are sometimes stolen or even fought over. It's almost as if the church or monastery or abbey with the most relics is the winner in the end."

"I think we need to look into the gravedigger some more," suggested Zachariah.

"I agree. I also think someone is lying, and I am getting pretty tired of it," Vivienne told him. "We need to find some answers soon, Sheriff, because I am really longing to get back home to Mablethorpe to see my son. To go back where we truly belong."

"Me too." He held up the bottle of red wine and smiled. "Will you join me for a drink, my lady?"

"Why not?" she asked. "I think we both could use a drink about right now to ease all the frustration. Mayhap if nothing else, it'll help us both sleep soundly tonight."

Chapter Seventeen

Zachariah walked into the refectory the next morning, having been so tired that he overslept. His biggest regret was that he hoped he hadn't missed breakfast, as meager as it would be. His stomach was growling like crazy and his head ached. That wine must have been stronger than he'd thought. Of course, drinking the entire bottle of wine with Lady Vivienne last night before she returned to her own room might have been part of the reason for the headache. He wondered how she felt today.

He more than agreed with what Lady Vivienne said last night. He longed to go back to Mablethorpe to see his daughter. Back to his own town. It seemed to him like he'd been here in Maltby le Marsh forever.

As soon as he walked into the refectory, he noticed something going on by the scullery. He headed over, sticking his head into the small room.

"What am I missing?" he asked, seeing Brothers Cedric and Grayson stacking bricks from a wagon onto a table by the hole in the wall. A lay monk walked in with buckets of mortar as well as trowels.

"We are getting things ready for the workers to brick this hole back up," Brother Cedric explained.

"Why? The investigation is far from finished. I didn't tell anyone to brick it back up yet."

"Constable Erikson gave us the order," relayed Brother Grayson.

Damn the constable. Was he taking matters into his own hands? Zachariah would have to have a talk with him since he was in charge of this investigation, being sheriff. "Don't do anything until I give the word."

"The constable said Brother Harold told him to do it." Brother Cedric seemed worried about not following orders.

"Brother Harold?" Why would the abbot give that order without consulting Zachariah first? And why wouldn't the constable have come to him, waking him from even the deepest sleep to ask him about all this? Things just weren't adding up. Everyone was starting to act odd lately.

The bells rang out from the church then, the tone being heard all the way inside the scullery since it was so loud.

"Hold up," Brother Cedric told the other monks with his hand in the air. "It is time for Tierce. We will continue directly after the prayer session. Brother Harold wants this hole totally bricked up by noon."

"Tierce?" asked Zachariah. "Don't you mean Prime?"

"Nay, I mean Tierce," said Brother Cedric. "Prime was two hours ago."

"What?" Zachariah scratched his head, not able to believe this. He had never been affected so severely by a bottle of wine to have slept that long! Mayhap the stress of this unsolved case was making him addled as well.

The monks left, and Zachariah walked over and looked into the hole in the wall once more. It was such a small space for a person. So confined. When the bricks were in place, he was sure the air flow stopped quickly. Poor Sabina must have been so frightened. Being bound and gagged the way she was, and most likely beaten, she had to have been so helpless. This woman was someone's daughter. He thought of Starah, wanting even more to protect her now. Even if someone had found Sabina hours after her immurement, Zachariah wasn't sure she could have survived after being left there to die. What a waste. What a shame. This angered him and made him even more determined to find and punish the girl's killer.

A small shiver ran through him. No one should have to die that way. Especially when they thought they were safe and protected inside the walls of the abbey. He decided he needed to step up this investigation and do everything in his power to find the murderer quickly. The problem was, he had no proof that the killer was someone at Maltby le Marsh abbey, even though it seemed likely to him. And if the murderer was a nun or monk from here, were they still here or did they leave two years ago? If only he could start getting some definite answers. Why was this investigation so difficult? He'd never had so much trouble with a murder case in his entire life.

Zachariah's stomach growled again in hunger. He decided to go find something in the kitchen to eat or mayhap take a walk out to the orchard to look for a few apples. Right now he needed to quell the hunger in his stomach and clear his aching head.

VIVIENNE HEARD A LOUD RAPPING NOISE, dragging her from her deep sleep. She opened one eye and then the other, now hearing Grunt barking as well. It only took her a moment to realize that someone was pounding on her door.

"Just a moment," she called out, jumping out of bed. She was about to get dressed when she realized that she must have been so tired last night after sharing the bottle of wine with the sheriff that she fell asleep before even changing out of her clothes. Running her hands over her mussed hair, she hurried over and pulled open the door. "Sister Ernestine?" she asked in surprise, seeing the deaf mute standing there. "Are you here by yourself? Isn't Maleine with you?" Vivienne looked up and down the cloistered walkway, finally seeing someone else but it wasn't Maleine. It was Zachariah's sister, Magdalena.

The deaf woman's hands waved around like wild as she tried to relay a message in her language of gestures to Vivienne, but unfortunately, Vivienne didn't understand.

"Slow down, Sister Ernestine. I don't know what you are trying to say. I just started learning to speak with my hands and I'm not that good at it yet."

"Good morning, Lady Vivienne." Sister Magdalena came down the cloistered walkway with a smile on her face. She was a kind woman who usually seemed happy, even though the sheriff seemed to try to make her life miserable. "I was on my way to Tierce when I saw Sister Ernestine standing at your door. Did the two of you wish to join me?" She looked directly at Sister Ernestine when she spoke so the woman could read her lips.

"I don't know. I just awoke, and my head is hurting," said Vivienne, holding on to the doorjamb feeling a little dizzy. She must remember not to drink that much wine again. "Wait a minute, did you say Tierce? How late is it?"

"It's nine o'clock, my lady."

"I slept that late? How could I?"

Grunt hurried over to some shrubbery, relieving himself since he'd been locked in the room for so long.

"Slow down, Sister Ernestine," said Sister Magdalena, her face taking on a solemn look as she read the girl's hand gestures.

"What has her so excited this morning?" asked Vivienne with a yawn.

"She says she cannot find Maleine. Oh dear, she thinks the girl might be in trouble. I wondered where Maleine had disappeared to, and thought she was with you, Lady Vivienne."

"Nay, Maleine is not with me. I just woke up. Could she be at church?"

Once again, Sister Ernestine's hands and fingers moved back and forth.

"What is she saying?" Vivienne asked, starting to feel as if something really was wrong, after all.

"She said Maleine left early this morning to try to help you find the murderer."

"She did what?" gasped Vivienne. "Nay. She never came to my door. Or, at least, if she did, I didn't hear her."

"Perhaps she knocked but you were sleeping?" asked Sister Magdalena.

"No, I don't believe so. If that were the case, Grunt would have barked and woken me up. Just like he did now when Sister Ernestine knocked at my door."

"Where do you think Maleine went?" asked Sister Magdalena, looking around as she spoke.

"I have no idea." Vivienne rubbed her face in her hands, a thought popping into her head. "Wait a minute. I think I might know where Maleine would have gone. I'm going to go look for her, but I can't take Grunt with me. Sister Magdalena, can you find your brother and bring Grunt to him for now? And please, tell Sheriff Fitch what is happening."

"Where should I say you are going?" asked Sister Magdalena curiously.

"Well, the first place I am visiting is the garderobe. Then I am going to catch a killer. I have a feeling that there is evidence that we have missed, and I swear that today I am going to find it."

~

Zachariah walked through the orchard, chomping on an apple and holding a loaf of bread under his arm. He had thought he'd find Vivienne out here with Maleine, since the postulant girl was always working and she hadn't been in the kitchen. Mayhap they were down by the creek. After all, Maleine had spent a good amount of time yesterday washing out the nuns' clothes at the water's edge.

He had just sat down under a tree and was about to eat the bread when he heard Grunt barking in the distance. "Of course," he mumbled, taking a big bite, thinking Grunt probably smelled the food and followed his trail. He half expected to see Vivienne with the hound, but as Grunt approached, he realized it was Magdalena and Sister Ernestine with the dog instead. He thought that was odd, since Vivienne never seemed to go anywhere without Grunt.

He stood up and brushed the crumbs from his lap, saving a little piece of bread for the dog. If not, Grunt would be following him around all day begging for food.

"Good morning," he called out, walking over to meet them. Grunt jumped up on him, the dog's slobbery tongue licking his hand. "Get down and I'll give you some bread."

Grunt sat at his feet. Zachariah fed the dog the bread and proceeded to pet him on his head. Grunt seemed to smile.

"Brother, we've been looking everywhere for you," said his sister. "When we couldn't find you in your room, the ossuary, or the kitchen, Sister Ernestine suggested we look out here in the orchard." She looked over at the deaf nun and spoke. "You were right, Sister Ernestine. You have good instincts."

Sister Ernestine nodded and smiled, just like the hound.

"You didn't think to check the church? Why the hell not?" Zachariah asked with a grin. "After all, I could have been there."

"Zachariah, this is no time to make ill jests. Everyone knows you'd never be in church by your own will." Magdalena seemed overly worried. He knew something had to be wrong when his sister didn't reprimand him for cursing.

"What is it, Magdalena?" he asked. "Is something wrong?" Vivienne popped into his mind. "I see Grunt but where is Lady Vivienne? Why isn't she with you?"

"Sister Ernestine says Maleine has been missing all morning," Magdalena informed him.

"So, did Lady Vivienne go to look for her? Is that where she is?"

"Yes."

"Well, where did she go?"

"She didn't say."

"I see." He rubbed his aching head and yawned. "I wouldn't worry too much about it. I'm sure Maleine is just off doing another chore. The nuns seem to keep her quite busy. I'm sure Lady Vivienne will be able to locate her soon."

Sister Ernestine's hands waved around in the air again.

"Is she saying something?" asked Zachariah, not having the slightest idea how to interpret hand language.

"Yes. She said I forgot to tell you what Lady Vivienne said."

"Well?" He crossed his arms over his chest and waited. "What is it?"

"Lady Vivienne said she was going to the garderobe, and then to catch a killer. She thinks someone has been lying to her."

Sister Ernestine shook her head and once again her hands moved.

"Oh, yes, that's right," said Magdalena. "My mistake." She turned back to Zachariah. "Actually, what she said was that she had a feeling that there was evidence that you two were missing and that she intended to find it."

"I think I might know where she is," Zachariah told them.

"Where?" asked his sister.

"She probably went to the sacristy."

"The sacristy? Why would she go there?"

Zachariah had a moment of concern. He didn't know if he could really trust Magdalena or for that matter, Sister Ernestine. He wanted to keep the secret room to himself for now. Until he knew more. But then he realized that he needed to start accepting and trusting his sister again, just like Vivienne told him to do. Mayhap this would be the start of making amends. He supposed it was long overdue.

"There is a secret room in the sacristy that hides all the real relics," he told them.

"The real relics? What does that mean?" asked Magdalena. "Of course, they are real."

"No, they are not. Actually, fake relics are put out for veneration, because Mother Superior and Brother Silas are afraid that the real ones will be stolen."

"I can't believe that!" Magdalena seemed heartbroken to hear this, and he couldn't blame her. "So we've been lied to? By our own leaders?"

"I'm sure they have good reason, Magdalena. By the way, have either of you seen Constable Erikson or Brother Harold today? I need to speak with them immediately."

"Brother Harold is probably in the church," said Magdalena, but Sister Ernestine shook her head and said something else.

"What is it?" asked Zachariah.

"Sister Ernestine said she read Brother Harold's lips earlier when he was talking with Constable Erikson at breakfast."

"What did they say?"

Magdalena took a minute to watch the young woman's hand gestures before answering. "She says they were talking about the necklace that Brother Harold told you he gave to Brother Benedict."

"What about it?" asked Zachariah.

A few more hand gestures and his sister relayed what else Ernestine was saying.

"She says that Brother Harold was looking for you. He made a mistake about something. Something to do with Brother Benedict's necklace."

"I'd better find them and see what this is all about." Zachariah started back toward the abbey, and Grunt was right at his side.

"What about Lady Vivienne?" asked his sister.

"She can take care of herself. I'm not worried about her. She'll be just fine."

"Well, what about Maleine then? Mayhap she's in trouble. Zachariah, Sister Ernestine is really upset. I think you should help us look for her. I have a terrible feeling that something bad has happened."

"All right," he finally agreed, not thinking there was anything wrong, but just wanting his sister to stop pestering him. "I'll look for Vivienne and Maleine after I find Brother Harold and the constable to tell them not to brick up the wall yet because I am not done investigating."

"Thank you, Zachariah. May God be with you." His sister made a big deal about blessing herself and then making the sign of the cross in the air to protect him as well.

"God's teeth, I cannot wait to get home," he said under his breath.

"Zachariah, I heard that," said Magdalena in a scolding tone. "Now I'll have to pray even harder for you so God will forgive you."

"You do that," said Zachariah, taking off at a run for the abbey just to make distance between them. Grunt barked playfully, nipping at his feet thinking it was all a game. Zachariah's head throbbed and his stomach still growled from hunger. Why the hell did the thought of fighting off rats on Rotten Row seem so desirable, compared to being here right now?

Chapter Eighteen

Vivienne sneaked into the church and over to the sacristy, wondering how she was going to get into the locked-up room. But when she noticed the door ajar, she realized someone was already in there. She looked around the church and saw Brother Silas and Mother Superior in the front row, so she knew it had to be someone else. Silently pushing the door open, she stepped inside the room and closed the door behind her.

"Maleine?" she whispered. "Are you in here?"

"Oh, my lady, it's you!" Maleine emerged from behind the table that held the reliquary.

"What are you doing here? And how did you get into the room? Wasn't it locked?"

Maleine smiled and held up the sharp end of a brooch. "I picked the lock with this."

"Where did you get that?"

"I found it in Mother Superior's room."

"You what?" gasped Vivienne, hurrying over to Maleine. "Let me see that," she said in thought, holding out her hand. When Maleine handed it to her, she realized it looked a lot like the cloak brooch that they'd found in the wall with Sabina. It had the same two snakes on it with the ruby red eyes. It made her wonder what it stood for and what was going on here. Why would Mother Superior even have this?

"I came to try to find out if there is something hidden behind the bookcase," explained Maleine. "I couldn't stop thinking about it."

"You should have spoken to me first," scolded Vivienne. "What you are doing is very dangerous. If you're caught you could be punished for it."

"You live surrounded by danger all the time, my lady. Your life is exciting, mine isn't. I need to feel alive."

"Enough of this nonsensical talk. I already know that there is a secret room behind the bookcase."

"You do?"

"Yes. It's small and has the real relics in it. Brother Silas showed it to me and the sheriff, too."

"The real relics? Then what are those?" Maleine pointed to the reliquary.

"I will explain later. Don't worry about it for now. Maleine, you need to leave this room right now."

"All right, but can I look at the secret room first? Please? I really want to see it."

Vivienne knew she had very little time and that prayers would be ending soon. She was going to object to the request, but didn't want to disappoint Maleine. After all, the girl was doing everything she could to help Vivienne find the murderer. Vivienne needed to show her gratitude somehow. "I suppose it would be all right," she answered with a sigh, looking back at the door that was still closed. "But we'll have to hurry. Brother Silas will be back as soon as the prayer session ends, I'm sure."

"I'll look fast, I promise. Oh, this is so exciting! I cannot wait to see it." The smile that graced Maleine's face was precious. Vivienne had never seen her look this alive or so happy before.

After all the terrible things Maleine had been through, she deserved a little happiness in her life, and Vivienne wanted to be the one to help her find it.

"All right. This way. But hurry." Vivienne rushed over to the bookcase, pulling on the shelf where she'd seen Brother Silas touch it to make it move. Slowly, the bookcase swung out, revealing the hidden room behind it.

"Oh my, this is fantastic." Maleine walked in, snatched a box off the shelf and opened it, peering inside.

"Careful, Maleine," Vivienne warned her, looking back at the door once more. "Those are valuable relics and we don't want to break anything."

"Valuable? There's nothing in here!" Maleine held out the empty box for Vivienne to see.

"What? Nay, that can't be right. Brother Silas showed us the relics earlier." She went over and looked into the box and, sure enough, it was empty. She took another box off the shelf and it was empty too. "I don't understand," she said aloud.

"Which boxes did Brother Silas show you that had relics in them?" asked Maleine.

"Well, I believe this was one." She opened a different box and smiled. "Yes. There it is. The hair of Saint Agnes. See it?"

"Let me take a look," said Maleine, picking up the hair inside the box and studying it closely in the light shining in from the main room.

"Careful, Maleine. That is the hair of a saint. We need to treat it respectfully."

Maleine started laughing and pulled the veil off her head. "Nay, it isn't. This is my hair! Look." she held it up to her head and the color and texture of soft curls matched perfectly.

"It's just a coincidence, I'm sure. Maleine, you must have the same color hair that Saint Agnes did. What an honor."

"It's not the saint's hair, I tell you. I'm sure of it." Maleine rubbed the hair between her fingers. "It's sticky," she said. "Remember, I told you that I spilled honey and then got it on my hair when I was working in the kitchen?"

"Yes."

"Well, Mother Superior was so angry that I wasted the honey that she hacked off all my hair as a punishment. She must have saved some of my locks. Just look at the curls and you'll know the hair is mine."

"Let me see that." Vivienne took the hair and sniffed it. A sticky residue was left on her fingers. She boldly licked one of her fingers. Sure enough, it was honey, just like Maleine said. "You are right, Maleine. This hair does have honey on it."

"I don't think honey would still be sticky after all these years if it were from an ancient saint, do you?"

"Nay. I don't think so either," said Vivienne, wondering exactly what was going on here.

"I think I found something!" Maleine pointed to the back of the shelf and pulled out a pair of shears. "These shears have the handles painted red. They are the exact shears Mother Superior used to chop off my hair."

"Oh, Maleine, I cannot believe this. They've been lying to us all along."

"What's in here?" Maleine opened another box, the one that supposedly held a piece of the cross that Jesus died upon. "Oh, it's a piece of the handle from the bread paddle that I broke the first day I got here. I didn't realize how hot the ovens were and dropped the paddle as well as several loaves of bread onto the kitchen floor. Sister Roberta was angry about that, as well as the Reverend Mother."

"That's right. You said they took away your meal as a punishment."

"They did."

"Maleine, are you sure that is really part of the wooden

paddle you dropped?" asked Vivienne. "It's not from the cross that Jesus was crucified upon?"

Maleine made a face. "Not unless Jesus was eating bread when he died. Look. I see a few bread crumbs on the wood. It must have happened when the paddle hit the floor."

Sure enough, Vivienne saw the crumbs too, just like Maleine said.

"Maleine, you are good at finding hints."

"Thank you, my lady. I like doing it."

"I'm getting a really bad feeling about all this." Vivienne hurriedly opened all the other boxes, but each of the rest of them was empty. "I need to give this information to the sheriff. There is no way Brother Silas showed the real relics to the bishop, because there aren't any in here to show him. Brother Silas must have lied about that too." She put a hand to her aching head. "And something tells me that he might have put something in that bottle of wine that he gave the sheriff and I to share."

"What's this?" asked Maleine, reaching up to the top shelf and pulling on something wedged there. All of a sudden, they heard a scraping sound and the shelving unit seemed to release and move.

"Maleine, I think you found something," said Vivienne excitedly. She pushed on the unit and it swung open. Another room appeared behind it.

"There's another secret room." Maleine's eyes grew wide.

"It's dark in there," said Vivienne, peering inside.

"I'll get a candle." Maleine ran back out into the main room and returned with a lit candle. "Lady Vivienne, this is like searching for treasure. It's fun." Her eyes danced with enjoyment, lighting up in the glow from the candle she held.

"Nay, it's not fun," she corrected the girl. "It is dangerous and we shouldn't be here. There might be a murderer or mayhap more than one killer on the loose. We'll just take a quick look and then we need to leave. Do you understand me?"

"Aye, my lady." Maleine couldn't stop smiling. "Let's see what's inside. I can't wait."

They both entered the second hidden room and stopped in their tracks. Their jaws dropped as they looked around. This room contained a lot of wealth and riches. Trunks were spilling over with gowns made from taffeta and velvet and trimmed in fine lace. Silk tunics and embroidered soft shoes were scattered on the floor. Woolen cloaks lined with ermine were folded neatly and stacked up in one corner.

"Those are the clothes of nobles, aren't they?" asked Maleine.

"Yes, I believe so." Vivienne walked over and touched a soft ermine-lined cloak. "These must be the belongings from the nuns and monks that they gave up when they entered the order."

"Ooooo, I like this." Maleine put a gemstone crown on her head, sticking her nose in the air, acting like a queen. The crown glittered with green and red stones. There was an etching around the gold that looked wavy. She couldn't see it well since the room was still semi-dark, but had a feeling it was two snakes with ruby eyes to match the brooches they'd found. Things were looking even more suspicious for the sacrist and the abbess right now.

"There is so much jewelry in here." Vivienne picked up piece after piece, inspecting them all. The hidden room held some of the finest jewelry she'd ever seen. There were necklaces, bracelets, rings, and even ornate metal circlets as worn on the heads of noblewomen. She also saw bags stuffed full of money.

"Oh my, there is even a sword that looks like it belonged to a knight," said Maleine, putting the crown back and hurrying over to the other side of the room. "And a battle-ax too. Where did all these things come from?"

"I have a feeling this is at least part, if not all, of the dowries that the nobles donated when their sons and daughters entered the abbey."

"Aren't these things supposed to be sold? To help support and run the abbey?"

"I would think so," answered Vivienne. "However, I am getting the distinct feeling that someone is not doing their job properly."

"I hear something," whispered Maleine, nearly dropping the sword as she put it back. "Lady Vivienne, I think someone is coming!"

"Quickly, blow out the candle," instructed Vivienne. "We need to get out of here fast and close up the wall before we're discovered."

"Aye," said Maleine, blowing out the candle. "Let's go."

Vivienne couldn't see in the dark, and tripped on something, landing on the floor. "Oomph!"

"Are you all right, my lady?"

"I'm fine."

"My lady, hurry," came Maleine's frantic whisper. "We're about to be discovered."

"Just go," she whispered back. "I'll be right behind you." The problem was, when Vivienne got up, she realized her dress was caught on something, keeping her from moving. She tugged at it, but it was stuck hard and she couldn't get loose.

"Who's in there? And what are you doing?" came a man's angry growl.

"I ... I'm sorry," she heard Maleine say from the antechamber, sounding very scared. "I was just curious, that's all."

"Is someone with you?"

"Nay," Maleine quickly answered. "I am alone. I won't do it again, I promise. And I won't say a word about what I saw."

"You're damned right you won't, because I'm not going to let you get a chance to tell anyone."

"W-what do you mean? Please, don't hurt me."

"You won't feel a thing, I promise."

Vivienne heard a thud followed by a big crashing noise that sounded like a body hitting the ground. Then the secret door started to move as the wall was slid back into place, closing her in. The sound of the wood sliding across the floor was like a death sentence to Vivienne. She realized that she was now trapped inside with no way to escape!

"Nay," she mumbled, finally ripping her gown to get loose. She ran to the door of the secret room, but in the dark she couldn't figure out how to open it. Then she thought she heard another voice but it was muffled through the wall. More wood sliding, and she realized the outer bookshelf was being put back into place as well. And then, everything was not only pitch black but deathly silent. "Nay. Let me out," she cried, pounding on the wall and pushing and pulling but it wouldn't budge. "Maleine!" she shouted. "Please, don't hurt her," she cried, but there was no answer because they couldn't hear her. She figured whoever was in the room must have left, and now she was all alone.

Her heart raced and fear coursed through her. What would they do to Maleine? Did they leave her here or take her with them? Was she hurt? And was she even still alive? Would the poor girl be the next postulant they found murdered? God's eyes, she hoped not. Vivienne felt like poor Sabina, being locked up inside a wall. What would happen to her when they discovered her inside the secret room? Or even worse, what if she was never discovered at all? How would she ever get out? Would she mayhap end up dying in here?

"Zachariah, please find me. Find Maleine. Grunt, where are you when I need you?" Panic filled her. She needed to get out of this room. Not only to help herself, but because no one but she knew how much trouble Maleine was in right now. Vivienne's stomach lurched, telling her that she was right. This was bad. Really bad. She had no doubt that poor Maleine's life was in real danger.

She stopped pounding on the hidden door, closed her eyes, and laid her forehead against the wood. She hoped she wouldn't run out of air before she was released from this confinement. She had to have faith in Zachariah, that he would discover what was going on. That he would find her. Hopefully he would at least find and help Maleine before it was too late.

Vivienne felt the tears welling up in her eyes. She sat down, thinking about Martin. She'd finally found her son after seven long years of mourning. What if she never had the chance to see him again? All she wanted to do was to hold him, hug him, and kiss him. To tell Martin how much she truly loved him. And most of all, how sorry she was that they'd been apart for so long and that she hadn't been able to find him sooner. Losing him again would hurt them both, and she didn't want her little boy to suffer in any way. He deserved better than that!

Next, Vivienne did something that she hadn't really done since the night her family was taken from her and her parents were murdered. She folded her hands and took a deep breath ... and prayed.

Chapter Nineteen

"There you are, Constable Erikson," said Zachariah, entering the ossuary, followed by Grunt. "I've been looking all over for you."

"I've been searching for you as well, Sheriff," the constable answered. Leaning over the body of Brother Benedict, he stood up straight when Zachariah entered. He held something in his hand.

"What's going on?" asked Zachariah.

"I had a little talk with Brother Harold this morning."

"About Brother Benedict's necklace?"

"Yes." The constable frowned. "How did you know?"

"Never mind that. What exactly was the talk about?" He took a few steps into the room.

"Brother Harold took a closer look at Brother Benedict's cross necklace and realized he made a mistake."

"What kind of mistake?" Zachariah walked over to the table. Grunt followed.

"He thought this was the necklace that he'd given Brother Benedict, but he was wrong."

"Wrong? How so?" Zachariah held out his open palm and the constable dropped the necklace into it.

"Brother Harold was here this morning, inspecting Brother Benedict's body with me. He took a closer look at the necklace."

"So you've said. Move the story along, Constable. I have a lot to do today."

"Aye, Sheriff Fitch. It seems that the necklace that the abbot gave the monk didn't have a green stone on it the way this one does. Brother Harold said this necklace is much more valuable and ornate than the ones handed out to the monks, or even the one that he gave him."

"And Brother Harold didn't remember that until now?" Zachariah found this odd.

"Yes. That's what he said. He also told me that he didn't know where this necklace even came from and that he'd never seen it before."

"Did he happen to say anything else about the monks who buried Brother Theodore when he died?" asked Zachariah.

"Yes, he did."

"Tell me."

"It was the gravedigger, Brother Grayson, Brother Cedric, Brother Silas, and Brother Harold who put the body of Brother Theodore into the ground."

"Yes, he already told me that. I was hoping to find out more. This doesn't help us narrow down the suspects, at all."

"It was raining that day, just as we suspected."

"Aye, so he said. Brother Harold explained that Brother Grayson left the body and waited until the storm was over to bury it."

"True. It seems that they all left until the rain subsided, and then returned and continued to bury the monk. All except Brother Harold, that is."

"What do you mean? He said he went down to the creek."

"Brother Harold told me that when he returned, he decided to stay there to watch over the body."

"Interesting that he didn't mention that to me," said Zachariah. Things weren't looking good for the abbot. "Did Brother Harold say he saw anything suspicious at all while he was waiting out the storm?"

"Not that he mentioned. Do you think it was the abbot who dumped Brother Benedict's body into the hole before Brother Theodore could be set in the ground?" asked the constable.

"It is looking pretty suspicious, I must admit. Especially since Brother Harold changed his story about the necklace."

"Is that enough to arrest him, Sheriff?"

"Nay, not really. Constable, I'd like you to find Brother Harold and keep a close eye on him until I return."

"Where are you going?"

Zachariah looked over at Grunt who was sniffing Brother Benedict's foot with the missing toe again. It gave him an idea.

"I'm going to retrieve the toe relic from the sacristy."

"Why?"

"Because, if it proves to be the toe of Brother Benedict, then that means the murderer is the one who probably took the toe in the first place."

"The murderer? Do you mean the gravedigger, Brother Grayson, or are you talking about Brother Harold?"

"I'm not sure yet. Brother Silas did tell me that Brother Grayson gave him the body parts from the cemetery to use as fake relics, so it could be him."

"Mayhap Brother Harold and Brother Grayson killed Brother Benedict together."

"Anything is possible. However, I need to know their motives. And how all this is related to the murder of Sabina."

"Well, at least I feel like we are getting closer."

"Constable, go to the scullery and have someone guard the

hole in the wall. I don't want any of the monks bricking it up until I can take another look inside. Mayhap there is something we missed."

"Aye, Sheriff."

"I'll come for you at the scullery. Oh, have you seen Lady Vivienne or Maleine this morning by any chance? They both seem to be missing."

"Nay, I haven't, Sheriff. Did you want me to hunt them down too?"

"Don't bother. I have a feeling I know where they are."

Zachariah left the charnel house and walked over to the church. He pushed open the large wooden door, finding it quiet and void of monks or nuns inside. That didn't surprise him, as the prayer session had ended recently and he was sure everyone was already busy going about their chores for the day, since they always seemed to have so many to do.

Grunt whined, looking around the church.

"Come on, Grunt. I might need your nose." Zachariah made his way to the sacristy and knocked softly upon the door. No answer. That meant it was empty. Good. He wore his dagger at his side, even though he'd left his sword back in his room. Even though Mother Superior told him no weapons were allowed in church, he was a sheriff and needed to carry a blade at all times for protection. He was about to try picking the lock with the tip of his dagger when Grunt jumped up, putting his paws on the door. To his surprise, the door swung open.

"What? It wasn't locked?" he said to himself. Zachariah found that odd, since he knew how protective Brother Silas was over the things in this room. He'd never leave it unlocked as well as unattended. Something was not right here.

Grunt hurried into the room and Zachariah followed, holding his dagger gripped in his hand should he need to use it. "Hello?" he said softly, walking into the room, leaving the door open. "Is anyone in here?" It was quiet inside, and no one seemed to be present. He made his way over to the reliquary, using his blade to pick the lock. He opened the metal door, pulled out the box with the toe bone in it, and opened it to peer inside. The toe bone was still there. He stuck the whole box into his pouch and closed up the reliquary again.

He had hoped to find Vivienne and Maleine in here, but it looked like they hadn't come to the sacristy, after all.

"All right, let's go, Grunt." He headed to the door but stopped when he saw Grunt sit down by the bookshelf instead of following him out of the room. "Come on, Grunt. We need to leave before we're discovered." Still, the dog didn't move. "What are you doing?"

Grunt whined and pawed at the shelf.

"I don't have time for games." He hurried over and grabbed the dog by the collar. He tried to pull Grunt to the door, but the dog actually growled and snapped at him. Zachariah quickly released the hound and stood up straight, looking down at him in thought. Grunt loved him. Why in heaven's name was he acting this way? He had never growled and snapped at him before.

Grunt always begged at Zachariah's feet every time he ate a meal. This was some odd behavior indeed. The dog didn't want to leave the room for some reason. Something was wrong here, but he just didn't know what. "What is it, Grunt? Show me," he said, using the words he'd heard Vivienne tell her dog on more than one occasion when she wanted the bloodhound to lead her somewhere. Once again, Grunt sat down and whined and pawed at the shelf. "All right, let's see what this is all about."

Zachariah pulled and pushed on the shelf, trying to remember where Brother Silas had touched it to make the bookcase swing open to reveal the secret chamber. Finally, it worked. He yanked the bookshelf open and when he did, Grunt rushed into the small opening, and started to howl. Bloodhounds often howled to alert their handler that they've tracked a scent.

Zachariah looked around inside the small area, not knowing what was wrong with the dog since nothing seemed to be amiss and there was no one else there. "Enough, Grunt. Now, come on. We need to go." He turned to leave and stopped in his tracks when he thought he heard a muffled noise. He listened closely, hearing a louder, thudding noise now. It almost seemed as if it was coming from behind the wall. "Hello? Is someone there?"

Next, Zachariah heard what sounded like a very muffled voice. Grunt barked furiously, standing on his back paws trying to climb the shelving, or so it seemed. Finally, it dawned on Zachariah what was going on here. "Lady Vivienne? Is that you?"

Grunt continued to howl and bark, both.

"Quiet, Grunt. I need to listen. Sure enough, with his head cocked, Zachariah heard a voice coming from behind the wall and could just make out some words.

"It's me, Zachariah. Help me! I'm trapped inside a secret room."

It sounded like Vivienne! What had she got herself into now?

"Vivienne, I'm here," he shouted. "But I don't know how to open the door."

More muffled words were masked by the dog's commotion.

"Hush, boy," said Zachariah, but the dog wouldn't stop whining and barking. Zachariah dug into his pouch and found part of a crust of bread. He held it up so the hound could see it. "Sit, Grunt." Thankfully, the dog sat, his attention focused on the food in Zachariah's hand instead of Vivienne behind the wall. "Say it again, Vivienne," he called out. "I couldn't understand you." He handed Grunt the bread and at the same time, listened closely.

"On the top shelf," she shouted from the other side of the wall. Grunt gulped down the bread and barked again, hearing Vivienne's voice and becoming excited. Then the dog jumped up, trying to help.

Zachariah reached up and felt around on the top shelf, finally finding something odd. It felt like a lever. He pulled it, and slowly the door, which was really the entire wall, creaked and moved a little. He pushed it open wider to find Vivienne standing there with a sword in her hands.

"Vivienne? What are you doing in there?" he asked.

Grunt ran over to her, wagging his tail and licking her hand joyfully, happy to have found her at last. Her face looked flushed and worry creased her brow.

"Zachariah! Thank goodness, you found me." She dropped the sword, sending it clattering to the floor. Then she rushed forward and fell against him. His arms encircled her and he held her trembling body tightly. She was very frightened, and this wasn't like her since she always put up a strong exterior. "I thought I would die in there," she told him, her face pressed up against his chest.

"You might have died if it hadn't been for Grunt," he replied. "He was the one who alerted me to your presence. It was all him."

"Grunt? Do you mean, you weren't looking for me?" She stepped back and eyed him up, seeming very disappointed.

Zachariah wanted to retract his words, but couldn't. He didn't want to lie to Vivienne. "My lady, I have to admit, I wasn't looking for you. Not really."

"Why not?" Now she almost seemed angry about it.

"I wasn't looking for you, because I didn't know anything was wrong. Plus, I know you can take care of yourself, so I wasn't worried."

"Then why are you even here?" She crossed her arms over

her chest in a huff. Her mood changed so suddenly that he started wondering if he'd done something wrong. Mayhap he should have just told her what she wanted to hear, after all.

"I came to get the toe bone of Saint Gerard to prove that it was really taken off of Brother Benedict's body." He looked past her into the darkened room. "What's in there, anyway? And how did you come to be locked inside?"

"Maleine and I found another secret room." Her anger seemed to be replaced by excitement when she relayed the information. "Sheriff, it is filled with money and jewels and the clothing and weapons of nobles. I think it is from the dowries that were given to the abbey. It seems they were never sold to support the church and abbey, after all."

"Interesting. I'd like to take a look in there." He stepped forward but she pushed him back.

"Nay. Not now. First, we need to get Maleine."

"Is she in there too?" He continued to try to see into the hidden room.

"Nay, she's not! She was here with me earlier, but we were almost caught. She managed to leave the room, but I got stuck inside it." She pointed to her torn gown.

"Oh. I see. I think." He wasn't exactly sure what her torn gown meant but was afraid to ask. If he did, her mood might swing back the other way again, and he didn't want that right now. "So, where is Maleine, and why did she leave you here locked inside the wall?"

"She didn't! Don't you understand?" She glared at him in frustration.

"Obviously not, my lady. So ... why don't you tell me?"

"Someone abducted her! They didn't know I was in here and that is why I got closed inside the secret room."

"Abducted? Who took her?"

"I don't know. I heard what sounded like a man's voice, and

then another voice but it was muffled. I couldn't tell who they were."

"Who's here? What's going on?" called out someone from the outer room.

"Come on," he said, taking her by the arm and pulling her out into the main chamber. Grunt followed.

"Brother Silas. Mother Superior," said Zachariah with a nod to greet them. He wasn't really surprised to see them standing there. It was just a shame that he and Vivienne got caught and would most likely be reprimanded now by Mother Superior's sharp tongue.

"Sheriff Fitch and Lady Vivienne, what are you doing in the sacristy?" Mother Superior demanded to know.

"I was trapped inside a secret room," said Vivienne. "One that holds a bountiful amount of wealth." She crossed her arms over her chest. "Would either of you like to tell us about that?"

"That secret room is where we store the dowries and donations we receive," said Brother Silas. "To keep them safe until they are sold."

"That's right," agreed Mother Superior. "We can't take the chance of such wealth being stolen."

"I thought this abbey was so broke that it was at risk of being closed down by the bishop," said Zachariah. "Why haven't you just sold the dowries by now to pay for the upkeep and for what was needed?"

"We have sold some," said the nun.

"By the looks of that secret room, I'd say you haven't," sniffed Vivienne, making her suspicions of them known.

"You don't understand." Mother Superior shook her head. "Those items are not from dowries. The dowries have already been sold through the years, most of it to buy relics. Brother Silas secured the wealth you saw from a rich noble just recently."

"Yes, the abbey was given a very generous donation," Brother Silas explained.

"Indeed, I'd say so. And who would that be who gave you such a generous donation?" asked Zachariah, searching for a name.

"It was from the widow of a baron," said Mother Superior, looking over at the monk.

"Who?" asked Vivienne.

"She requested to remain anonymous," the monk answered.

"We need to know," insisted Zachariah in a firm voice.

"Yes, you have to tell us. It's important," added Vivienne.

"You'd better tell him, Brother Silas," Mother Superior told the monk. "After all, Zachariah is the sheriff. We don't want to be accused of holding back information."

"Of course not," said Brother Silas. "It was the Baroness Alnwick who gave us that sizeable donation."

"The Baroness Alnwick? From Northumberland?" asked Zachariah.

"Yes. Do you know her?" asked Mother Superior. "I've never met her, but Brother Silas has."

"Nay, I don't know her," said Zachariah.

"Neither do I," admitted Vivienne.

"She's a very kind lady," said the monk. "Mayhap someday I can arrange a meeting between you."

"Why wouldn't the baroness make a donation to an abbey near her instead of one so far away like Maltby le Marsh?" asked the sheriff.

"Because of her daughter. She used to be a nun here. Many years ago, before I came to his abbey," said Mother Superior.

"So she's not here now?" asked Vivienne.

"Nay. She died about a year before the abbess arrived," said Brother Silas. "The baroness was doing it to honor her dead daughter as well as her newly departed husband."

"Then the abbey will no longer be at risk of closing down," said Vivienne. "You'll most likely sell those items and use the money to keep the abbey open?"

"Of course," said Brother Silas. "That is our plan."

"Did you tell this to the bishop upon his visit?" asked Zachariah.

"Yes, of course I mentioned it," said Brother Silas. "He was more than pleased, but did not have time to peruse the donation goods on this visit."

Zachariah thought about the bishop's visit and what he'd heard about the abbey still at risk of being closed down. This story wasn't adding up.

"How did you know about the second secret room?" asked Mother Superior, changing the subject.

"The real question is, why didn't you tell us about it when you showed us the first secret room?" asked Zachariah. "It seems as if you two have kept things from us that could be beneficial in this murder investigation."

"Heaven's sake, you don't think either of us had anything to do with the murders, do you?" asked Mother Superior, her hand going to her heart.

When Zachariah looked like he was about to admit his suspicion, Vivienne spoke up instead.

"Of course not, Mother Superior," she said. "Why would we ever think that?" Until they had the proper evidence they needed, they must try to keep their suspicions to themselves.

Zachariah looked at her in question. She glanced at him from the corner of her eye, hoping he'd go along with whatever she said.

"How did you get in here?" Brother Silas eyed *them* suspiciously now. "I had the door locked."

"Nay. It was open when I got here," said Vivienne.

"Me, too," added Zachariah.

"Well, how did you find the second secret room?" Mother Superior asked the question once again.

"Maleine found it," Vivienne admitted.

"Maleine? That troublesome postulant?" asked Mother Superior. "She is always putting her nose where it doesn't belong. Where is she? She'll need to be punished for this."

"She's not here," Zachariah told her.

"Someone came in and abducted her," Vivienne explained, watching for their reaction.

"Abducted? What are you saying?" Brother Silas wandered around the room, busying himself with straightening things rather than to look directly at her.

"We believe that Maleine's life is in danger, and that she was taken by the murderer," said Vivienne. "We need to find her, and quickly."

Grunt trotted over and started sniffing Brother Silas's leg.

"Stop that," said the monk, kicking his foot and sending Grunt running back to Vivienne. When he did so, Vivienne noticed some white dust near the bottom of his long brown robe.

"We'll help you look for Maleine, but it'll have to wait until the next prayer session is over," said Mother Superior. "It is time for it to start."

"Nay! Enough with the prayers already," snapped Zachariah. "Nothing else is going to slow us down."

"The sheriff is right. We can't wait," Vivienne told them. "I have a feeling something awful has happened to Maleine. We have to find her right away."

"Did either of you see anyone doing anything suspicious on your way up here?" asked Zachariah.

"Nay," said Mother Superior.

"Aye," answered Brother Silas. "I noticed Brother Harold and Sister Roberta meeting and talking in hushed whispers in the shadows of the cloisters."

"You did?" asked the Reverend Mother. "Why didn't you tell me about such behavior immediately? There is no talking allowed between them at this time."

"I was going to mention it, but didn't want to get anyone in trouble."

"Where are they now?" asked Zachariah.

"I think I saw them going toward the ossuary," Brother Silas told them.

"I don't like the sound of this. Let's go find them." Zachariah led the way to the door with Grunt right behind him.

When they were outside, Vivienne hurried to Zachariah's side, speaking softly so the others couldn't hear them.

"What do you think?" she asked.

"They're hiding something," he responded.

"I agree. I think they are both lying, even though they seem to have an answer to every one of our questions."

"I don't trust them. And neither do I trust Brother Harold," said Zachariah.

"Me either. And from the way I'm feeling this morning, I'd say there was something put into our wine."

"I wouldn't doubt it," he told her. "I've never had such strong reactions to drinking wine before."

"Sheriff, Maleine and I discovered that half the boxes that supposedly were containing the true relics are really empty. The rest of the relics in the secret room are fakes as well."

"What do you mean?"

"The *real relic* hair of Saint Agnes that they showed us was actually Maleine's hair."

"What? Nay. How could that be?"

"It was. She proved it to me. And that wood that is supposedly part of Christ's crucifixion cross is really from the handle of a bread paddle that Maleine broke while working in the kitchen."

"Are you sure about all this? I mean, accusing a sacrist and an abbess is not a small issue."

"I'm positive. The wood had bread crumbs on it. And the hair had honey on it that Maleine spilled in the kitchen. Sheriff, these two are not to be trusted, no matter who they are or what they say. I wouldn't doubt they are lying about that big donation they are keeping in that secret room, too."

"I'm getting the same feeling."

"Do you think they murdered anyone?"

"Hard telling. However, Brother Harold is starting to seem more suspicious right now as well as the gravedigger, Brother Grayson. Mayhap it was one of them. We just don't yet have enough evidence to make a proper accusation."

"I trust Brother Harold and Brother Grayson more than I do those two." Vivienne looked quickly over her shoulder to see Mother Superior and Brother Silas speaking in hushed tones as well. "Do you think they are the ones who abducted Maleine?"

"I suppose it's possible," he said. "But they seemed surprised to see us in the sacristy."

"The abductor didn't know I was in the secret room, so he or she *would* be surprised. I think it was them, Zachariah. I feel it in my gut."

"We need proof, Vivienne. Hard proof. Right now, all I have is a toe bone, a brooch, a rosary, and a monk's cross necklace. None of those items prove a blasted thing. Plus there were four monks in the graveyard the day Brother Theodore was buried who are under suspicion too."

"And Brother Silas is one of them."

"Aye. The constable discovered that they left the body with only Brother Harold watching over it."

"Does that make Brother Harold the murderer?"

"I'm not sure, but Brother Harold did tell the constable that he was mistaken about Brother Benedict's necklace. He changed his story and said he didn't give it to him, after all."

"What? How could he forget a thing like that? It makes no sense."

"That's what I said." He pulled the cross necklace out of his pouch, inspecting it. "Brother Harold claims the necklace he gave Brother Benedict didn't have a green gemstone embedded on it."

"Let me see that." She took it and looked it over. "This is the same type of green gemstone that the rosary was made of that was found on Sabina."

"Yes, it seems so."

"I've seen this gemstone somewhere else too. It was on a crown in the secret room."

"Really. Suspicious indeed."

"I'd say the evidence against those two is adding up quickly." Once again, Vivienne glanced back, just to make sure Brother Silas and Mother Superior weren't listening to her conversation with the sheriff.

"There's also this brooch which has me stumped." Zachariah removed the brooch from his pouch next.

"Oh, I didn't tell you. Maleine had a brooch very similar to this one with the snakes on it."

"Maleine had a brooch?" He looked up in surprise. "What was she doing with it?"

"She used it to pick the lock in the sacristy. She told me she took it from Mother Superior's room."

"God's teeth, is the girl stealing now? Lady Vivienne, Maleine is proving to be no better than her father."

"Nay, you don't understand," protested Vivienne. "The brooch she had matches this brooch that was found on Sabina. The one that we think belongs to the killer. And that crown in the secret room had the same snakes on it."

"So, all the items have the same origin," said Zachariah. "Yet, the brooch has been in the wall for two years."

"That's right," said Vivienne. "That means that the jewels and things in the secret room weren't really from a donation that came recently."

"And if they had those treasures for at least the past two years, why weren't they sold off to try to save the abbey?" asked the sheriff.

"Suspicious enough to accuse them both?" asked Vivienne. "Is it enough evidence to have them both arrested?"

"I don't know what to think right now," said Zachariah, shaking his head. "I don't trust either of them, but they seem to have an explanation for everything." He glanced back over his shoulder. "Ever since we got here, they have seemed to be doing things to slow down the murder investigation."

"They don't seem to have an answer why none of the relics are real," said Vivienne. "Then again, we didn't actually come right out and ask them, I suppose."

"Nay. Mayhap we should have."

"Well, whether we trust them or not will have to wait for the time being," said Vivienne. "Right now, our priority needs to be on finding Maleine. I'm afraid she might be hurt. Or she might already be dead. Zachariah, please. I am so frightened for her."

"We'll find her," he promised. He stopped and looked back at the two following them. "Mother Superior, I'd like you to call everyone to the refectory at once."

"What for? It isn't time to eat," she told him. "And everyone will be headed to the church to pray."

"Make an exception," he told her. "There is a girl missing and I will wait no longer in trying to find her. I am afraid the murderer might have struck again. I need everyone in the refectory immediately."

"What are you saying?" gasped the nun. "Do you really think Maleine might have been killed?"

"We're not sure, but we hope not," Vivienne told her. "It is crucial that we discover her whereabouts quickly."

"Yes, we must move fast," said Zachariah. "We need the help of each nun and monk in the abbey if we're going to find her. Alive. And if we don't all work together in harmony, we might just end up with another death on our hands. I swear to God I will not let that happen!"

Chapter Twenty

Fifteen minutes later, everyone was gathered in the refectory, confused as to why they were there at all. Zachariah paced the floor, still waiting for Constable Erikson to show his face. Where in the world was he?

"Shall we start?" asked Vivienne.

"Not yet," Zachariah told her. "Dammit, where is the constable? I could use him right now. Especially if we find our killer."

"I'll ask around if anyone has seen him." Vivienne was about to do just that when Constable Erikson stumbled into the refectory. He was holding his bleeding head. "Zachariah, look!" Vivienne cried, pointing at him. "Constable Erikson's been hurt."

"God's eyes, what happened?" Zachariah rushed over to his constable, taking his arm and helping him over to a bench to be seated. "Who did this to you?"

"I don't know. I was in the ossuary and someone hit me over the head from behind," said the constable. "I never saw who it was."

"Dammit, this is going to stop right now." Zachariah stormed up to the front of the room, holding up his hand.

"Someone has attacked our constable," he announced in a loud voice.

Gasps and mumbles went up from the crowd.

"One of the postulants is missing as well," he continued. "She is new here. Her name is Maleine. If anyone knows anything about the attack on Constable Erikson or the where-abouts of Maleine, I urge you to speak up now. And please, do it quickly."

Everyone remained quiet. Vivienne saw Zachariah look over to a table where Brother Harold sat with Brothers Cedric and Grayson. Then he glanced over to where his sister Magdalena sat with Sister Roberta and Sister Ernestine. Mother Superior stood near the entrance of the scullery with Brother Silas next to her. None of them said a word.

"It's all right to talk," Vivienne assured the nuns and monks in the room. "This is important. Has anyone seen Maleine? Please. She might be hurt. We need to find her. I think her life is in danger."

Grunt barked several times and Brother Silas became upset.

"Someone needs to remove this dog at once," said the sacrist almost seeming afraid of Grunt.

"Yes, the hound shouldn't be in the abbey at all, as I've said more than once now," added Mother Superior. "Lady Vivienne, control your dog."

"Come here, Grunt," said Vivienne, having an idea. The dog ran over to her. "Sheriff, give me the brooch."

"Vivienne, what are you doing?" asked Zachariah in a low voice.

"Trust me," she said, holding out her hand.

"All right," he said, handing her the brooch that they'd found in the wall with the body of Sabina.

"This brooch was found with the deceased postulant named Sabina," she said, holding it up so everyone could see it. "We believe it belongs to the person who murdered her, and that in her struggles Sabina pulled it off of the killer during the attack."

More hushed talking buzzed around the room.

"My dog is a bloodhound," said Vivienne. "All he has to do is sniff the brooch. Then, he'll be able to follow the scent of anyone who has had contact with it."

"But a lot of us have touched that brooch," said the constable, holding a rag to his head to try to stop the bleeding. "How is that going to help?"

"My dog will sniff out the scent of everyone who has ever touched it. That is, providing they are in this room right now." She held the brooch down by her leg. "Go ahead, Grunt. Take a sniff. Find anyone who touched this brooch."

"This is silly," complained Brother Cedric. "You can't find a murderer by using a dog."

"I agree," spoke up Sister Roberta. "And like the constable said, a lot of us have touched the brooch. Even if the hound points out who has touched it, it proves nothing. It is only going to make it look like we are all killers."

"Aye," agreed Brother Harold. "I don't want to be accused of murdering anyone."

"Why not?" Brother Silas spoke up. "After all, Brother Harold, you are the one who dumped Brother Benedict's body in the hole before Brother Theodore was buried, so just admit it."

"What? Nay!" cried Brother Harold, bolting up to a standing position. "I did no such thing. That's a lie, Sheriff. Don't believe him."

"Brother Harold told me he gave that cross necklace to the deceased, and then he changed his story all together," the constable said loud enough for everyone to hear him.

"Arrest the abbot, Sheriff," ordered Mother Superior. "It seems to me he is the only guilty one here."

"I'm not guilty, I tell you." Brother Harold started walking to the front of the room. Grunt was standing right there, but instead of stepping around the dog, the monk tripped on the hound and fell to the floor. Grunt quickly scurried away with his tail between his legs.

"Brother Harold!" Vivienne ran over and helped him to his feet.

"I must have tripped on something, how clumsy of me," mumbled the monk.

"It was my dog that you tripped over," Vivienne told him. "Brother Harold, Grunt is big enough that you should have noticed him standing there."

"I-I'm sorry," said Brother Harold. "I hope I didn't hurt Grunt."

"Nay, he'll be fine," she told him. "But thank you for your concern."

"Brother Harold didn't see the dog, because his eyesight is failing. Isn't that right?" asked Zachariah, walking over to the monk's side. "That is also why you mistook this cross necklace for the one you gave to Brother Benedict years ago." Zachariah held up the necklace for all of them to see. "You didn't notice the green stone on it until you inspected it closer while in the ossuary with Constable Erikson today."

"Is that right, Brother Harold?" asked Vivienne. "Is your eyesight failing?"

"Yes," he softly answered, looking downward. "I am ashamed to admit it, but it is true. Sheriff Fitch is correct in saying what he did. I pretended to look at the cross necklace when Brother Benedict's body was exhumed, but I really couldn't see it from where I stood. Please forgive me for being dishonest. I didn't want anyone to know about my failing sight." The monk looked as if he felt he had let them all down.

"Brother Harold? Why didn't you just tell us about not

being able to see well?" asked Brother Cedric, coming to his side. "We would have understood. You didn't have to hide it."

"I was ashamed," said Brother Harold. "You see, two years ago when I confessed to Mother Superior that I was attracted to Sabina, she told me that God would punish me for my lustful feelings. And she was right. My eyesight started failing right afterward."

"You were attracted to Sabina and Mother Superior knew about it?" asked Vivienne in surprise. This seemed to be one well-guarded secret.

"And neither of you said a word about this, although we are in the middle of investigating the murder of that poor girl?" asked Zachariah, shaking his head in disgust.

"I wanted to tell you," said Brother Harold. "But Mother Superior told me to keep quiet or you'd think I killed the girl."

"Is that right, Reverend Mother?" asked Zachariah, looking over to her still standing near the scullery.

"I was only trying to protect the abbot," said the nun.

"Why would you do that?" asked Vivienne.

"I did it because I didn't want his reputation ruined," continued Mother Superior. You see, Brother Harold never came out and admitted it to me, but I believe he is the one who got Sabina pregnant."

That brought about a lot of shocked gasps and mumbling from the group of nuns and monks listening.

"Nay!" cried Brother Harold. "That's not true at all. I was attracted to Sabina, I admit it. It was wrong and I pray daily for forgiveness. But I tell you, I never even touched the girl. I wasn't the one to get her pregnant, I swear it."

"He's telling the truth," said Brother Silas. "It was Brother Benedict who impregnated Sabina. Everyone knows that. But I believe that Brother Harold found out about it and he went crazy. That's why he killed both of them. Out of jealousy."

Vivienne was shocked to hear this accusation. She could tell by the sheriff's expression that he couldn't believe what he was hearing either.

"Shall I arrest Brother Harold, Sheriff?" The constable got to his feet. "I mean, it seems as if we've found our killer."

"Nay. I don't think it was him after all," said Vivienne, wanting to stop this nonsense before the abbot was arrested and hauled away. "After all, Brother Harold just worried about hurting my dog. Nobody who murdered two people would feel compassion toward an animal."

"She's right," agreed Zachariah. I don't believe Brother Harold is the murderer either. He was left to watch over the body of Brother Theodore during the rainstorm. But I believe that with his failing eyesight, he couldn't see the murderer dump Brother Benedict's body into the hole before Brother Theodore's was set inside."

"I did see someone out there in the rain," admitted Brother Harold. "But I had dozed off while sitting under a tree to keep dry, and was still not fully awake at the time. I figured it was just a dream. Then when the ghost started showing up, I thought mayhap I'd seen the ghost but didn't want to sound silly so I kept quiet."

"I saw the ghost." Magdalena stood up. "You wouldn't have sounded silly to me."

"Or me." Sister Roberta stood up as well. "I saw the ghost too."

"So did I," said Vivienne.

"What does this have to do with anything?" asked Brother Grayson.

"Have you ever seen the ghost in the graveyard, Brother Grayson? You are there all the time," said Zachariah. "I mean, you are the head gravedigger, are you not?"

"I am, but no, I haven't seen any ghost," the monk answered.

"I think these people are making up stories, trying to scare us all."

That caused more commotion and it took Zachariah a few minutes to calm everyone down.

"Sheriff, we need to find Maleine," Vivienne reminded him, loud enough for others to hear. "The longer it takes, the less chance there is that we will discover her still alive."

"Lady Vivienne, when I was in the scullery earlier, I thought I heard a voice." Sister Magdalena came over with Sister Ernestine following.

"The ghost?" asked Vivienne.

"Nay, I don't think so," said Sister Magdalena. "I looked around but couldn't find anyone. The voice seemed ... sort of muffled."

"Constable, search the scullery," commanded Zachariah.

"Aye," answered the constable, still holding his bleeding head as he got to his feet.

"I'll do it," offered Vivienne, hurrying past Mother Superior and Brother Silas as she entered the small room and stopped dead in her tracks. Reaching out to a side table, she hurriedly lit a candle, to verify what she thought she was seeing. "Sheriff, the wall is completely bricked back up. Did you know that?"

"Nay. It can't be." Zachariah came running. "I instructed the constable to tell Brother Harold not to brick up the wall until I was done with the investigation."

"No one told me that," cried Brother Harold.

"Sheriff, I was hit over the head before I could give Brother Harold the message." Constable Erikson stood outside the door of the scullery, looking in.

"Someone didn't want that wall to remain open," said Vivienne. "Oh, my God! Zachariah, I fear Maleine is in there."

"God's teeth, no! Out of the way," shouted Zachariah,

rushing into the room. "We need to get these bricks removed from the wall. Now!"

"Nay, it was just repaired," protested Brother Silas.

"Don't be destroying my abbey," commanded Mother Superior.

Grunt barked, pawing at the wall.

"Grunt is trying to tell me something. Everyone, be quiet." Vivienne ran to the bricked-up wall and put her ear to it. Sure enough, she could make out the faint sound of a woman's voice. It almost sounded as if she were calling out for help. "Maleine's in there! Zachariah, do something. Help her!"

"I need something to use to break down this wall." The sheriff looked around the room, trying to find something but there was nothing there but kitchen utensils and pots and pans.

Sister Roberta ran up, holding an iron pot in two hands. "Here. Use this. It's strong."

Zachariah grabbed the iron pot and with all his might kept hitting the bricks until they finally started to loosen. Still, it was taking much too long.

"Careful not to hurt her," shouted Vivienne.

"Men, I need help taking these bricks out of the wall," shouted Zachariah.

Brother Harold and Brother Cedric ran over and the three men started to remove the bricks but the mortar was already partially dry and holding them in tightly.

"Move aside. I've got this." Brother Grayson pushed his way into the room with a shovel in his grip, as well as a metal rake that had thick hooked prongs on the end. He was a big man and was used to digging graves and doing manual labor. He first used the shovel to hit the bricks to loosen them even more, and then the rake to pull them free from the wall. The rest of the men rushed in and collected the loosened bricks, tossing them to the floor.

"Grunt, get out of the way," warned Vivienne, pulling her hound to the side so he wouldn't be harmed by a flying brick.

"Maleine is in here, I see her," shouted Zachariah, reaching into the wall. With the help of Brother Grayson, he pulled the girl out. She was badly beaten, bruised, and bleeding. Her wrists and legs were tied tightly together with rope. There was a cloth gag in her mouth as well. Maleine's eyes started closing and before they could ask her anything, she passed out.

"Is she alive?" asked one of the nuns peeking into the room.

"Merciful saints, help her," said another.

Vivienne hunkered down to check on her. "Yes, she's alive but has passed out, probably from the pain. She is badly hurt."

"We need to get her to the infirmary at once," shouted Sister Roberta.

"Wait," said Zachariah. "Before anyone leaves, I need to know which monks bricked up this wall?"

Everyone looked around but said nothing.

"Brother Harold? Was it you?" asked the sheriff.

"Well, no," said Brother Harold. "I was instructed by Mother Superior to have the lay monks brick it up and I assumed they did the job. I wasn't here when the work was done."

One of the lay monks stepped forward. "We were going to do it, abbot, but when we arrived after the prayer session, it was already completed."

"Well, someone did it. So who was it?" shouted the sheriff.

Vivienne suddenly remembered that she saw something white on the bottom of Brother Silas's robe. Now she realized it must have been mortar. "It was Brother Silas," she said aloud. "He was the one who abducted Maleine as well. I'm sure of it."

"Brother Silas, where are you? Step forward," commanded Zachariah.

"I told him not to hurt her," cried Mother Superior dropping to her knees and folding her hands in prayer. "I tried to stop him, but I couldn't."

"You knew Maleine was in the wall and you didn't tell us?" Vivienne couldn't believe this.

"Constable, arrest Mother Superior," ordered Zachariah. "And someone find Brother Silas. His disappearance proves his guilt, along with the confession we just heard from the abbess. Brother Silas is the one who abducted Maleine, and it is my suspicion that he was the one to murder both Brother Benedict and Sabina as well."

"Brother Silas is not here," someone from the crowd informed him.

"I saw him run out the door," said another.

"Dammit, I'll find him myself," snarled Zachariah.

"I'll come with you, Sheriff." Constable Erikson started to move but he was still bleeding and would be of little help.

"Nay," said Zachariah. "You stay here and watch over Mother Superior so she doesn't escape as well."

"What did Mother Superior do to be arrested?" asked Brother Cedric.

"She knew about Maleine's abduction and stayed quiet. That makes her an accessory to the crime," said Vivienne.

"That's right," agreed Zachariah. "Also, Brother Silas and Mother Superior have been lying to all of you. There are no holy relics. They are all fakes."

This sent all the monks and nuns into a frenzy.

"Plus, I believe they were stealing the money and dowries from the abbey to keep it for themselves," added Vivienne.

"Nay," said Mother Superior, still crying and shaking her head from her position on the floor. Her eyes were focused on Maleine. "It was a donation from the widow, Baroness Alnwick. Brother Silas secured it just recently. He told me so."

"Was it really?" asked the sheriff. "Or are you just playing dumb to try to save your hide from being imprisoned?"

"The Baron of Alnwick is a good friend of my family and very much alive," said Sister Roberta. "I just saw them in town yesterday. His wife is not a widow at all and surely didn't donate anything to the abbey."

"I admit, we were lying about the relics," confessed Mother Superior as the constable pulled her up from the floor. "But Brother Silas had me fooled about the rest. I wanted this abbey to succeed, not to be closed down. Brother Silas told me he had a way to do it through selling fake relics. I didn't know he killed anyone, and that's the truth!"

"You still were part of a very deceptive plan," snapped Zachariah.

"And you didn't tell us he abducted Maleine," added Vivienne. "How could you keep that to yourself, knowing she would probably die?"

"I wanted to tell you, but I was frightened. I didn't want to go to jail. Brother Silas told me to keep quiet, that none of it mattered. He said if I didn't, he'd blame everything on me."

"The deaths of two people and the abduction of an innocent girl do matter." It was Brother Harold who spoke up now. "No relics, nor the state of an abbey is worth a human life."

"I agree," cried Mother Superior. "I swear, I knew nothing about who murdered that monk and poor girl. Brother Silas told me he sent them away and I believed him. I didn't murder anyone, I tell you."

"Get Maleine to the infirmary, now." said Zachariah. "This conversation will be continued later since I still think there are big chunks of the story missing. I'm going to go after Brother Silas, and when I find him, he'll wish to hell I hadn't."

"Wait, Sheriff," called out Vivienne, running after

Zachariah as he left the refectory. Grunt followed and so did Sister Ernestine. "I'm coming with you."

"Nay. Go back inside, Vivienne." The sheriff stormed across the cloistered walkway, talking to her over his shoulder. "I don't have time to go back to my room for my sword but I could really use it right now."

"Brother Silas is dangerous," cried Vivienne. "You will need something to defend yourself against him."

"I'll use my bare hands to strangle the life out of him, if need be, but he will not get away, I promise you that. Even if I have to kill him."

"Stop talking crazy, Zachariah," she said, finally catching up to him. "You are not going to kill anyone." He stopped and turned around to face her.

"What is *she* doing here?" He pointed to Sister Ernestine who was right behind Vivienne.

"Sister Ernestine, you need to go back to the refectory," said Vivienne, facing the nun when she spoke. The young woman used her hands, trying to say something. "Sheriff, she said Maleine is her friend and she wants to help us."

"How the hell is she going to help? She can't even talk." Zachariah threw his hands in the air.

"Sheriff! That was downright rude." Vivienne spun on her heel, glaring at him.

Grunt started barking, but Vivienne was too angry with Zachariah right now to even pay attention.

"I'm sorry, my lady, but this is work for the law enforcement, not a nun. Or you, for that matter."

She was about to argue with him when Sister Ernestine grabbed her by the arm. The nun pointed to the graveyard.

"What is it, Sister Ernestine? What's wrong?" Vivienne turned to look at the graveyard and her jaw dropped. She took hold of Zachariah's arm and spun him around as well. "Look! Tell me what you see."

"Vivienne, I don't have time for—oh, my God. Is that what I think it is?"

"Yes. It's the ghost, Sheriff Fitch. Now do you believe me?"

ZACHARIAH COULDN'T BELIEVE his eyes. It was broad daylight, yet he saw the ghost of a monk floating above the gravestones in the graveyard. So it seemed he was either going mad or that Vivienne and the others had really seen a ghost after all, even though he hadn't believed them.

"Sister Ernestine thinks we should follow the ghost. So do I," Vivienne told him.

"Why not," mumbled Zachariah, taking off at a run after a damned ghost. If the ghost had truly given those leads to Vivienne, then mayhap he was trying to do so now, too. He figured at this point, what did he have to lose? Vivienne followed him with Grunt barking as he ran along with them. Sister Ernestine trailed right behind them. When Zachariah got in front of the ossuary, the ghost suddenly disappeared. He stopped, taking that as a sign of some sort. "I know you're in there, Brother Silas," he shouted, not really sure but thinking mayhap the ghost was leading him to the killer after all. "Surrender. Come out with your hands above your head and you won't get hurt."

"That's where you're wrong, Sheriff." The door to the ossuary slowly squeaked open. Brother Silas stepped out, and Zachariah's heart almost stopped. The monk held Magdalena up against him and had a sharp blade pressed to her throat. "You will let me walk out of here right now and you will not follow, or I swear I'll slit your sister's throat from one ear to the other. And don't think I won't do it."

"Magdalena." Zachariah could barely speak since his mouth

was so dry. He felt his heart drumming in his ears. This couldn't really be happening. That murderer was threatening to kill his sister!

"Zachariah, he's going to kill Sister Magdalena." Vivienne came to a stop next to him.

"I can see that, Vivienne. I am not blind." He kept his eyes focused on his sister. She looked so frightened and he felt so helpless right now.

"Do something," she whispered.

"I'm working on it," he whispered back. "I'm open to suggestions."

"Zachariah, please, do as Brother Silas asks," begged Magdalena. "Let him pass."

"Throw down your knife and back away," ordered Brother Silas. "I'm leaving and you are not going to stop me."

Grunt growled lowly. Sister Ernestine caught up to them and stopped as well.

"All right. Just don't hurt her." Zachariah hunkered down and slowly placed his dagger on the ground.

"Now move away from the blade, and keep your hands in the air," commanded Brother Silas. "Back up, I tell you, or your sister dies!"

"I'm doing as you say. Just don't hurt her. Please." Zachariah backed up with his hands held high over his head.

"The women too. Hands in the air!" screamed Silas. "Nay, on second thought, send the deaf-mute one to the stable for a horse. At least I know she won't tell anyone."

"She can't understand you," said Vivienne. "I need to use my hands to tell her what you want."

"Then do it," he snarled, slowly moving down one step, still holding the dagger to Magdalena's neck.

If anything happened to his sister, Zachariah would never forgive himself. How did things get so out of hand?

Vivienne said something to Sister Ernestine using the hand gestures she'd learned. Zachariah only hoped the girl understood what she was trying to tell her to do. If not, they were all in trouble. Then the nun ran off toward the stables with Grunt following on her heels.

"Magdalena, I am so sorry for ever saying you were to blame for Margaret's death," Zachariah spoke up. "I know it wasn't your fault. Please, forgive me for being so angry and mean to you." He didn't want either of them to die before he had a chance to make amends. Damn, he was such a fool to hold a grudge for so long. Especially when it hadn't been anyone's fault, but just an act of God.

"I forgive you, Zachariah." Magdalena's voice was breathy, as she was not able to talk clearly with the blade pressed up against her throat.

"This isn't the time for stupid family reunions. Where is my horse?" shouted Silas. "I want one now!"

"Give Sister Ernestine a moment. She'll be back with your horse, I promise," said Vivienne.

"Why did you do it, Brother Silas?" asked Zachariah, trying to keep the man talking. "Why did you kill an innocent girl and a fellow monk? We know it was you."

"Hah! Sabina was far from innocent," laughed Brother Silas. "She loved Brother Benedict, but her curiosity got her in trouble. She discovered my plan regarding the fake relics as well as my secret room where I put the goods I stole from the abbey."

"You tried to bribe her to keep her quiet, didn't you?" asked Vivienne. "That is why you gave her that green gemstone rosary."

"Yes. She thought it was a true relic, but it wasn't," said Silas with a chuckle. "She promised to stay quiet if I gave it to her, but she lied. She told Brother Benedict about everything, and I had to try to bribe him too."

"The cross necklace with the green stone in it," said Zachariah.

"That's right. I gave it to him from the dowries I held. However, I knew the two of them wouldn't keep quiet for long. And I wasn't about to continue giving them more of my treasure."

"Your treasure? You mean possessions of the nobles that you stole," said Vivienne. "From the dowries of those who came to the abbey."

"Yes, that's right," the monk admitted. "You see, no one is really as pious as you think they are. We are all weak of flesh. Even Mother Superior."

"Did Mother Superior have anything to do with the murders?" asked Vivienne.

Brother Silas laughed. "Nay. She was too easy to fool and naught but my puppet. She had no idea I killed anyone. No one did. The Reverend Mother just wanted the wealth and riches and to be abbess of the best abbey around. Her pride was her main weakness. You see, she would do anything for me since I was the one with the brains. The only one who could give her what she really wanted."

"What about the brooch Maleine found in Mother Superior's room?" asked Vivienne.

"I put that there to frame her because you two were getting too close to discovering the truth," said Brother Silas.

"So Mother Superior wasn't stealing from the church?" asked Vivienne.

"Not regarding the dowries, nay," said the monk. "But she was a big part of selling fake relics and keeping the money, only using a little as was necessary so the bishop wouldn't close down the abbey."

"You tricked her," said Vivienne.

"She knew what she was doing," he snorted. "She is not free from guilt."

"Tell us more about the relics," said the sheriff.

"I made so much money on fake relics that it just makes those who bought them look even more than stupid. And to top it off, I convinced Mother Superior it wasn't a bad thing to do at all. I told her she would have her precious abbey restored and those who believed in the relics were no worse off than before. I convinced her it was for the good of all, and not a sin. I even started rumors of the relics we have creating miracles when the pilgrims touched them. For a penny, a pilgrim will claim anything, I swear. That made the relics even more valuable and sought after." He laughed liked a madman now. "Some people will believe anything if you lead them by their nose down the path you want them to take."

"Did you ever have any real relics?" asked Zachariah, trying to stall for time while he devised a plan to take the man down.

"Never. Each one of them was fake from the very beginning. And I'd keep replacing them and selling them over and over again."

"You got greedy. You never intended to give any of the money from the dowries to the church or abbey, did you?" asked Vivienne.

"Never. The funny part about getting things so easily, is that I always thought of it as a challenge to attain even more. I should have taken it all and run while I had the chance, but this abbey has been my kingdom for many years now. If I had thought for one minute that someone was going to find Sabina's body in the wall, I never would have stayed so long."

"Yet they did find her," said Vivienne.

"That was by pure accident."

"You never said why you killed Sabina." Zachariah tried to move closer without the man noticing.

"I wanted Sabina, but she rejected my advances. She only wanted Brother Benedict in that way," Brother Silas told them.

"So you killed Sabina because she wouldn't lie with you?" asked Zachariah.

"Oh, we coupled. I had her first, even if it was against her will." Brother Silas sounded proud by what he did.

"You raped her!" cried Vivienne. "How could you?"

"You were the one who impregnated her then," said Zachariah.

"That's right, I was." Brother Silas walked down the second step, still holding tightly to Magdalena. "I figured when Mother Superior found out the girl was pregnant, she'd want to hide the fact or her precious abbey's reputation would be ruined. It didn't take much convincing to get the abbess to agree to brick up Sabina in the wall to repent for her sins."

"Mother Superior knew Sabina was in the wall?" Vivienne had a hard time believing an abbess could be so evil.

"It's called immurement, my lady," explained Brother Silas. "Nuns are sometimes bricked up into walls to repent for their sins, especially if they broke their vow of chastity. Usually, they are taken out after a few days."

"Did Mother Superior know Sabina died in the wall?" asked the sheriff.

"Nay," he told them, moving to one side slowly, bringing Magdalena with him. "The foolish abbess must have felt guilty about her decision because she changed her mind at the last minute. Mother Superior told me not to put Sabina in the wall but to make her leave the abbey instead. However, it was too late. I already had her in the wall and I wasn't about to take her out."

"You sick, sick man," Vivienne hissed through her teeth.

"I told Mother Superior I sent the girl back home and

Brother Benedict left with her since they were in love. I told her that I watched them go and that they were happy to leave."

"But you didn't do that," said the sheriff.

"Nay, of course not. Brother Benedict came looking for Sabina when I had just finished closing her inside the wall. He attacked me. I had no choice but to kill him. Those sharp-edged trowels make a good weapon."

"That explains the broken rib we saw on Brother Benedict's body," said Vivienne.

"Yes. Not to mention, the bricks I used to hit him over the head." Brother Silas laughed some more.

"You didn't have to kill them," cried Vivienne.

"I sure did. The two of them weren't going to keep quiet about what they knew, and they needed to be silenced. Forever. They sealed their own fates, my lady."

"I hardly think that's true," snapped Vivienne.

Zachariah spoke next. "So, you dumped Brother Benedict's body in the grave before Brother Theodore was buried."

"Yes. I knew Brother Harold was going blind and wouldn't see me do it. Plus, he fell asleep when he was supposed to be guarding the body," Brother Silas told them.

"Why didn't you take back the rosary and the cross necklace instead of leaving them with the dead bodies?" asked Zachariah.

"I should have, and regretted it later. But I had to move fast and wasn't thinking about the possessions at the time. I just wanted to hide the bodies before I was discovered."

"You had the brooch on your cloak when you killed Sabina, didn't you?" asked Vivienne.

"Yes. I was hidden under a cloak. She put up a fight and must have grabbed it before I dumped her in the wall. I didn't even know she took it. I thought I just lost it somewhere. I was surprised to see it found in the wall with her body. It was a perfect plan," said Brother Silas, still chuckling. "That is, until the damned ghost of Brother Benedict kept showing up."

"You were the one in the scullery that Sister Magdalena saw," said Vivienne. "You were looking for the bones of Sabina's baby. Were you trying to hide them?"

"Not at all," said the monk. "I wanted to use them as one of my next relics. Just think how valuable it would be when I made up a story of the bones being of the unborn child of some saint or another."

"That was your own child," Zachariah ground out. "You truly are an evil and very sick man."

"The ghost of Brother Benedict wants justice for their deaths, and he is going to get it." Vivienne's words were confident and condemning at the same time.

"Sheriff, if your stupid sister had never gone to the constable in the first place, none of this would be happening right now."

"The ghost led me to the wall," squeaked out Magdalena. "Constable Erikson is my friend, and I told him I thought something was wrong. He was the one to look inside the damaged wall. He found Sabina. Because of Brother Benedict's ghost leading me there."

"You won't get away with this," warned Zachariah, his hands still in the air. He looked around the ground for a rock or anything to use to fight off Silas. The trouble was, it was all so risky. In the blink of an eye, he could lose his sister if he weren't careful. He had to play this out correctly, but wasn't sure exactly what to do.

"Where's that damned horse?" shouted Silas, with his dagger still at Magdalena's throat. "I'm going to cut into her neck a little for each minute it takes for the horse to get here."

Magdalena whimpered as the blade got closer, cutting her slightly and causing her neck to bleed.

"Nay, leave her alone!" screamed Zachariah. "If you want to hurt someone, come for me instead. I dare you."

"Here comes your horse now," announced Vivienne.

Zachariah looked from the side of his eye to see someone sitting atop the horse. They were totally covered by a hooded cloak. He knew the size of the nun, as she was tiny. This person was much larger. He had a feeling Vivienne had given Sister Ernestine instructions with her hands that only the two of them had understood. Hopefully, she had sent the girl for help.

"Good," said the monk, looking up. "Wait a minute. That's not the deaf girl on the horse. That's someone else. You crossed me!"

Grunt started barking like crazy from behind the ossuary. When Silas turned a little to look, Zachariah knew this was the only chance he might have to save his sister. He lunged forward, pushing Silas to the ground. "Vivienne, get Magdalena," he shouted, punching the monk in the jaw.

"I've got her," cried Vivienne. Grunt came over and started biting the monk on the foot.

Brother Silas still had his knife and lashed out at Zachariah as he kicked the dog. Zachariah dodged the end of the blade. They rolled over and over on the ground fighting. If only Zachariah could get the dagger from Silas, he'd have a fighting chance.

The monk was stronger than he'd expected, and Zachariah was thrown down face-first into the dirt. He rolled over only to find Silas standing above him with his dagger raised above his head, ready to plunge the blade into Zachariah's heart. Not at all what he wanted to see right now.

"You'll die too, Sheriff. So sorry. Nay, not really." Brother Silas started laughing until the end of a shovel crashed down over his head from behind him, causing him to drop his blade, knocking him to the ground. It was the gravedigger who had come to Zachariah's rescue.

"I'm tired of burying bodies, but wouldn't mind planting yours deep in the bowels of the earth," snarled Brother Grayson.

There was a small group of people with the gravedigger. When Silas went down, he had knocked into Sister Ernestine and she stumbled and fell to the ground, hitting her head on a boulder.

"Dammit, you are going to pay for all this." Zachariah jumped up and grabbed Silas around the neck with two hands, squeezing the life out of him.

"You're ... choking ... me," sputtered the monk, trying to fight back.

Zachariah was so angry that he honestly wanted to kill the monk. And he might have too, if Vivienne hadn't stopped him.

"It's over, Zachariah," came her calming words, floating on the breeze.

The constable hopped off the horse and flipped down his hood to reveal his identity. "I've got him, Sheriff Fitch." He shackled the monk's hands behind his back.

"How did all of you know we were here?" asked Zachariah.

Brother Grayson explained. "Thank goodness, Lady Vivienne told Sister Ernestine to get us, and that Sister Roberta was there to decipher what she said."

"Zachariah! Lady Vivienne, come quickly! It's Sister Ernestine," shouted Magdalena, on the ground and holding Sister Ernestine's head on her lap. Blood was coming from Sister Ernestine's ear.

"God's teeth, did her hurt her too?" snapped Zachariah.

"Brother, please watch your language," scolded Magdalena. "Sister Ernestine fell and hit her head on a rock, but she is just fine."

"More ... than ... fine," said Sister Ernestine with a smile.

"You can talk?" gasped Vivienne. "How can that be?"

"The hit to her head that took away her hearing and her speech as a child has been restored today by a miracle when she hit her head again," explained Sister Magdalena.

"It is ... a miracle." Sister Ernestine sat up and looked around, smiling at everyone and rubbing her head.

More and more people ran up from the refectory until just about everyone was there. They all talked aloud, and since Mother Superior had been arrested, as well as Brother Silas, there was no one there to tell them to keep quiet anymore.

"How is Maleine?" asked Vivienne, to no one in general.

"She's awake and is going to be just fine," said one of the nuns. "Sister Roberta is with her and putting herbal creams on Maleine's cuts and bruises. Maleine told us that Brother Silas did this to her."

"Magdalena? May I talk to you?" asked Zachariah.

"Of course, Zachariah." Magdalena left Sister Ernestine chatting with the others and came to his side.

"I'm so sorry," he said.

"About what?" she asked with a smile. "It wasn't your fault that lunatic tried to kill me, and Maleine as well."

"I'm talking about the way I've treated you. I was never so scared as when I thought Brother Silas was going to kill you."

"Well, he didn't, so you don't need to dwell on it any longer." She reached out and gently took his hand in hers.

"I've missed you, Magdalena. I've distanced myself from my entire family and only because of Lady Vivienne did I even question that I've been so wrong."

"I told you that I forgive you, Zachariah. Let's just leave it at that." Magdalena reached up and kissed him on the cheek.

"I wish you'd come back to Mablethorpe," he told his sister. "I feel like there is so much we need to catch up on. Plus, it would be nice for Starah too, since she's lost her mother and has no other family but me right now."

"I am a nun, Zachariah. I have been for many years. You know that. I've taken vows and committed my life to the abbey."

"You can leave the abbey. Get married and settle down," he told her.

She smiled and shook her head. "I appreciate what you're trying to do, my dear brother. But we both know I am too old to marry. Besides, I am already a bride of God."

"Right," he said, giving her a hug, still wishing that things could be different. But it was too late for Magdalena to change her entire life. And why should she do so, just for him? He'd made amends, but some things could never be reversed. His sister chose a life as a nun, and who was he to want to change that?

Chapter Twenty-One

Vivienne sat at Maleine's side in the infirmary two days later, having stayed at the abbey while Zachariah and the constable took care of things concerning the arrests of the Mother Superior and Brother Silas. She didn't want to leave Maltby le Marsh before she knew that Maleine was going to be all right. Both in body and mind.

"Thank you for saving my life, my lady," said Maleine, taking a sip of the broth that Vivienne had brought to her in a wooden cup. "I was never so frightened in my life."

"Why did you tell Brother Silas in the sacristy that you were alone right before he abducted you?"

"I didn't want him to know you were there and to hurt you, my lady. I was trying to protect you."

"Thank you, Maleine, but in doing so, you almost lost your life. And by the way, it wasn't just me who saved you. It was Sheriff Fitch, Brother Grayson, Brother Harold, as well as Grunt, too."

"Oh, Grunt, I'm going to miss you." Maleine reached out to pet the dog who had his chin resting on the side of Maleine's bed. The dog looked up at her with big, sad eyes. "Lady Vivienne, I heard bits and pieces about what happened, but some things are still not clear to me."

"Like what?" asked Vivienne. "Perhaps I can explain."

"The brooch found in the wall with Sabina. Was that from Silas?"

"Yes. Brother Silas admitted that Sabina fought him when he tried to kill her. He often roamed the abbey at night covered in a cloak from head to toe. He used a brooch from the treasures he stole to hold it closed. Sabina pulled it off of him in the struggle. She was about five or six months pregnant with Brother Silas's child. He forced himself on her. And of course, you know that the baby died in the wall too."

"Yes. This is all so awful. Poor Sabina." Maleine shook her head sadly. "I know now how terrifying it was in that wall and I wouldn't wish such a horrible end on anyone."

"You're safe now, Maleine. And I am so thankful we found you in time."

"Did Brother Silas kill Brother Benedict too?"

"Yes. I'm afraid he did."

"This is such a sad story."

"It is. Especially since this is a holy place with holy people. Or so we thought. It seems even good people can end up tempted and turn bad."

"What about the fake relics? I know where they got some of them, but where did the rest come from?"

"Brother Silas was getting them from the cemetery. He told us that Brother Grayson gave him the bones and hair, but Brother Grayson knew nothing about it. The toe bone that was supposed to be from a saint, Brother Silas took right off Brother Benedict's body before he threw him into the grave."

"And Mother Superior knew nothing about the murders? She was only involved in stealing the dowries and the selling of fake relics?"

"She wasn't involved in the killings, but she did find Brother Silas abducting you in the sacristy and she didn't tell us."

"Yes, I saw her just before Brother Silas hit me over the head with something and knocked me out."

"Mother Superior holding back this information won't win her any favors regarding her sentence."

"Will she be imprisoned?"

"Yes. They both will. And Brother Silas will most likely be sentenced to death."

"I'm so confused, Lady Vivienne. I thought life in the abbey would be safe," said Maleine. "But I see now that bad things can happen anywhere, not just in my little town of Mablethorpe."

"Yes, they can and they do. Maleine, you said you wanted to join the abbey to atone for your father's sins. But be honest with me. Were you coming here because you thought it would be a safe haven?"

"It was a little of both, I guess," said Maleine, taking a sip of the broth, holding the cup in two hands. She was badly bruised and had one eye still swollen, but her spirit seemed healed already, and that was what truly counted. "Lady Vivienne, what would you say if I told you that I might have had a change of heart about being a nun, after all?"

"We'd say, it's the right decision," came a woman's voice from behind them. Sister Magdalena walked into the room along with Zachariah. Grunt ran from the bed with his tail wagging, right over to greet the sheriff.

"You and the sheriff think that leaving the abbey is the right decision?" asked Maleine.

"Not only us, but the abbot, as well as the new abbess, also agree that mayhap the abbey is not the place for you," said Sister Magdalena.

"The abbey has a new abbess? Who is it?" asked Maleine, putting down the cup on her lap, but still holding on to it.

"Sister Roberta has been voted in by the other nuns and monks to take Mother Superior's place as abbess," said Sister Magdalena. "And the first thing she'll do is contact the bishop so the abbey won't be closed down. She is going to sell all the treasures from the dowries that are in the secret room you found to pay for the upkeep of the abbey and the church as well."

"How nice," said Maleine. "Does that mean you'll be the new prioress then, Sister Magdalena?"

"Nay," said Magdalena. "Maleine, I've also decided to leave Maltby le Marsh Abbey."

"You have?" Maleine's eyes opened wide. "You mean you're not going to be a nun anymore?" Maleine was so surprised at hearing this announcement she almost spilled her broth.

"Oh, I didn't say that, Maleine." Magdalena's face lit up and she looked over at Zachariah. "I decided to transfer so I can be closer to my brother and spend more time with him and Starah. I am going to continue being a nun, but at Mablethorpe Abbey instead."

"That's great. I'm happy to hear that," said Maleine. "But if I am not suited to be a nun, and neither do I want to be one anymore, what will happen to me?"

"Maleine, my offer still holds about you coming back to Mablethorpe Castle with me," said Vivienne, watching the girl's eyes rise up in surprise.

"Really?"

"Really," Vivienne answered.

"What would I do there?" Maleine wanted to know.

"Well, I could really use a handmaid, since I don't have one. That is, if you will accept the position."

"My lady, I would love to, but sadly, I don't know anything about being a handmaid."

"It doesn't matter, Maleine," Vivienne told her. "Because I am going to teach you."

"Are you sure you want me as your handmaid? I can't even read or write, my lady."

"You'll learn that too. And since you were so helpful in this murder investigation I ..."

"Lady Vivienne," the sheriff stopped her, with a warning tone to his voice. "What are you doing? I already have you helping me investigate. I am not looking for anyone else."

"Relax, Sheriff. I just wanted to tell Maleine that I would always listen to her opinions on any case we might be trying to solve. She has proven to be a very good investigator, you realize."

"Thank you, my lady. That means a lot to me, coming from you." Maleine's face lit up. "I think I would like to take you up on your offer after all, and come to the castle to be your handmaid."

"Excellent," said Vivienne, with a happy feeling engulfing her. "That is exactly what I wanted to hear. I am sure you will be very happy there."

"I think so, too," Maleine answered.

"We'll leave first thing in the morning." Vivienne stood up and looked back over her shoulder. "I am sure Wymond will be happy to see you."

The girl blushed. "I'll be happy to see him, too," she said softly, once again sipping her broth. "I mean, because I miss Chomp and Snuff, of course."

"Of course," repeated Vivienne with a wink.

"The ferrets?" said Zachariah, making a face. "She misses the ferrets?"

"Sheriff Fitch, sometimes you need to listen a bit more deeply, to find out the true meaning of a woman's words," Vivienne told him with a sly smile.

"Nay, my lady," Zachariah answered. "Even if I knew how to talk using those hand gestures, I swear, I would never understand what goes through a female's head, as long as I live."

Chapter Twenty-Two

Vivienne never felt better as their wagon rolled toward Mablethorpe Castle the next day. The sun was shining, the birds were singing, and she felt so alive that it almost made her want to get up and dance. Of course, part of the reason could be that they had finally solved the murder mystery, and she was now headed back to be with Martin. She missed her son so much that she couldn't wait to see him again.

Maleine was in the back of the wagon with Grunt and Sister Magdalena. They'd be taking Magdalena to Mablethorpe Abbey, but not until the next morning. Zachariah convinced his sister to stay in town with him overnight, so they could spend time together. He drove the wagon, and Vivienne sat on the bench seat next to him.

"That murder case was anything but easy," Vivienne commented. "I'm glad it is over."

"I agree," the sheriff answered. "And I'm telling you right now that I don't ever want to have to investigate at an abbey again."

"Too much silence?" she asked.

"At first, yes. But since Sister Ernestine got her voice back, I swear all she does is talk. I was actually glad to leave, just to find a little peace and quiet from all that chatter."

"Sheriff Fitch, you really need to learn to make up your mind. You either like the silence or you don't. Which is it?" she asked him.

"It depends on who's talking, I suppose." He glanced over, giving her a wry smile. The man looked as handsome as ever, and she was glad he was her friend.

"It'll be good to see the children again, don't you agree?" she asked him.

"Aye. And I want to thank you for urging me to make amends with Magdalena. It feels good to have part of my family back again. She'll be close enough now at Mablethorpe Abbey that Starah and I can visit her whenever we want."

"I am happy for you, Zachariah. And I only hope you can someday make amends with Isaac and Cassandra, too."

"One sibling at a time, my lady," he told her. "Right now, I'm not in a hurry to do anything but get home to rest and relax."

As they got closer to the castle, Vivienne noticed knights and their traveling parties on the road. There seemed to be more travelers than usual. She didn't think much about it until they approached the castle and she saw tents going up just outside the castle wall.

"What is going on here?" she asked, stretching her neck and looking around. Why were so many people gathering outside her uncle's castle?

"Why don't you ask someone?" suggested Zachariah.

"All right, I will. Excuse me," she said, waving over a knight on a horse. "Can I ask you what is going on here?"

"Aren't you Lady Vivienne from Mablethorpe Castle?" asked the knight.

"I am."

"Then I'd think you'd already know."

"Know what?"

"That a tournament is taking place right here at your castle in a fortnight, and the king is coming, as well."

"It is? He is?" Her stomach fluttered. "King Edward is really coming here?"

"Yes, that's right. Have you never met the king, my lady? You seem so nervous about it."

"Nay, I've not met him. Not yet." She wrapped her arms around her, feeling suddenly insecure.

"If the tournament is in a fortnight, why are tents already going up?" asked Zachariah.

"Everyone wants to be sure to secure a good spot for the tournament," said the knight. "After all, not only is the king going to be here, but word has it that so will the Legendary Bastards of the Crown, so I've heard."

"Really?" Now Vivienne's heart almost stopped. She'd heard about the Legendary Bastards of the Crown. They were bastard triplets of the king that he'd ordered killed at birth. That made them her half-brothers. She wondered if King Edward had ever wanted her killed as well. Or if he would give that command as soon as he found out she was his bastard child too. Her hand caressed the king's ring she wore on a chain around her neck, hidden under her clothes. So many questions she had for King Edward. So many answers she was scared to know. Vivienne only wished her mother had told her all about this before the woman died in her arms.

"This is a huge event, my lady. I hear the winner of the tournament will win the grand prize."

"A grand prize?" She couldn't believe it would be that good. After all, her uncle wasn't considered rich. Actually, he was cheaper than anyone she knew. "What prize is that? Has the king offered something of great value?"

"Surely you jest, my lady," said the man with a broad grin.

"After all, I am sure you know that the competitors chosen for the tournament are all single men. And also that the winner gets you as his wife."

"Me? Wife? Nay! You've heard wrong, Sir Knight." Her anger grew inside. She knew this was all her uncle's doing and she didn't like it in the least. "Please spread the word that I will not be marrying anyone. Winner, loser, or other."

"Of course, my lady." The knight looked at her oddly and stopped as the wagon continued to roll.

"Vivienne, are you really getting married?" asked Zachariah under his breath.

"Nay! You know that I'm not. Why do you even ask such a preposterous question?"

"I only ask because if the king is coming, and your uncle has already promised your hand in marriage as the grand prize, then I don't see how you'll get out of it."

"I will, don't worry. King or no king, I don't care. I won't marry until I'm ready and it'll only be to a man of my choosing."

Zachariah was very quiet, not saying a word.

"Don't you believe me?"

"Of course, I believe you, my lady. But I also know that this tournament will be very important. If Lord Mablethorpe already agreed to marry you off to the winner because that is what the king wanted, then how can you fight that? This is the king we're talking about, Vivienne. His word is law."

"I know that," she said, biting at her bottom lip. What Zachariah didn't know was that King Edward was her true father, and she was about to meet him for the first time. In her mind, it already seemed like the meeting was going to be one of fury. "Leave that to me," she told him. "And mark my words, I am not afraid of anyone. Not even King Edward."

The wagon stopped inside the courtyard, and Vivienne saw Martin and Starah coming to greet them. Grunt noticed them too, and jumped over the side of the wagon, running to them, barking.

"Mother!" shouted Martin.

"Father!" yelled Starah.

"Wee ones, slow down," hollered Nairnie, waddling as fast as her short, fat legs could carry her as she tried to keep up with the children.

Vivienne held out her arms and scooped up Martin, hugging him and kissing him, so happy to be with her son once again. She looked over to see Zachariah holding Starah on his hip.

"I missed you so much," said Vivienne, never wanting to let her son go.

"Mother, did you hear? The king is coming and there is going to be a big tournament with a joust and everything."

"I heard," she said. She noticed Zachariah going back to the wagon with his daughter, helping Magdalena get out. She also noticed Wymond with his crutch hobbling over to the wagon with his ferrets on the ground trailing after him. Maleine took Wymond's hand as he helped her to the ground.

Of course, Grunt saw Chomp and Snuff and bedlam broke loose. The dog barked and chased the ferrets around the wagon, managing to spook the horse. Zachariah had to reach up and grab the reins so the horse wouldn't run off.

"Lady Vivienne?" called out Zachariah, balancing Starah in one arm and trying to hold back the spooked horse with the other. "Can you collect your dog, please?"

"I'll get him," said Martin, almost falling as he tried to get out of her arms.

"Father, I'll catch the ferrets." Starah squirmed out of Zachariah's hold too. Nairnie tried to catch the children, rambling on in her Scottish burr about how things here were even more chaotic than living with pirates.

Vivienne strolled over and took Zachariah's arm. "Let's take a walk," she said.

"Gladly. But only if we can go somewhere quiet."

"I have just the place, but we're going to need to take the horse and wagon to get there."

"All right. But are you going to tell me where we're going?"

"Nay. Not until we get there."

It wasn't long before they reached the graveyard outside the church in town.

"The graveyard?" Zachariah arched one brow. "After everything we've been through lately, you wanted to come here? Really?"

"You said you wanted to go somewhere quiet, didn't you?"

"I suppose you have a point, even if this isn't what I had in mind." He got off the wagon and helped her to the ground. "Anywhere in particular you'd like to amble?"

"Yes. I'd like to stop by Margaret's grave, if you don't mind."

"Nay," he said, suddenly hesitant to do so.

"Zachariah, you've made amends with Magdalena, and now I think we need to let Margaret know that everything is fine between the two of you."

"This is silly."

"Come on." She took his hand and led him over to his wife's grave. When they got there, he just stared at the ground. "Tell her," said Vivienne.

"Don't make me do this."

"Do it!" She wasn't going to take *no* for an answer. This was part of the healing process for him, and she knew he'd thank her for it later. She'd seen how hard it was for him to make amends with Magdalena until he thought her life was about to be snuffed away. He seemed better since he and his sister were talking again, but his inner wounds were far from healed.

"All right, all right." Zachariah looked to the ground and

folded his hands together. Then he cleared his throat about three times before he could bring himself to say a word. "Margaret," he finally said in not much more than a whisper. "I've made amends with Magdalena. I know now that it wasn't her fault you died."

"Tell Margaret that you forgive her too. For ministering to Magdalena when she was sick with the pox."

"Vivienne, this is stupid."

"Is it?" She raised a brow now. "What if Margaret went to her grave thinking you were cross with her for helping your sister in the first place?"

"Nay. I'm not cross with her."

"Tell *her*, not me." Vivienne pointed to the grave.

"I understand what you did, and I thank you. For helping Magdalena," he said aloud, looking at Margaret's headstone. "No one knew you could contract the pox twice. It is no one's fault. You did the right thing."

"Good," said Vivienne. "Now tell her you love her and then you're free to go."

"What?" That seemed to make him really uncomfortable. Mayhap since she was standing right there? After all, they had an unspoken attraction to each other even if they both insisted they were just friends.

"You heard me. Tell Margaret you love her," she insisted.

"I love you," he whispered, and for some reason Vivienne had the odd feeling he was saying it to her and not his dead wife, but that could just be her imagination.

"Very good. We can go now, Sheriff Fitch." She turned to leave and movement from the other end of the graveyard took her attention. "Do you ... see that?" Her heart jumped into her throat.

"See what?" Zachariah looked up, and by the expression on his face it was apparent that he saw it too.

Brother Benedict's ghost floated across the graveyard and this time he was not alone. This time there was another ghost with him. It looked like a woman in a long cloak with a short veil on her head. She was holding a bouquet of flowers. Vivienne knew without a doubt who it was.

"Benedict. And Sabina," she said with a smile. "They are together again at last. They are thanking us for helping them and for giving them both a proper burial." Before they had left the abbey, Vivienne had made sure that the bones of both Sabina and Brother Benedict were buried in the church's grave-yard where they belonged. That is, buried together.

"I don't know what you're talking about," said Zachariah, not wanting to admit he saw them.

"You see their ghosts, too, so just admit it."

"Nay. No matter what you say, I do not see a monk and woman with a bouquet of flowers."

"Really," she said slyly. "You do realize that I didn't say anything about her holding flowers."

"You didn't?"

She shook her head. "So how did you know she had flowers if you didn't see the ghosts too?" She stopped and smiled play-fully, looking directly into his alluring eyes. There was no way he could get out of this now. He would have to admit that he saw the ghosts.

"Did I ever tell you I can read minds?" He had a dung-eating grin on his face as he took her arm and escorted her back to the wagon.

"You can read minds," she repeated.

"Uh huh. That's right."

"Well, then, Sheriff Fitch, if you can read my mind, tell me what I'm about to do right now."

"Huh?" He turned to look at her but not before she reached out and ruffled his hair and turned around laughing, and running through the graveyard with him chasing right behind her.

Yes, Vivienne never felt better than she did today. But this feeling was going to leave her quickly if she couldn't do anything to reverse her uncle's stupid promise to the king that she was going to marry the tournament winner.

From the Author

I hope you enjoyed Murder at Maltby le Marsh and will take a moment to leave a review for me. This is an ongoing story about the lives of Lady Vivienne Harlowe and Sheriff Zachariah Fitch and the murder investigations they tackle together as a team.

Immurement, as horrific as it sounds, was something that truly happened, dating all the way back to ancient Rome. In medieval times, I hate to even say, my research shows that the Roman Catholic Church would brick up nuns or monks in a wall if they'd broken their vows of chastity or expressed heretical ideas.

Supposedly, they would be put alive into this type of tomb to punish them by keeping them away from the outside world. There was a small opening which food and water was dropped into in order to keep them alive. Of course, sometimes they were put there to die, as what happened in my book. I've even read that at times small children were put into the wall with the nuns.

Those who actually chose to be immured of their own free will, and live this gruesome way, were called Anchorites or Anchoresses. And sadly, in other periods of history, walling up people was used as a form of human sacrifice, supposedly to bring good luck to those who put them there.

Yes, the Dark Ages could certainly be very dark and more horrible than any of us could ever imagine.

If you haven't already read the **Harlowe and Fitch Historical Mysteries** that came before this, please be sure to do so. It is always best to read them in order so no surprises will be ruined.

Book 4 in my mystery series is next and focusses on a tournament at Mablethorpe Castle with their special guest being the king. It is called **Murder at the Joust**. Will Lady Vivienne finally meet King Edward, her real father? Will she tell him she's his bastard child, and can she once again dodge her uncle trying to marry her off? And will she finally meet her half-brothers, the Legendary Bastards of the Crown?

As in most of my books, I like to have recurring characters or ones who make guest appearances from some of my other series. My **Legendary Bastards of the Crown Series** is historical romance and about the triplets, Rowen the Restless, Rook the Ruthless, and Reed the Reckless. Be sure to read this series to find out more.

Another of my historical romances that is one of my favorites and also involves life and mystery at an abbey is **Amber,** Book 3 of my **Daughters of the Dagger Series**.

To see more of my books (over 100 and counting), please stop by and visit my **Website** at **http://elizabethrosenovels.com.** You can also follow me on **Instagram, Amazon, Bookbub, Goodreads, Facebook, Bluesky, TikTok,** and **Twitter**. I also have a **Private Readers' Group** on Facebook that I invite you to join.

Until next time,
   Elizabeth Rose

I'd like to leave you now with an excerpt from ***Amber, Daughters of the Dagger***.

Bowerwood Abbey and Monastery, England, 1357

Vespers had just finished, and Amber de Burgh of Blackpool, novice of the Sisters of St. Ermengild, blessed herself as the doors to the church slammed open, and in entered the devil himself.

All heads of the congregation of praying nuns and monks turned toward the door. Father Armand who was conducting the service looked up sharply in surprise.

"Lucifer!" he cried out, startling everyone inside the church. "Bid the devil."

Commotion broke out and the occupants of the church parted like the Red Sea. The nuns huddled together in a hurry, quickly blessing themselves and praying aloud. The monks gathered together at the other side of the church, conversing in hushed whispers.

Amber raised her chin, looking over the heads of the nuns, surprised to see a man standing in the doorway instead of the horned and hoofed demon she expected to find. A bedraggled man with a chain around his neck and chains on his wrists stood in the entranceway. His legs were spread, and his hands raised to stop the doors of the church as they hit the wall and swung back toward him. Lightning illuminated him from behind and thunder boomed from outside. Rain pelted down like a barrage of arrows from the sky, crashing against the stone steps of the church directly behind him.

"Father," the man said in a low voice through clenched teeth, and Amber realized he was speaking to Father Armand. "I will see you in Hell before I do your bidding again, you bloody bastard!"

Cries of shock went up from the group around Amber. One of the nuns swooned, ending up prone on the floor in a tangle of her black robes and long veil. Several of the sisters rushed over to assist her. The monks at the other end of the church continued talking to each other behind their hands. Amber curiously made her way from the wooden bench at the front of the church closer to the door to gaze upon this spawn of the devil.

"You are naught but the devil," shouted the priest. "Lord Jesus Christ, we beg your forgiveness for this possessed man who has entered into your house of worship." The priest made his way down the steps of the dais, raising his book of prayer to the sky as he walked a straight line toward the angry man.

"God's eyes, look what you've done to me," spat the devil man in the doorway. That's when Amber noticed the gashing wound in his side and the trail of blood behind him as he took a step forward.

"You will not use blasphemy in the house of the Lord," reprimanded Father Armand. "And you will remove yourself from these premises immediately."

"I will not!" shouted the man the priest had called Lucifer, stumbling forward. Catching himself on the edge of a bench, he bent over. "I seek refuge and ministrations, and dammit, I will get what I came for and not be sent away again." His words were filled with anger and venom. Amber felt the fear in the room, as the nuns cowered together watching with wide eyes, and the monks huddled together in the shadows. The priest grabbed hold of a tall, freestanding iron candleholder, slowly making his way toward the wounded man.

Also by Elizabeth Rose

Mystery Series:

Harlowe & Fitch Historical Mystery Series

Murder on Rotten Row

Murder at Maltby le Marsh

Murder at the Joust

Medieval Series:

Below the Salt

Legendary Bastards of the Crown Series

Seasons of Fortitude Series

Secrets of the Heart Series

Legacy of the Blade Series

Daughters of the Dagger Series

MadMan MacKeefe Series

Barons of the Cinque Ports Series

Holiday Knights Series

Highland Chronicles Series

Pirate Lords Series

Highland Outcasts

Medieval/Paranormal Series:

Elemental Magick Series

Greek Myth Fantasy Series

Tangled Tales Series

Portals of Destiny

Contemporary Series:

Tarnished Saints Series

Working Man Series

Western Series:

Cowboys of the Old West Series

And More!

Please visit http://elizabethrosenovels.com

About Elizabeth

Elizabeth Rose is an award-winning, bestselling author of over 100 books and counting. She writes medieval, historical, contemporary, paranormal, and western romance. Her books are available as EBooks, paperbacks, and some audiobooks as well.

Her favorite characters in her works include dark, dangerous and tortured heroes, and feisty, independent heroines who know how to wield a sword. She loves writing 14th century medieval novels, and is well-known for her many series.

Elizabeth loves the outdoors. In the summertime, you can find her in her secret garden with her laptop, swinging in her hammock working on her next book. Elizabeth is a born storyteller and passionate about sharing her works with her readers.

Please be sure to visit her website at **Elizabethrosenovels.com** to read excerpts from any of her novels and get sneak peeks at covers of upcoming books. You can follow her on **Twitter, Facebook**, **Goodreads** or **BookBub.** Join Elizabeth's **newsletter** so you don't miss out on new releases or upcoming events.

9 781648 399558